Deny Me, The Nightshade Boy

Book 1 in The Heartwood Trilogy

Mary VanAlstine

DREAMING IN COLOR

CONTENTS

Dedication

THIS BOOK MUST BY point of fact be dedicated to my father, Guy Stewart. You have been a tireless and devoted writer longer than I've been alive, and you have worked just as hard to inspire me to write, too. And it worked. You've allowed me to chart my own course and you've always put my whims first. Thank you for being my inspiration to be unapologetically myself.

CONTENT WARNING

THIS BOOK CONTAINS DEPICTIONS of self-harm, depictions of psychosis, depictions of depression and anxiety, implied substance abuse, implied sexual assault, and instances of magical violence. Reader discretion is advised.

Chapter One

The Artwork

Andrew Vidasche was much too nerdy to be hunting faeries in Lilydale.

What he'd have preferred to be doing was sipping tea and watching documentaries in sweatpants while he cuddled his cat. Nerds like him shouldn't be walking into faerieland. But if he wanted to keep his sanity (what was left of it), he didn't have a choice. The solitude had gotten too heavy, and with it, the weight of the rift between him and his estranged mother.

In a park overlooking downtown Saint Paul, Andrew made his way to the Brickyard Trail, the easiest place to get off the Path and into the bluffs where the Folk lived. Lilydale was untamed: steep sprawling limestone crags hung over the eastern banks of the Mississippi, haggard trees clinging desperately to the soil between the stones. Once, they'd tried to put a brickyard in the hills, but its massive kiln had exploded and killed everyone working. Not too long ago, some kids on a field trip got washed away in a mudslide while hunting for fossils, and the bluffs had been prohibited ever since. It seemed to Andrew that nature was trying to keep people out.

For as wild as it was, magic foods made by the Folk still got out of the bluffs and into the hands of humans, which Andrew never would have known about if not for how open his mum had been about her struggle with addiction. In Andrew's teens, his mum's pill addiction had culminated in such Fae-spelled foods. He remembered the foods to be unassuming: apple chunks in plastic baggies or heels of dark rye bread, once a little vial of golden liquid. But a single bite would leave his mum out of touch for days, hallucinating that she was being strangled by vines, turning on all the gas burners on the stove because she liked the smell, or convinced she was a princess on the better days. She'd be covered in sweat with a hummingbird heartbeat and blue skin around her lips.

The visions of her during and after taking those enchanted foods haunted Andrew. Using the stove made him hyperventilate. Irish brogue accents brought tears to his eyes. He wanted to both hug and slap any red-haired woman he saw. It seemed like the only way to get relief from his memories was to find her again, to rebuild their relationship. To try to reconcile.

Because his mum hadn't had a phone since he was fourteen, his first step to tracking her down was to get a hold of her oldest friend. Kate's phone number was still written on a scrap of paper buried in a box of Andrew's childhood things. When they met, she'd confirmed his suspicions that Fae-spelled foods might have been his mum's downfall. She blamed the Folk: dangerous, ambivalent faeries living in the river bluffs over the city. She tried to talk him out of going up there, but if there was some chance his mum was up there—captured by the faeries that got her addicted—then he was going to find her. So here he was. What would these supposed faeries even look like? Tinkerbell? Legolas? He wouldn't mind Legolas, if he were being honest...

Late afternoon in October was Andrew's favorite time in Minnesota. He savored the faint chill in the air and the explosion of sunset-colored leaves. They littered the black asphalt and clung stubbornly to branches, quivering in the breeze that made loose auburn hair from Andrew's ponytail tickle his cheeks. He zipped his fleece pullover higher as he stepped into cooler shadows. Packed wood chips skittered under his boots. Fearful of a magical ambush, he jumped at every snap and rustle of leaves.

Andrew peered southward through the trees. Thighs shaking, breathing shallow, he climbed off the marked path and into the underbrush. His heavy Doc Martens made him sound like he was tromping forth in a full suit of armor. Despite them, he tried to duck under branches, weave around thistles, gently bend stalks of feathery grasses out of his path. How many of the wildflowers coloring the scraggly hillside could kill him? He imagined some waist-high winged child shoving poisonous flowers down his throat, and he snorted.

Maybe there wasn't even anything out here except turkeys and deer.

West of him, far below, the dark Mississippi ran relentlessly toward the equator, yawning under the interstate bridge in the distance. There wasn't much that would protect him from tumbling headfirst into the river; the bluffs were jagged and dropped sharply into limestone cliffs with seemingly no warning. If he fell, Andrew wasn't sure anyone would notice he was gone.

"I think it's time to hire a shop assistant," he muttered.

Wiping sweat from his brow, he blinked away a flash of panic. It was going to be just as much work to get back to the park. The kind of hiking the Brickyard trail demanded was much different than his usual tame running routine. He wasn't sure on his feet. Maybe if he lost his footing, he'd be impaled on a branch before he hit the river.

Andrew paused at a fallen tree obscured beneath scaly moss, leaning his palm against the flaky bark of an oak while anxiety needled his spine. He scanned the way forward again, but nothing looked like it would house mythical little faeries. It would be easier to just go home, take a bath, get drunk on whiskey.

But he was stubborn, and more than a little curious. Climbing onto the decaying log, he allowed stubbornness to guide him further into danger. He hauled his leg over, boot scraping off dry bark and crusty white moss.

Then he froze, sucking in a sharp gasp. His boot was a sliver away from stepping on a *body*.

Slowly, slowly, slowly, Andrew pulled his foot back and planted it in the loose dirt. Heart in his throat, he leaned down toward the body, which *was* pallid enough to be a corpse. Pillowed in silky grasses with a halo of tiny white wildflowers was a woman more art than human. Sharp in the manner of an uncut diamond, she was a specimen that even Andrew recognized as beautiful. Her complexion was snow-white with arched brows, long lashes, and deep red lips. She had shining burgundy curls falling back from her forehead. With long, elegant fingers, she clutched a clay pitcher in the crook of her elbow, which sloshed softly with her every breath.

Ah...breath. Not dead then, so that was good.

As Andrew tried to figure out what to do, her eyes snapped open.

They were blood red.

The woman moved with alarming speed, and her beauty was replaced with a silent snarl and fire in her eyes. She was above him before his back even slammed into the ground. As she lunged at him, Andrew fumbled for his pocket knife, flipped up the blade, and thrust his arm out.

The woman's weight bore down on the knife. She dropped her pitcher, where it shattered on the log as she spun away with a cry.

Andrew scrambled to his feet, patting himself over and checking he still had all he needed on him. "Oh my god! I'm sorry!" He pulled out a folded canvas first aid kit from his back pocket. Extending it to her, he said, "Here, please! That looks...smokey? Why are you smoking?"

The cut on her sternum oozed blood—and smoke, as if the wound were made of tinder. She wiped at the blood and hissed, looking down, baring wolf-sharp teeth.

He dropped the kit onto the log between them. "I didn't mean to hurt you. You scared me," Andrew said, closing his blade and pocketing it before holding his hands up, palms out. "I...I'm looking for someone."

The woman's head flicked to the side. Her sharp profile caught a streak of afternoon sun, silver-bright. She swayed as she clenched her fists and panted.

"Wow. You can't be human," he breathed. "I must be near Lilydale. You...you must be a faerie."

"Go away," the woman growled, still not looking at him.

Remembering his purpose, he went on quickly, "I have concerns about these Fae-spelled foods, you see, and I'm afraid that my mum—"

"I don't care," the woman interrupted, "about your concerns or your fears."

"Do you have human prisoners?" Andrew demanded, indignant over the woman's apathy. "Are you wrangling humans that eat your foods and—"

"No!" Swallowing visibly, she shook herself like a dog

and stepped toward him. Though Andrew's height was substantial, this woman saw him eye-to-eye. "You know nothing of me, but I will tell you this. Human affairs are no concern of mine. I do not take prisoners. But if humans seek food from my people, I do not get in their way."

"You ruined my mother's life," Andrew said, a tremble in his voice. "I—I know," he added quickly, when the faerie opened her perfect crimson lips, "you don't care. But I can't be the only one in the city whose loved ones are hurt by your ambivalence. One of these days, someone's going to make you pay for that."

"Ah, yes?" Her eyes glinted with a hard light. She wiped the fresh blood off her chest. Andrew stiffened. Reaching a stained hand toward him, the woman smudged her thumb over Andrew's forehead and said softly, "*I* will make you pay for drawing my blood."

Then she pulled on a shadow and vanished.

CHAPTER TWO
THE FOX

"So, YEAH," SAID ANDREW, rolling the corner of Sam Larson's resume between his fingers. "Two weeks ago I was hiking alone and realized nobody would probably notice if I died."

Sam's smile took on a strained quality. He nudged his round tortoiseshell glasses up into his fluffy bangs. "That can't be true..."

Shrugging, Andrew continued, "That—you at least being aware if I suddenly go missing, you know—would just be a cursory gain from having an assistant. You'd have, um...other tasks." He glanced past Sam to the park across the street. Magic's Computer Repair peered out of a little rectangular building with an old red door and three cloudy window panes. At least the view of the park was typically serene, and he could watch the softball games happening if he got bored. But he had no serenity today. Things felt...charged, like the atmosphere before a storm. "What else? Oh, customer correspondence. Don't like that." The hairs on his arms were standing on end; he scratched anxiously at them, still looking out the front windows. "And...getting more customers would be, uh..."

Sam fussed with his pride tie striped pink, white, and baby blue. "Hey..." Andrew spared him a quick glance. "You good, Mr. Viadsche?"

"Ah—sure." His head twitched in something akin to a nod. When he looked back toward the door, he—

He lurched to his feet, his desk chair tipping and clattering into Sam's legs. Lightning bolts of terror lanced ice-cold down Andrew's spine, freezing him in place with his back against the wall.

Sam swiveled toward the door. "What's wrong?"

Through the front window, luminous scarlet eyes bored into Andrew. A wicked smile curved like a scythe on her lips, showed teeth gleaming like broken glass. The faerie's skin was almost transparent in the afternoon light, which seemed to fall *through* her like she was an apparition. Her burgundy hair was dotted with red poppies that looked like blood splatters in a Tarantino movie. Raising her long hand, she tapped her sharp black nails against the glass.

Tink.

Andrew flinched.

Tink.

Andrew slapped his hand over his mouth to stifle a scream.

Tink.

The dark slashes of her eyebrows rose, and then she vanished.

Andrew blinked and lowered his trembling hand, taking a stumbling step past Sam to scan the trees and every inch of the windows. For good measure, he pushed open the door and leaned outside. But there was no sign of the faerie from the bluffs. He let the door close on his heels as he turned back around.

Sam wore several expressions jumbled together on his blemished face. When Andrew met his eyes, Sam hunched up with an awkward little laugh.

"You didn't see anything?" Andrew gestured with a quavering hand. "Out the window?"

"Er." Sam blushed, his eyes darting away. "Nope. But I could be, I mean, maybe my glasses—"

A little strangled laugh squeezed from Andrew's chest.

So she just manifested especially for him.

This was it. He made that damned beautiful woman bleed, and now she was haunting him. Or maybe she'd kill him eventually. But she seemed the type of predator who would toy with him first. Like orcas did, tossing seals into the air and catching them in their teeth a dozen times before ripping off one flipper at a time.

Pressing his hands over his face, Andrew held his breath for as long as he could before forcing the air out of his nostrils in one elongated sigh. "Well," he said. He came stiffly back to the long desk where Sam sat fidgeting. After fixing his desk chair, he lowered himself carefully into the seat. Adrenaline pumping in his veins helped him muster an easy, sardonic smile as he said to Sam, "Want to bail, Mr. Larson? I've got a sneaking suspicion that my life is ruined, and I may only get crazier from here on out. You are an excellent candidate for an assistant or whatever else you end up wanting to do here, but in no way will I presume to be an excellent employer when I'm...crazy."

Sam leaned back in his desk chair. His hazel eyes roved the little store front with its neat aisle of computer hardware. The desk where Andrew sat was tidily kept with cords wrapped with zip-ties, a cup of tea near Andrew's elbow somehow having endured his awkward and dramatic display.

Sam looked back at Andrew and smiled kindly. "Unless you start taking your crazy out on me, I can't judge you for going through stuff. Your shop looks really nice, and it's close to the buses that go back to campus." He shrugged. "And I definitely appreciate that you've gotten my pronouns right."

Andrew blinked. "Correctly identifying you seems like a given."

"You'd be surprised." Sam raised his brows and looked away.

"Well. Shall we continue, then?"

Nodding, Sam looked back with a smile.

"You said you have people skills, right?"

"Oh, for sure!"

"Good grief. Native Minnesotan, aren't you?" Andrew glanced past Sam again, but there was nothing out of place outside.

"Yeah. Speaking of, your accent is seriously so great," Sam blurted. "Cheerio and stuff." Andrew gave him a look, which made him blush. "Sorry. I'm just glad you reached out. I didn't think those emails to alumni would actually lead to a job—er, presumably—but this shop seems like a perfect place for me while I finish the computer sciences program at the U of M. I still have a year and a half left, but I have certificates in three coding languages..."

Eyes still fixed on the trees, Andrew nodded absent-mindedly and said, "The last half of that program is hellish. You said you want to start at twenty hours, but if that's too much—like around finals season—you need to tell me. And I fully expect you to do whatever you wish when things are quiet, be it homework or whatever else you kids do." He scraped his hair back from his face, his fingers getting tangled near the nape of his neck.

"Crunking, mostly," said Sam.

"I'm sorry, what? Crumpets?"

They both laughed.

Rubbing his neck, Andrew said with eyes downcast, "And I'm, ah...sorry. For my odd behavior."

"Really, Mr. Vidasche, it's okay." Sam straightened.

"You can just call me Andrew," he said. He raised a brow

at the eager look on Sam's face. "Oh. Would you like the job?"

"Yes, please!"

"Splendid. I can give you a ride back to campus. I have some research to do at the library. Do you think they have a section on faeries?"

One year passed. Then another.

Night after night, season after season, the uncanny, scarlet-eyed faerie haunted Andrew's dreams. And his days...and his nerves...and all his thoughts. He was a husk of a person filled up with fears that, at any moment, *she* would form from the shadows and slash him open with her sinister nails, laughing as he bled out at her feet.

She was...everywhere, but only out of the corner of his eye. Only where the shadows grew longer. Only to turn his cup of tea into flower petals right when he took a drink at a cafe. Only as a soft sigh in his ear when he was alone in a room. Sometimes it was a second pair of feet running in time with him on a trail when nobody else was in sight, or a tinkling laugh drifting by on the wind. He flinched when dogs barked or a bird flapped outside his window, or when his cat's tail brushed his calves when he went to the restroom in the dark.

His resting heart rate jumped from fifty to ninety; his skin always tingled with needles of heat. He'd changed his medication four times, but not even the highest doses or the strongest tranquilizers brought him relief.

Hoping to find relief in information, Andrew pored over Folk literature in the years that came. Inspired by his mum's Druid practices, he began his research in the pages of Celtic books.

"Whatcha looking at?" asked Sam, two years since he started at Magic's, comfortable now asking Andrew questions since he knew Andrew would tell him to mind his business if he needed to. As far as Sam could tell, Andrew had always been a little unhinged. Sam had been in the shop, after all, when the sword Andrew had bought off eBay showed up. It was an iron Viking-era replica of a straight sword the length of his forearm called a seax. The lie was easy enough—Andrew had been a History minor, and had always wanted to start a sword collection. Sam *didn't* know that Andrew was taking swordplay lessons and wearing a holster around his chest under his clothes where he could slip the sword if he felt particularly harried. But the academic excuse seemed to work well enough for most of Andrew's paranoia, since Sam was too polite to criticize.

"Um, it's a Druid folktales book," Andrew answered. "I always check antique bookshops for stuff like this. Found this one on West Seventh."

"Druid? Like the Dungeons and Dragons class?" Sam grinned as if he knew that wasn't what Andrew meant.

With a patient shake of his head, Andrew said, "It's actually a really old practice. My mum is Irish. She called herself a Druid. I learned a bit here and there when I was a kid."

"Isn't that just, like, a witch?"

Andrew turned a page in his book and smoothed his hand over an intricate letterpress drawing of a tree dense with Celtic knots. "Not exactly. The Druids don't do spells or curses. They celebrate and revere nature. They want balance. They want to be mindful of the magic they believe is already in the world. Um, anyway, can you call on the Janssen order and let them know it's ready?"

"You got it, boss." Sam's carefree smile spread on his lips as he stood up and went to the cabinets next to their desk.

Andrew picked up a pen to start sketching the tree in his little ring-bound notebook. This was the third notebook of its kind he'd filled up. He jotted down notes from the book on Faerieland while Sam made the call. Over the last two years, he had amassed a mostly consistent understanding of the scarlet-eyed faerie and other beings like her.

The fair Folk were weak to iron—like his switch-blade—but little else. Though they could be killed, they were otherwise immortal, and were all different races, from tall, elegant elves like the one he met, to small gnomes and tricky goblins. All were bound to speak only truths, but used riddles and omissions in order to mislead.

Throughout history, humans and the Folk had a tumultuous relationship. The Folk would spirit humans away to
their beautiful liminal realms, or spoil crops or water supplies for their own entertainment. But some texts proposed
that some kind of fragile stalemate was possible. Sometimes, faeries even bestowed gifts on humans, or would
enter into relatively equal bargains.

This scarlet-eyed faerie never confronted him explicitly,
and was always nonviolent, but Andrew hardly felt neutrally about her. She sometimes left him alone for a month
or two, once even for ten months. She let him think he
was free of her. But it was always worse when she would
reappear. Then, she would leave a row of dead sparrows
on his windowsill. Or he would see her on a rooftop when
he walked to the store, and she would just...watch him,
gargoyle-still, grinning, while Andrew scampered out of
sight like a rabbit in the crosshairs of a hawk.

Another year, another, and another passed. When autumn came, it would be the fifth year since Andrew was in
the bluffs and drew the blood of his vengeful faerie stalker.

It was high summer now, and it had been a few weeks
since he'd seen his pale specter lurking behind a tree or
found her handprint in the dust on his windshield. But
that didn't come as a relief to him. It made him more on
edge, more certain that at any moment, she would make
her presence known again. Fortunately, Andrew's Celtic

books gave him a handful of ways to protect himself. He warded his apartment with runes etched on his door frame. He made himself invulnerable to falling under Fae charm by wearing an iron necklace with rowan berries called a *géas*.

"Hello," sang Sam, waving his hand in front of Andrew's face. "You in there, Andy?"

Andrew blinked, pressing his thumb and forefinger into his eyes. "Yes. Yeah. Sorry." The pair sat at the long desk at the back of their shop, each stationed in front of large desktop computers bookending spots to hook up computer towers, a little shelf of tools including tiny screwdrivers and a flashlight, and a manual Andrew had written up to help with orders.

"That kind of day for you, huh?" asked Sam. He was twenty-four now, but his shaggy hair still obscured his forehead and still had streaks of bleach and color in it - currently red.

"What kind of day?" Andrew asked.

"When you seem somehow both spacey *and* jumpy at the same time. What's that called? Dissociated?" Sam said. His computer chimed musically as it shut down.

"Oh. Yeah. According to my therapist," said Andrew with a humorless laugh. He'd stopped making progress in therapy after his trip to the bluffs. He suspected he'd get a new diagnosis in his chart if he told his therapist that he was being stalked by a faerie from Lilydale.

"Well, how about we go out for drinks?" said Sam. "Try to loosen you up a bit."

"Do you actually want me to go out with you, or do you just feel sorry for me?"

Sam snorted. He shoved his shaggy hair behind a pierced ear. "I don't feel sorry for you. I am very well aware your solitude is a choice. Remember over Christmas when that girl from the U asked if you wanted to go out for coffee, and you were just like, 'I don't drink coffee,' and stared at her till she left?"

"Indeed," said Andrew with a sniff. He pushed away from the desk and stood up, arching his long, lithe spine and touching his fingers together.

"Brag," muttered Sam, about a head and a half shorter than him. He squeezed past Andrew and unbuttoned his collar as he crossed to the shop door. "Can we go to The Squire? It's been, like, a month."

"Do we go anywhere else?"

"*Touché.*" Sam turned his attention to his phone as they stepped outside into the humidity. He was very good at picking up on Andrew's cues that silence was preferred over small talk, and always seemed able to comfortably ignore Andrew.

The horizon southwest to them was glowing with a fading sunset. The Squire was about half a mile down West Seventh, which on a Friday evening was densely populated with restaurant diners and people making their way to shows or events at the convention center. Sam and Andrew enjoyed the walk, and it was easier to leave their cars in the tiny lot behind Magic's instead of hunting for street parking.

Already feeling his shoulder-length hair sticking to the back of his neck, Andrew snapped an elastic band off his wrist and tied his hair back. "You have friends, right, Sam?"

"Er, yes," Sam laughed. "I have four roommates."

"But you want to spend your Friday night with me."

"I'm an only child, and my mom deadnames me all the time. So you feel like spending time with family. The right kind of family."

Andrew smiled faintly. "Agreed."

As they stepped into The Squire ten minutes later, Andrew muttered, "Ugh, there's a show here tonight." Behind the host stand, a crowd clustered around the plain little stage with its two speakers and row of spotlights currently aimed at a woman crooning about heartbreak next to a man playing a banjo. The bar's tin ceilings reverberated the music a thousand times, making sure Andrew always left with a migraine on show nights. It truly must take a special kind of extrovert to enjoy such a tiny, noisy show at a hole-in-the-wall bar. There was a little blonde woman who certainly seemed to be getting into it, arm hooked through the elbow of a man wearing a forced smile on his light brown face. Andrew's gaze lingered on his strong, squared jaw and cheery apple cheeks until his head started to turn as if sensing Andrew staring. When Andrew quick-ly looked away, he found Sam fixing him with a bemused smirk and a raised eyebrow.

"Shut up," muttered Andrew, giving Sam a push.

Mercifully, The Squire had a second room through a green telephone booth door past the stage. Sam cut confi-dently through the handful of people standing around the stage, Andrew slipping silently after him until they made it into the second room. It wasn't totally peaceful with the show going on, but it was more tolerable.

Framed by a glinting rainbow of bottles and crystal glasses, the bartender caught Andrew's eye when they came through the door, giving him an obliging nod. Kate was broad and heavily tattooed, with thick plastic glasses on the end of her nose, and a mop of short, salt-and-pepper hair. She pointed her thumb toward a small table near the bar with two chairs, not quite cleared yet, but the only empty spot in the room. Andrew grabbed Sam's elbow and led them to the table as Kate joined him and swept the crumbs off the table with a damp, dirty rag.

"You, here, on a night with a show?" asked Kate with a *tsk*. "So many people."

Andrew grunted.

"It's my fault," laughed Sam. "I'm a rascal."

"You're an angel, kid," said Kate. "We have a raspberry cider on tap right now. You interested?"

Sam nodded vigorously. "Oh, yes please."

"And an Old Fashioned for you, sir?"

"Of course. The perfect drink for an old man like me."

Kate shot Andrew a nasty look that screwed up her features. "Aren't you thirty?"

Andrew cast his eyes to the tin ceiling. "Thirty-*two*," he said with a sigh.

Disdainfully shaking her head, Kate sauntered back to the bar. The thrum of the music and the press of other patrons laughing and arguing around the bar plucked them out of time and space until only the bar existed.

"She knew your mom, right?" Sam asked as he stuck his tongue out at his phone and nodded in satisfaction, tapping away, and then lifting it to snap a photo of Andrew. Hurriedly, Andrew slapped his palm against the lens with a glare. Sam grinned, undaunted, setting his phone aside. "Didn't even have the camera open," he said with a glint in his hazel eyes.

"Yes, I saw a lot of her in my teens," Andrew confirmed with a nod toward the bartender. "She'd check on me and my mum a lot. I called her when my mum almost blew up our apartment."

Sam raised his brows. "She what?"

"Don't do drugs, kid."

"Wow," Sam breathed. "Sorry, you just don't usually mention your mom. I guess I get why now."

Kate squeezed back around the bar and delivered their drinks. "Food?"

Andrew shrugged. "Maybe in a bit?" She nodded and left them. He watched her leave with a furrow in his brow. He seemed to come to The Squire primarily to torment himself, given Kate always made him think of his mum, and thinking of his mum was like swallowing knives. Maybe being haunted by the scarlet-eyed faerie wasn't that bad, since it was a welcome distraction from his childhood.

Sam watched the crowds with a feline smile curling his lips, taking small sips of his drink, the can lights turning to magical gleams in his glasses. Andrew took a larger drink than necessary from his own glass, clearing his throat as the liquid seared its way into his belly like a flamethrower.

"Dude," said Sam, his eyes tracking someone making their way to Kate's bar. He blinked, turning in his seat. "I think I know her." He cut a sidelong glance at Andrew and said slyly, "And *you* look like you want to know her *friend*."

"Mind your own business," he grumbled as Sam leapt from his seat and moved toward the short blonde girl Andrew had seen a moment ago. She had her meaty fingers still wrapped around a light brown bicep that belonged to the man with the square jaw. His lips were stretched in an uncomfortable grimace as he lightly pawed at the girl's grip on him.

"I really don't drink much, I swear," Micah Stillwater was saying to the short blonde girl whose fingers dug into his bicep. It was her social media post that had led him to The Squire, but he wasn't expecting her to...attach herself to him. She was a younger girl, not much over twenty-one, and still acting like a teenager. Cirrus was leaning into the popularity of the witchy aesthetic more than when he'd seen her last, Micah noted. She was wearing a choker with an amethyst crescent moon, a black dress, and heavy eye makeup around her doe-brown eyes. She even had a large, fresh grayscale lantern tattoo above her prominently displayed cleavage.

"Really, it's on me," said Cirrus. "I didn't think I'd ever see you again! You were around all the time after I graduated high school, but then you literally vanished, like a figment of my imagination. You still 'like' my music posts and stuff, but you're never at any of the shows anymore."

Micah shrugged, wincing as she ordered him something random from the bespectacled bartender. The gray-blue gaze of the bartender stayed fixed on Micah a little longer than he was comfortable with.

"IDs, please," said the bartender.

"Oh." Micah's heart lurched. He hesitated, watching Cirrus easily flash her card as he started to fumble with his wallet. He cautiously held his card out to the woman, who took it and stared at it, then him, then it again.

She grunted, handing it back with a slight shake of her head. "Older than you look."

Micah remained silent, his stomach clenching. His father was going to get an *earful* about all this. Micah hated having to show his ID, and if Julian had just let him stay at home, he wouldn't have needed to. But no, Julian insisted Micah needed to get out of the house, trying to claim Micah was too young to be around for the brownstone bingo night Julian was hosting. That could hardly be true, but Julian knew he needed an ironclad excuse to get Micah out of the house when he wasn't working. But what was so bad about wanting to make sure his father was okay? Julian's fits were unpredictable, random, and often violent. It had taken a long time for Micah to figure out how to help him through them.

"It's his hair," laughed Cirrus. "Anyway, *Micah*, why did you vanish? What are you up to?" She took a drink from her electric blue cocktail.

"I'm not doing a whole lot besides work," he said, finally tearing his eyes off the suspicious bartender.

"You sound like you're forty," the girl said as she pressed a canned seltzer into his hand.

Feigning a drink, Micah choked on a strangled groan.

"Cirrus?"

The blonde spun around as a small shaggy-haired person broke into a beaming smile. They squealed and embraced each other while Micah held the seltzer up over Cirrus's shoulder as she knocked into his chest. Someone at the table in the corner was watching the embrace with red eyebrows raised sardonically, likely similar to the face Micah was making.

Glad to have Cirrus's attention deflected, he edged

around the pair as they chattered happily, with enthusiasm only young adults could still muster. Half tempted to drop the seltzer in a bin bursting with dirty dishes and empty cans near the bathrooms, Micah was ready to make his way back to the stage when he felt the tingle of someone's eyes on him. It was the owner of the sardonic eyebrows, whose sharp gaze held him with curiosity until Micah noticed. An angular profile appeared when the pale man looked quickly away, hunching, fingers curling around his tumbler. Micah barely had to squint to notice the brush of color on the man's high cheekbones. It brought a grin to his face and made his gait falter; he slowed, turning toward the table in the corner. Heavens, that man was a *lithe* form—even though he was hunched up like a fox in the forest dreading to be seen, he was all long lines, long hair, long and slender neck.

From his seat, Andrew took a shaky drink of his Old Fashioned as the pair of checkered sneakers turned toward him. He knew he'd been staring too long, but hoped it would go unnoticed. Alas. It was noticed. After a moment, he steeled himself and glanced up as he said, "I saw my bespectacled friend knows your—" Friend didn't seem to describe the way that girl had been grabbing him. "Blonde...companion."

With an easy smile on his plush lips, the man nodded. His skin was warm brown like sunbaked sandstone, and his eyes were some midtone that had to be blue or gray or green or...honestly, they looked a bit violet. "Little bouncy balls of energy, aren't they? Ah, to be young again." He was soft-spoken with a tenor voice like a breeze rustling prairie grasses.

"Absolutely cannot relate," Andrew said. "I have always operated on a thin reserve of energy that depletes with the slightest provocation." He blinked, surprised at his own ability to generate a coherent thought to a stranger. This man must have something special in his blood.

Snickering and nodding, he said, "I'm Micah."

"Andrew. You can take Sam's spot." He gestured to the seat opposite him.

"I don't know. If she fights me for it, I'll probably lose."

"He," corrected Andrew.

"Oh. Apologies."

"He doesn't correct people that often, but I will. Doesn't mean you can't take his spot though." Andrew kept talking—rambling, really. Very out of character. "I'm his boss, so I can decide that for him."

Micah's eyes sparkled. "If you insist."

Andrew glanced at the bar where Sam was still gesticulating excitedly. "Those two haven't stopped talking since he went over there. Who is that?"

"Uh, I don't know much about Cirrus besides her name." Micah sank into the spot opposite Andrew. "We run into each other at shows like this a lot."

"Ah." Andrew trailed a finger around the lip of his glass.

"So you're part of the reason my peaceful little hole in the wall is so rowdy tonight."

"Hey, now, don't lump me in with the kids over there. I was also forced to socialize tonight." He grimaced. A little dimple stood out on his cheek. "Do I detect a bit of a British accent on you there, Andrew?"

"I can never seem to scrub the Scouse off me altogether," Andrew agreed with a nod.

"Sorry, Scotch?" Micah blinked.

"Scouse. I'm from Liverpool," Andrew explained.

"Oh, so like, you got a Cockney thing going on?" Micah imitated the lilt that might have been garnered from watching the *Newsies* movie.

With a tired sigh, Andrew shook his head and said, "No, sir, that's south London. Liverpool is in the east. Think of it like the *Fargo* accent among Minnesotans."

"Got it." Micah smiled like this was the best thing he'd ever heard.

After posing for a photo with Cirrus, Sam rushed over to the table with her in tow and said, "Dude, Andrew, Cirrus did tech crew with me at the U. I haven't seen her in, like, five years! Isn't that nuts?" He paused. Pushing up his glasses, he glanced several times between Andrew and Micah before finally saying with a sly crease appearing under his eye, "Well, hello there, Andy's new friend. What's your name?"

"Sorry I took your spot," began Micah, starting to stand,

but then Cirrus leaned an arm on his shoulder.

"You're good, babycakes," said the young woman. Confused incredulity wrinkled Micah's brow. His lips formed the word 'babycakes' like it tasted bad. Cirrus didn't notice. Andrew brought his glass to his lips to hide his grin.

Sam picked up his cider and took a swig. "I can't believe Andrew let you sit down. Most people would get hissed at."

"Sam," Andrew hissed.

Sam winked at him before returning his attention to Micah. "Look at your dope gauges. How long have you been stretching them?"

"Oh," laughed Micah, trying to roll his shoulder and slide Cirrus's arm off him. It didn't work. "I'm not the one to ask. There was a lot of excess force involved." He tugged on the emerald in his earlobe.

"That's the badass way to do that," said Cirrus with a gleam in her eye.

"I assure you," Micah said, shaking his head, "It is not. It is the stupid way. I wish I'd done it as slowly as you're supposed to."

Andrew settled back into his seat, realizing as his heart sank that obviously Sam and Cirrus were preferred company over himself. And what was his heart getting all fluttery for, anyway? He wasn't the type to make a romantic connection at all, let alone at a *bar*. And *especially* not with someone as charismatic and attractive as Micah.

Micah's eyes strayed back to Andrew, so he wasn't looking when Cirrus dropped herself onto his knee. His eyes bugged but he managed to stay silent by gripping the edge of the table as hard as he could.

"I think," sang Cirrus, "that we should go down the street to that speakeasy in the basement of those artist lofts." She cast Micah a hooded glance over her shoulder as she sipped from her drink.

Sam exclaimed, "Dude, I've heard about that place!"

"You haven't *been*?" demanded Cirrus, clicking her tongue. "Babe, where have you been living since college? Under a rock with *this* nerd?" She jabbed her thumb in Andrew's direction.

Andrew, to his credit, didn't give her any other response besides a slow, indifferent blink as he took a sip of his drink.

"Hey," Sam cautioned, putting his hand on Andrew's shoulder, "this is my boss. And my friend. Don't be a jerk."

"Yeah, yeah, my bad and everything." Cirrus finished off her drink in one swig and a little shudder. "Anyway, let's do it. The speakeasy. It's killer, trust me." She stood up from Micah's knee and fixed the tight hem of her dress, checking her teeth in her phone reflection. "C'mon, boys."

Sam and Andrew had a lengthy, wordless exchange while Sam carefully scrutinized Andrew's face. Andrew sighed slightly, scratching at his shirt collar and exposing a chain necklace. With a louder sigh, Sam said, "You really don't wanna come?"

"I'll stay here," Andrew said patiently. "You go and just

text me when you get home."

"Oh, no." Cirrus pressed her hand to her cheek. "You don't want to come? So sad." She stuck out her lip in a quick pout before waving cheerily. "Bye. Come on, Micah."

Grimacing, Micah said slowly, "I'm good. I came for the show, so...yeah, just not really feeling—"

"What! I haven't seen you in like, four years, and we all know you're gonna go back into hiding," whined Cirrus. "Please? Please?"

"Sorry, Cirrus," Micah said, a bit more firmly. "You go on."

Leaning over Andrew, Sam was mid-sentence in a whisper when Andrew batted at Sam's bangs like a cat until Sam straightened with a scowl. Cirrus sneered at Andrew, hooked her arm around Sam's neck, and hauled him away through the telephone booth doorway.

"She's fun." Andrew sipped his drink.

"Not my type of person," said Micah.

Andrew's umber eyes flicked toward Micah, and then away, curiosity pinching a crease between his eyebrows. "What's your type of person?"

"Cats."

Disarmed, a grin and a chuckle escaped Andrew before he ducked his head. The sound was reminiscent of lonely library halls, sheltering a wealth of knowledge if one only had the patience to stay.

"But, anyway," Micah added, shifting on his seat, "that

was technically true. I did come for the show, so I can leave you—"

"Oh." The warmth slipped away from Andrew's expression, leaving something carefully neutral in its place. "Right."

Micah cleared his throat, awkward. The offer was meant to provoke him to ask him to stay, but it seemingly backfired. Determined to get clarity, Micah said carefully, "I could stay. If you'd like." They held each other's gaze for several silent moments, the voice of the singer from the other room soaring as she begged her wayward lover to come home.

"I feel a bit silly," Andrew admitted.

"Why's that?" asked Micah.

Andrew turned the glass in his hands, watching the amber liquid swirl gently. "Generally most people I meet are sort of a bore," he said slowly, his accent particularly apparent on the last word, "but I find the thought of you leaving so soon to be painful."

A grin spread across Micah's lips, his neck heating up as he asked with a laugh, "Do you always talk so formally?"

"Kind of, yeah." The curves of Andrew's ears were dark red as he rubbed his chin and took a deep drink from his glass.

Micah's grin widened. "It's cute."

The bartender appeared so suddenly at Micah's shoulder that he jumped. She set a glass of water in front of him and pointed at the seltzer. "You want me to take that?"

"Ah." Micah frowned. "Yeah, I won't drink it. Thank you."

"You sober or something?" asked Andrew.

Shrugging, Micah said, "Mostly. And I don't drink shitty drinks." Andrew grinned. "No offense," Micah added to the bartender.

"Oh, no," she said with her gray-flecked brows raised, "you're absolutely correct." She picked up the can and then propped her other hand on her hip. "Food, now?" she asked Andrew.

"I should probably eat," Andrew said.

They both ordered, conversation gradually becoming easier as Andrew nursed his drink without replacing it with more, his shoulders relaxing and his eyes more often meeting Micah's. Their matching veggie wraps arrived quickly, but Micah could only feign interest in his food since his company was so much more captivating than the meal.

Andrew tugged the elastic out of his hair and let the locks fall to his shoulders. Transfixed, Micah stared as Andrew teased apart the tangles with his fingers. He blinked and looked back up at Andrew, whose slender peach lips quirked in the corners as he set his chin on his hand.

"Who forced you to socialize?" asked Andrew. "You said earlier."

"Oh." Micah hurriedly swallowed a bite of food, wiped

the corners of his mouth, and told him, "I'm usually just staying home with my dad, but he kicked me out tonight. Told me to hang out with people my own age."

"Well," said Andrew, "they left." He pointed his thumb toward the phone booth door.

Micah grinned. "You think you're older than me?"

"Hm," was all Andrew said, and Micah sagged with relief when he didn't have any additional comments.

"Why do you hate Liverpool?" Micah asked. "I'd love to be from England."

"I guess I don't hate Liverpool. Just my dad. He's a psychopath."

"Oh. Sure. My mother's a psychopath, so I get that. We love some good family trauma, right?"

They shared a bitter laugh.

"It adds flavor." Andrew smirked.

Micah felt he could devour that sly expression on Andrew's narrow face without a second thought. Leaning back in his seat, he crossed his arms on the tabletop and curled his fingers into his forearms, trying not to get ahead of himself, trying not to make it obvious how he was imagining twining Andrew's hair around his fingers while they...

"Runes," said Andrew with his gravelly voice rising in excitement, pointing a long finger at Micah's knuckles. He tilted his head. "*Ingwaz* is 'abundance,' and...um, what's the M one here?" He tapped Micah's right pointer finger.

"*Mannaz*. Kind of a sexist one, 'man,' technically, but more broadly, the self," Micah explained. "You didn't strike me as someone who would recognize runic symbols."

Uncertainty flashed across Andrew's features. "I'm well-read," he said after a moment.

"Evidently," said Micah with a placating smile.

"Did you do them yourself?"

"Oh, no," said Micah, staring at the ceiling. "That would be stupid and reckless, not at all what I was like when I was younger with too much time on my hands." He looked down to find Andrew smirking at him again. It made Micah's toes tingle as he cautioned, "Andrew, you gotta be careful with that look."

"What? Why's that?"

"It's making me very much wish we were kissing." The words fell out of Micah's mouth on an impulse, but the effect on Andrew was immediate: his cheeks and ears flamed brightly, and his eyes went round and then quickly downcast.

The bartender snuck up on Micah again with a receipt booklet in hand. He jumped, and then quickly handed her his card before Andrew had even collected himself. He gave the bartender a little smile, but her eyes were on Andrew, a furrow in her brow.

Clearing his throat, Andrew glanced up at her and then at Micah's card in her hand. He blinked and then made a noise of protest, and it was enough to dismiss the bartender, who shook her head and moved over to the register behind the bar.

"I don't think she likes me," Micah observed.

Andrew paused, looking briefly dazed, and then said, "Nah, she's all right. She just knew me as a teenager. Protective, or something."

"That I can respect," Micah said. It didn't explain why she'd looked so suspicious about Micah's ID, but he was at least slightly more accustomed to that. "Does she need to protect you?"

Andrew studied Micah with such intensity that heat rose to Micah's cheeks. As he was about to answer, the bartender dropped the receipt booklet in front of Micah and said to neither of them in particular, "Be good."

As Micah slid his card back into his wallet, Andrew let out a shallow breath through his nostrils and cocked his head silently toward the exit. As they slithered through the crowd and waiters and the host stand, Andrew reached back and clasped Micah's hand. His palm was cool and callused, the grip of his fingers sure and strong. A hummingbird pulse drummed against Micah's hand.

Outside, the indigo sky was at the threshold between dusk and nightfall, dark enough for the streetlamps to be glowing incandescent overhead, and neon lights to cast strange shadows from The Squire's windows.

Releasing his hand, Andrew turned and said in a rush, "I didn't really have a plan, once we were out of there. I walked." He pointed north, toward the silhouetted skyline of the city.

"Me, too," said Micah, sliding his hands into his jeans and pulling out his phone. "Let me order a car."

"I like to walk," Andrew said. Under the kaleidoscope lighting, Andrew's pupils were enormous, his bark-brown irises almost gone as if in a solar eclipse.

"Whoa." Micah frowned. "Your pupils—"

Hooking a finger through Micah's belt loop, Andrew bumped them into the brick wall under the bar's awning. His hands slid onto Micah's cheeks, and he stooped to bridge their slight height difference and pressed their lips together. Micah jolted. Andrew's mouth was feverishly hot.

After a beat, Micah lightly pushed him back, swallowed, and said, "Are you okay? You're so hot."

Andrew's fluttering lashes glinted like copper. "I—I'm sorry, I thought you had said—" He dropped a hand off Micah's face.

"Hey," Micah murmured. "I'm just making sure."

It was a relief to Andrew when Micah's muscled forearm slid around his waist. Andrew caught a glimpse of syrupy lilac-colored irises before he let the press of Micah's lips envelop him, tasting sweet like mulberries before everything beneath Andrew's skin seemed to spin like a tumbling leaf in the autumn.

Andrew grew heavy and almost limp against Micah; he pulled back with a frown. "Let's get you home," he said quietly, cupping Andrew's scalding neck with his fingers. His palm brushed against Andrew's necklace, which shocked him like static. Micah dropped his hands immediately, frowning more deeply.

Andrew blinked down at Micah, untangling his arms from his shoulders and straightening. One of his knees buckled, and he slumped against the wall for a moment, pressing the heel of his hand to his forehead. "Yeah," Andrew said.

Taking a small step away, Micah said, "Where are we going?"

"Magic's," said Andrew. He crossed his arms over his stomach and started off at a clipped pace, a muscle spasming in his angular jaw.

Hurrying after him, Micah blinked. "Where are we going?" he repeated.

Andrew laughed, glancing back at Micah. When the streetlights flashed in his eyes, his irises were back, now the color of antique gold. It allowed Micah to relax again, reminding himself that they both had to walk this way, that nothing was happening right now except an evening walk.

Andrew explained, "My shop is called Magic's. Computer Repair. And Programming, since Sam does that now. The sign was there when I opened my shop, so it seemed serendipitous."

They crossed under an enormous, knotty-rooted maple tree, cicadas buzzing noisily from the branches.

Staring at the sky, Andrew said more softly, "Kind of like tonight." Andrew blinked, as if surprised to hear himself speak.

Grinning, Micah bumped their elbows together. "Yeah." After a few minutes, as they headed westward off the main road past a seedy gas station, Micah said, "Dude, I live, like, two minutes from here."

"Ah, yeah?" Andrew looked where Micah pointed east toward the river. "Funny we've never met before."

"Maybe not directly," Micah said softly. "But maybe we've crossed paths."

They went across the quiet street and approached a faded black and white sign in splintering wood that read MAGIC'S. Micah followed Andrew around to the rear of the small brick building. The second story windows were all open, cloaked with fluttering red curtains. A white flood light flashed on, spilling over them in a garish play of light and shadow.

In The Squire, Micah had felt the desire to kiss Andrew like fire in his veins. It was almost like the spark had jumped from him to Andrew, blazing like a wildfire that was extinguished the moment Micah stepped back from him outside the bar. But Andrew seemed okay while they walked. Maybe he...didn't hold his liquor well. Or maybe the kiss had been a reckless impulse. Micah certainly understood *that*. But those weren't the only options. They were just the only ones Micah wanted to think about.

Fumbling with his keys, Andrew fit one in the lock in the solid metal door. His back was to a small crumbling lot with just two cars parked, and a dilapidated plank fence wrapping around two of the sides. Using his shoe to prop open the door, Andrew braced himself in the doorway and gave Micah a long, silent look.

"What is that face for?" Micah asked in a hush, as if afraid to frighten away a skittish animal.

Blinking, his lashes shadowing his high cheekbones, Andrew ran the tip of his pink tongue over his lips and said softly, "I want to kiss you again. I want it so bad it's like you have me under a spell."

Micah's stomach clenched. He managed an awkward half laugh and a dismissive shrug, but Andrew remained serious, his cheeks ruddy as if with fever. He gently picked up Andrew's hand, which was like touching a steel radiator. When Andrew had taken his hand on their way out of the bar, it hadn't felt like this. Then, it was a shadow, cool and comforting.

Andrew stared intently at their joined hands, jostling Micah back into the moment. He lifted Andrew's hand to his mouth and brushed his lips against his prominent knuckles. "Why don't I come back tomorrow?"

His breath catching and falling in a shuddering sigh, Andrew leaned more heavily on the doorframe. He nodded, silent.

"I work in the morning. I manage a bubble tea shop. I'll come over when I get off, okay? You like tea, right? You're British, so I assume so."

A smile flickered on Andrew's face and then disappeared. He nodded again.

"Get some sleep," said Micah, stepping back again, digging his nails into his palms. Andrew didn't move but to lift his head and watch as Micah continued to retreat, his cheeks pink and odd against the deep shadows of his jaw and eye sockets, the flood lights shining too brightly in his dark eyes. Unsettled and distracted, Micah almost ran into a car parked on the curb before he finally looked away from Andrew. Goosebumps rose on his arms as he hurried back toward West Seventh, chewing on the inside of his cheek, furrowing his brow deeply enough that it hurt his head.

As he stepped through the trunks of the linden trees outside the stairs to his brownstone, the leaves overhead rustled with the whisper of his name. He jumped, spinning in a tight circle, but there was nobody there but someone walking their dog at the other end of the block.

To the voice in the trees and the tingle between his shoulder blades, Micah growled, "Dude, go away! Leave me alone. I'm not in the mood." He stood in place, waiting until the breeze died down, waiting until that feeling of being watched abated. When he was sure he was alone, Micah marched up the iron steps to his brownstone, pausing outside the door to gaze down the street as if hoping he could see Magic's storefront from his front door. Maybe then he could keep an eye on Andrew, make sure he was okay, and not...charmed.

CHAPTER THREE
THE GÉAS

THOUGH ANDREW FELL ASLEEP smiling, he woke up screaming. He toppled out of bed, landing heavily on his knee.
Fumbling with the clasp of his *géas*, Andrew ended up
snapping the chain and tossing it across his bedroom floor.
Gasping, he rubbed his neck, kneeling next to his bed,
sounds from the street muffled by the horrified pulsing of
his blood in his ears. He staggered to his feet and into his
bathroom, flipping on the light to glare at his reflection.
There were gray circles under his eyes—worse than usual—and around his neck was a faint rash in the shape of
the chain from the *géas*.

"What the hell," Andrew muttered. "What the—"

Last night.

What...happened? A quick glance out his bathroom door
showed no extra shoes by the door across from the kitchen,
no extra lights on. Everything was tidy except that it
looked like his cat had knocked over his stack of books from
the arm of the couch. *That* culprit sat on the edge of the

kitchen island, blinking at him. Arwen Undómeow's fluffy chest rose in a silent meow, her tail flicking where it curled delicately around her feet.

"Save the judgment," he said to her with a growl. "And get off the counter."

She blinked again, ambivalent. Arwen would be hiding if anyone else besides Sam were in the house, so...he was alone.

But he couldn't remember *anything* after leaving The Squire. Nothing outside except...except lips, and the sickly sweet taste of mulberries, and a warm arm pressing around his waist. The smell of the charged air before a storm was somewhere in his mind's memories as well. Violet eyes fixed on him outside the building in the parking lot, fading into nightfall, but lingering like a thumbprint on Andrew's heart long into the night.

Okay.

So...so Micah kissed him. That had to have been the extent of it, at least. But it should *not* have felt so fragmented, so feverish in his mind, not after drinking a single Old Fashioned over two hours.

Andrew's knees went weak so suddenly that he slid onto the closed toilet next to the sink, a shiver crawling up his spine.

"Did I get drugged?" he asked his cat. She blinked at him, impassive. "Fucking figures," he spat. "God forbid I have a normal romantic experience." He dropped his head into his hands, cold with anger and burning with humiliation.

And what the hell happened with his *géas*? He pulled himself back to his feet, peering in the mirror at the irritated skin on his neck, grimacing. It had certainly done *something* last night, adding to his fear and confusion around what had transpired in the gaps in his memory.

Hurrying back into his bedroom, he went to retrieve his phone off his nightstand, but...the charging cord dangled empty over the edge of the table. Andrew frowned, searching for the jeans he'd been wearing where they were crumpled on the floor by his closet. He dug out his phone from the pocket of his pants.

"Shit," he muttered. "It's noon already." He was always a naturally early riser, sleeping maybe until nine on a luxurious day. Flipping through his notifications brought him little clarity about the previous night. Junk email, work email, work email, several texts from Sam, but that was it. He pulled up his contacts, disappointed but not surprised to find that he hadn't added Micah's number to his phone.

Andrew pulled on the same jeans, which smelled like bar food and alcohol, but he didn't care. Ignoring his unread messages, he sent a text to Sam telling his assistant to stay home. Andrew needed space to think.

Taking several steps toward the door, he paused, looking up into his slightly open closet. Andrew stretched and pulled down his small metal crossbow. The bag of bolts fell out with it; he caught it and stuffed it in the waistband of his jeans. It had been a year or so since his last time practicing with it, but he hadn't forgotten how to use it.

Without eating, without steeping his usual cup of tea, Andrew slipped on his moccasins, locked his apartment behind him, and thumped down the narrow stairwell. The right-hand door led outside to the parking lot. He unlocked the door on his left and let himself into Magic's storefront. He dropped the crossbow and bolts on Sam's chair, and then ran the pad of his thumb over the rune scratched into the doorframe as a way to try to soothe himself. Leaving the lights off, Andrew started to pace, arms crossed, wracking his brain for any details that were skimming in and out of his awareness.

Mulberries.

Mulberries.

A sweet-tasting kiss he barely remembered, coarse bricks snagging on his shirt.

"Come on," groaned Andrew, thumping his fists against his forehead, squeezing his eyes shut. "You're supposed to be problem-solving, not *pining*."

Lowering his hands, turning toward the front door, Andrew tried to take a long breath. Then a flash of turquoise appeared in the window, a brown face beneath...someone new, here to haunt him.

Micah could hear Andrew yell from outside Magic's storefront. The jolt of fear made him almost drop his phone—and his bubble tea, but he was less concerned about that. He took a small step closer to the window in the door and saw a spark of orange hair inside the shadowy store.

Then Andrew threw open the door, his face bright red as he said sharply, "What are you doing here? Didn't you do enough last night?"

As Micah's brows rose and his lips parted, Andrew jolted with uncertainty. Micah said carefully, "You don't remember that we talked about it?"

Andrew took a stumbling step back into the shop. He was in the same black button-down he wore the night before, and when he rubbed his collar, he exposed a blotchy pink rash ringing his neck. Micah remembered the shock from a necklace Andrew wore the night before, and now it was gone, with a rash in its place. Andrew's nostrils flared, his chest heaving as he looked past Micah toward the trees across the street.

He said without conviction, "You—you did something to me. You must have. I—I don't remember anything after we got outside. Er, I mean, I do—" His ears turned bright red.

He glanced at Micah, whose eyes were wide and dark even though the midday sky reflected within them like a microcosmic world. The man looked even better in daylight than he had the night before. He wore a slim-cut button-down, a bronze leaf necklace poking out from the undone collar, with fitted joggers hugging his muscled thighs. It was almost painful to look at him, to try to marry the way he made Andrew feel with everything that might have happened when he couldn't remember.

Micah's throat bobbed. "I'm sorry," he whispered. "I thought something seemed wrong. Outside. We—we did kiss, and I understand if it felt like you—well, with your memory failing—" He trailed off, turning away, pinching the bridge of his nose. "Sorry." His voice quavered. Micah kept thinking about his father, over and over, sweat rising on the small of his back. Pressing the heels of his hands into his eyes, Micah said breathlessly, "Consent is really critical to me, and if you at all feel..." He dropped his hands to steal a look at Andrew, who was frozen like a fox caught in headlights. "If you at all feel like I took advantage of you, I respect that, and I apologize, and...I'll walk away and that'll be that. Okay?" He reached into the pocket of his joggers and pulled out a plastic cup with a vacuum-sealed lid. It was one of those cups you pierced with a straw large enough to suck up tapioca pearls. "Black tea with a touch of honey. Er, I made it for you, so I—"

Andrew held out a trembling hand toward the tea, but he didn't come any closer.

When Micah took a small step toward him to give him the tea, Andrew's chest tightened, his stomach lurching. He swiped the tea out of Micah's hand and stepped back into the safety of Magic's doorway. "I'm sorry," Andrew said. "I've drank four times that much and remembered it all. It scares me, and I've got some baggage I will definitely admit has made me...paranoid."

Micah nodded. He looked away down the street, frowning. "I should have known better," he finally said.

"What do you mean?"

"I've got baggage, too," said Micah. "Sitting down with you was the first time in years I've tried to connect with anybody. I should have known it wouldn't go well."

Andrew's hands tingled with the temptation to indulge Micah's sharing, to acknowledge how it seemed like they had common ground. But all those visions of the scarlet-eyed faerie stopped his tongue, kept him behind his icy walls. He asked bluntly, "Did you drug me?"

A harsh, breathless laugh slipped between Micah's lips as he scraped his turquoise hair back from his forehead. "No, Andrew, I did not drug you." He turned away from the store, eastward toward West Seventh. "Look, I'm gonna get out of here." Micah glanced back and met Andrew's eyes with moisture clinging to his lower lashes, which were puffy and flushed. "I'm so, so sorry for all of this." Not expecting a reply, Micah started off down the sidewalk as he blinked to clear his swimming vision. He wiped the tears from his eyes with his wrist, grinding his cheek between his teeth, his chest tight, face crumpling. He barely waited for the crosswalk to turn to let him pass before he briskly strode through the intersection.

Micah tapped through his phone and lifted it to his ear. Unsurprisingly, the call went to voicemail. He said into the silence, "Hey, uh, something happened and I—want to bounce some suspicions off you. I know you probably won't wanna, but I'm pretty bummed, and kinda freaked out, and...yeah. You're the only person I feel safe talking to about this. Stop by if you want."

Within the hour, she did.

The night at the Squire became buried by day after mundane day. Six days had passed when Micah stood beside his slightly shorter father in a crowded co-op grocer half a mile from their brownstone. Julian flipped his reading glasses onto his nose and squinted at the label on a package of tofu. Then he sighed noisily, his shoulders sagging and bumping into Micah's chest.

"Micah."

"What?"

Sticking an elbow into Micah's stomach, Julian grumbled, "You're in my bubble. Go pick out a plant or something."

"Trying to get rid of me, Dad?"

"Yes. Nothing is going to happen to me in the produce section." Julian dropped the tofu into his mostly empty cart and then pushed it determinedly away from him.

Shaking his head, Micah slipped his hands into his pockets and went toward the plant display by the registers. The plants at the co-op were always stunning. They were the freshest, greenest, and happiest plants being sold any-where in the Twin Cities—and Micah had been *every-where*. Syabira, the flower vendor for the co-op, was a mentor to Micah, but she wasn't here this late in the day. She liked to flit in and out when even the first shoppers and the cashiers were bleary-eyed.

Her signature chalkboard signage read with a flourish,

> *There is always*
> *a need for flowers.*
> *Close your eyes*
> *and choose!*

With or without her around, her selection was as mag-nificent as always. He pushed the noise of the shoppers and the beeping of the registers into the background. Eyes closed, he inhaled the perfume of the blossoms balanced by the earthen soil, which loosened the knots in his stomach at once. He picked up a large bromeliad with lemon-yellow leaves growing up in the center, turning it around to in-spect the health of the oldest and largest leaves but finding no fault.

Rather than adding it to Julian's cart, which he would insist on paying for using his disability money, Micah went through a self check-out so he could buy the plant himself. He slid the receipt into the space between the soil and the plastic pot and then turned back to the produce section.

A slender man slightly taller than Micah blocked his path, walnut-brown eyes wary and calculating.

Micah jumped. "A-Andrew?"

Fox-faced Andrew stood in front of him, lips pressed together in a skeptical line. He wore a V-neck tee showing his sharp clavicle and the edge of his metal chain necklace.

"Uh," Micah began, heat creeping up his neck, "Hey. It's, er, did I—"

Andrew mercifully cut him off. "I noticed your colorful hair. Curiosity got the best of me." He had a hand basket dangling from his spindly fingers. All that was in it so far was tins of tea.

Over Andrew's shoulder, Micah saw Julian pause with a mango in his hand to watch this interaction like it was one of the dramas they watched together.

Hugging the bromeliad in the crook of his elbow, Micah said, "I—don't wanna say the wrong thing. I'm, er...I'm glad. That we bumped into each other."

Andrew smiled slightly. It looked like his lips weren't used to curving like that. "Me too."

He was embarrassingly delighted to be talking to Andrew again. Things ended so bitterly the morning after The Squire, and he'd tried to just forget about it. But Andrew just kept returning to his thoughts. He passed The Squire when he went to work, and the kiss under the neon lights out front replayed in his head every time. If only...if only it had happened without that razor edge of dread. Dread that everything Micah had been avoiding about himself for twenty years might be slipping back into his life, demanding action. He'd gotten some advice after he'd left Magic's the last time, but the advice...had not been reassuring.

"Look," began Micah, "I want you to know—"

Andrew lifted his hand, quickly and briefly, and Micah fell silent. Bright color rose on Andrew's high, pale cheekbones as he said, "I don't think you assaulted me. I don't think I ever did." His pink tongue flicked out briefly between his teeth. "I was scared. I hadn't kissed anyone in quite a few years, and I didn't want it to be like that."

Micah swallowed. His eyes burned, and he blinked several times.

Andrew frowned. "Are you going to cry?"

Sniffing, Micah quickly shook his head. "Nah, man, who does that?" His voice was thick. "I just feel the same as you, that's all."

Silent, Andrew nodded, chewing on his nail and looking away.

On an impulse, Micah thrust the plant toward Andrew. "Here. It's a bromeliad. Con—consider it an apology gift. It's non-toxic to cats, but mine try to chew on it."

Staring at the plant, Andrew asked, "How do you know I have a cat?"

Micah bit his lip. Then he picked off a short black hair from Andrew's shirt and held it up. "Evidence."

"Ah." Andrew turned crimson. "Yes. Well, um. Thanks. For this. I gotta...run away now." He bobbed like he was bowing and then turned so fast on his heel that his shoe squeaked.

Micah blinked, feeling dazed, like the encounter was a dream. He looked over at Julian, whose expression mirrored his own bewilderment.

"Who do you keep looking for?" Sam asked.

Andrew blinked and looked over at his assistant just as Sam took an enormous bite of his foil-wrapped burrito. A chunk of cilantro lime rice fell out and plopped onto the silver counter.

"You on' usua'y peo'o wa'," said Sam with his mouth full. He swept up the spilled rice with a paper napkin. Andrew stared dryly at him. Chipmunking his food, Sam repeated, "You don't usually people-watch."

It had been a week or two since Andrew ran into Micah at the co-op. And then ran *from* Micah at the co-op. If that was the last time he saw Micah...Andrew cringed at the thought. He kept thinking about that leaf necklace Micah had on at the co-op; it looked like a real little leaf that had been dipped in copper. He'd had a hunch and ended up looking up what the leaf from a mulberry tree looked like and, sure enough, it had matched the curvy segmented shape that had rested just below Micah's sharp collarbones. The shape had enchanted him so much he'd caught himself doodling the leaf on post-its and order forms several times. "I am not looking for anyone," he lied.

"It must be a boy." Sam beamed.

"You have cilantro in your teeth."

"Don't be embarrassed." Sam used his phone camera to pick at his teeth with a painted fingernail. "You said you haven't dated since college."

"I don't know how. Hookup culture is lost on me," said Andrew. He flipped a piece of lettuce in his taco salad with his fork. "It's just...you remember at The Squire, the guy that was with your rude friend? With the green hair. Micah?" Hoping to avoid Sam's intense look, Andrew turned back on the video on his phone. His favorite swordmaster had released a new video showing a swordplay technique that combined the speed of fighting with a saber with the bold strikes of the Viking seax blade like the one he had.

Sam nudged their elbows together and waggled his eyebrows so they disappeared under the curtain of his hair. "What about him, Andy?"

Eyes firmly on his phone, Andrew, mumbled, "So, that night, we kind of...kissed."

"Andrew!" exclaimed Sam. "How could you not tell me?"

"Because it felt like it wasn't really me, I guess. You know, I *was* incredibly attracted to him. That wasn't the problem.

But for as rarely as I try to get to know people, why did it go that way? It was wrong."

Sam rested his cheek on his fist. "Ah. That makes sense. So you're just waiting to run into him again, huh? Have a sweeter encounter? Andrew's a little smitten."

"I ran into him again at the co-op." Andrew paused his video and then stabbed a piece of carnitas and then scraped it off on the side of his bowl.

"Oh my god! Did *he* give you that plant you have in the shop?"

Cringing, he nodded.

"God. No wonder. Here I was worried you were gonna turn into a plant dad."

Andrew ignored the jibe. "It was nice seeing him again. But I wish things had started differently."

Sam remarked with a shrug, "Everything's gotta start somewhere."

Chapter Four

The Rescue

Andy where are you

Sorry. I woke up early and went to The Bean Factory. I should be back by 10.

Bring me coffee

Yes your grace.

7:23am

Andrew set his phone on a heavy book on the tabletop, lifting his teacup to waft the complex fragrance under his nose. He wrote today's date in his spiral notepad and then leaned over the yellow book pages, chewing absently on a strand of his unbound hair. Someone laughed pleasantly near the register. Footsteps passed near him, paused, and then carried on more slowly. Andrew glanced up as he brought his teacup to his lips. He gasped, inhaled, and choked and spluttered on tea.

"Oh, jeeze," said Micah, turning toward the two-chair table where Andrew sat. "Are you okay?"

"Yeah, yes, yes," Andrew rasped as Micah hurried up to him from the bakecase. Wiping tears from his lashes, he said, "I just can't believe we ran into each other again. Are you following me?" If not for the scarlet-eyed faerie, it would've been a flirty joke. Maybe.

"I swear I'm not. My tea shop is down the block," Micah said hurriedly. He tilted the black binder in his hands towards Andrew. It read QUARTERLY REPORTS. "I wanted to get some work done here."

"I guess if you work over here, I must be the one following you," said Andrew. He tried an awkward little laugh, hoping to dissolve Micah's obvious discomfort. If only he knew how much Andrew had been thinking about him. It was harder to identify times when he *hadn't* been thinking about him in the month that had passed since that night at The Squire. "What's your shop again? To a Tea?"

Micah blinked. "That's the one. How'd you know?"

Andrew felt his ears grow warm. "That's what it said on the cup of tea you brought me."

One side of Micah's mouth curled in a crooked grin. "Oh, yeah. I wasn't sure you would have drank it. Fear of rohypnol or something."

His ears felt close to boiling. Andrew *had* been concerned there was something akin to a date-rape drug in that sealed tea. "I actually didn't drink it," said Andrew. "Sorry."

Micah's eyes crinkled. "No need."

Andrew pushed his hair behind his ear.

Dressed in a plaid collared shirt with the top several buttons undone, Micah glanced at the table and tilted his head so his silky bangs curtained over his brow. The mulberry leaf jingled softly on its polished copper chain. "What're you reading? *The Nature of Faerie Cha...*" Micah's voice halted on a strangled note. "Charm."

Slamming the book closed so the blank back cover faced the ceiling, Andrew resisted the instinct to hide his face. How mortifying to be a grown man reading about faeries. "I'm, er, eclectic." He stole a glance up at Micah.

Micah's face was pale. He slowly ran the tip of his tongue over his top lip, blinking several times. His eyes seemed to flicker like a lightbulb dimming. He managed, "It's all good."

Suspicion licked at a corner of Andrew's mind. "Seems like it isn't," Andrew said coolly. His phone vibrated several times on the table, and he used the opportunity to collect his thoughts as he picked it up.

Ok my friend Cirrus texted
me and since I'm alone and
bored she's gonna take me
with her to cechk out this
place up by Cherokee

*check

I think it's called Lilydale

Be back by 11, promise

Andrew gasped, "Oh, shit." He swept the book into his arm and sprang to his feet, his chair clattering. "I gotta go. Sorry." He started trying to write back to Sam, but his thumb was trembling too much.

Micah stepped back to give Andrew clearance. "What's wrong? Are you okay?"

"It's that crazy blonde girl you were with. I think she's up to no good. My assistant Sam—" Andrew paused. He ventured, "Have you heard about Lilydale?"

Micah's complexion paled further. He was the same color as a sandy beach in the winter. His dark eyebrows rose. Then he schooled his expression, a neutral mask sliding into place as he opened his mouth to reply.

"I'm going to take that as a yes," said Andrew. He tapped the phone icon and lifted it to his ear. Sam's phone went straight to voicemail. Swearing again, he took a wide step toward the door of the café.

"I can come with you," Micah blurted. "I—I can help."

Admittedly, Andrew was terrified to return to the bluffs. But he'd been practicing with his sword, and he had his iron knife strapped to his ankle any time he left the house, and he already wore his *géas* everywhere he went. And Sam didn't have any of those things.

"How, and why, would you help?" asked Andrew, clutching his book as he dialed Sam's number again, to no avail.

Micah looked toward the door so the early morning sunlight glinted in his eyes, turning his irises violet. He clearly wasn't wearing contacts; Andrew was too close, and would be able to see lenses. So if Micah's eyes were naturally that floral hue...

Leaning down, Andrew asked in barely a whisper, "Are you even human?"

Micah flinched, keeping his gaze obstinately on the door. His throat bobbed. He answered flatly, "Yeah."

Curling his fingers around his book, Andrew glanced from the cover back at Micah as a muscle jumped in his tawny jaw. This and several other old texts on the Folk told him that Fae beings were incapable of lying. If Micah was Fae, he wouldn't be able to say he was human.

"Look," said Andrew. "I'm not good at feelings. I was really happy when we met at The Squire, though we can agree there was something off-key about kissing there. But Sam told me everything has to start somewhere."

Micah finally tore his eyes off the door to look up at

Andrew. Hope parted his lips as his eyebrows rose.

Andrew went on, "I suspect that both of us wish the night at The Squire had gone better. I suspect we're both capable of better than that. And I could use company going up to the bluffs, anyway. I don't feel safe up there."

"You shouldn't," said Micah, and then he clamped his mouth shut. "Er—"

"Right, but I kind of know what I'm doing. Sam doesn't. He definitely isn't safe up there, so I need to go. You can come, if you want. As long as you know what you're getting into." He hoped his implication was as clear as he could make it without outright saying he believed there were faeries in the bluffs.

Micah nodded. "I do." He pulled his own phone out of his pocket as Andrew tried Sam one more time. Micah's phone made the *whoosh* sound of a sending message. He glanced up seriously and said to Andrew, "I can drive."

Andrew's sword was in his backseat. He shook his head. "I got it. Come on." Then he snapped an elastic off his wrist and bound his hair in a messy ponytail on the back of his head. The pair of them left the café swiftly and in silence.

Micah fidgeted with the warped corner of his three-ring binder, focusing on the car vibrating under the soles of his sneakers. He'd been happy to avoid Lilydale for this long...maybe five years. But if some young kids like Sam and Cirrus were wandering into the bluffs intent to find a party or Fae-spelled foods, Micah had to do something about it. He knew nobody else from Lilydale would. It was very possible that going with Andrew was going to reveal quite a bit more than he hoped most humans in Minnesota would know about him. It was very possible that his efforts to look normal and discrete were about to go to waste. Julian wouldn't be happy about that. But to Micah, less hiding sounded like a relief. Even if it would end with him being rejected again.

He glanced at Andrew, who chewed on a cuticle with a furrowed brow while he drove. He'd missed a bit of auburn hair at the nape of his neck when he put his hair up. Micah found the oversight quite endearing.

He knew the answer, but he asked anyway, "Why'd you ask if I'm human? Did you think I might be a hobbit or something?"

Andrew's walnut-brown eyes flicked toward Micah, and then back to the road. "Do you want me to play dumb? You saw the book I was reading. You didn't make fun of me. You must know what I do about Lilydale."

Sighing through his nose, Micah hoped Andrew knew less than him. "I like playing dumb."

"Okay. Then it was a slip of the tongue. Of course you're human."

"Of course," said Micah softly.

Micah's tone was so tragic that Andrew almost felt sorry for him. Micah wasn't looking at him, with the kind of fierce intensity that told Andrew he was avoiding his gaze on purpose. It all but confirmed to him that he was hiding something. But the details weren't as important to Andrew as getting Sam out of the bluffs and away from any potential Fae encounter. Sighing, Andrew looked back at the road. On the sidewalks lining the bridge, ascetic runners and bikers trudged joylessly up and down the bridge's lantern-lined walkway. After the bridge ended, Andrew hung a sharp right to follow the steep drop-off of the bluffs.

"Looks like you know the way," Micah said.

Andrew paused. "I go running in Cherokee."

"Well, that makes my suspicion sound real dumb."

Andrew allowed him a slight grin.

The lush greenery was held back only by a bike path and intermittent wooden benches. The houses along Cherokee Avenue transitioned from shabby to chic as the neighborhood aged. A large tennis court was busy with early morning players beating the heat of the day. He pulled up to the curb near the city's overlook and his car lurched into park. He slid out of his seat and into the open air, which had cooled slightly now that they were upwind from the river. Andrew spent a moment gazing at the skyline on the northwestern side of the water, cool sepia in the first few hours of light, with the cathedral a mere mirage in the west.

Andrew began to ground himself the way his therapist taught him. Five things he could see. Leaves, skyscrapers, blue sky, his knuckles, the river. Four things he could hear. Children's laughter, wind rustling, his heartbeat, cars crunching on asphalt. Three things he could touch. His iron necklace, his hair, the cool glass window. Two things he could smell. Grass, and tea clinging to his shirt where he'd spilled it. One thing he could taste.

Mulberries on Micah's lips.

As the sensation of that kiss at The Squire returned to him, all the grounding unraveled.

"Grounding yourself?" asked Micah, his sweet-tasting lips quirking into a grin as he popped into Andrew's line of sight.

The breeze licked at Micah's hair, which gleamed like jeweled blades of grass over his brow. Typically, Andrew felt underwhelmed by the fashion hair colors people had adopted in the last decade. But the unnatural hue suited Micah perfectly, even if it made him seem even less likely to be human.

What would Andrew do if he learned Micah was Fae after all? Five years being haunted by the scarlet-eyed faerie had run him straight into the arms of another one of the dangers he'd been training himself to avoid.

"You know about grounding?" Andrew asked.

"Yeah. It helps my dad." Micah looked past him at the rolling hills scattered with trees. Families meandered on the grassy expanse and people threw tennis balls down hills for excitedly stumbling dogs. Several groups of picnickers were spread on large plaid blankets. When he first came to Minnesota, he loved this park. It felt like the border between two worlds, both human and not. The love faded as his relationship with the city changed, as he became rooted in humanity with school, degrees, property.

Micah looked distracted. Swiftly, Andrew bent and reached behind his driver's seat. He grabbed the hilt of a short sword in a black sheath and slid it into the holster he wore under his shirt.

Clearing his throat, eyes back on Andrew, Micah said, "Was that a sword?"

Andrew flushed from his neck to his scalp. "What?" He slammed his car door shut. "What are you talking about?"

Micah stared at him.

Andrew squirmed. "I thought we liked playing dumb."

"Not about weapons," said Micah with a frown.

He kept his hands on the roof of the car, like he was being arrested. "I can't—I *won't* go in there without it."

Micah pursed his lips as he looked at the sky. After a few beats, he asked, "What's it for?"

"People who can't protect themselves."

Guarded, Micah's gaze dropped down to meet Andrew's eyes. "Are you going to hurt me?"

Andrew's stomach turned over. "Why would I need to?"

For a heated moment, they stared at one another over the

hood of the Saturn, at an impasse.

With a knot of shame, hunching in embarrassment, Andrew shook his head slightly. "I'm sorry. I know I'm a disaster. I'm, um—I'm gonna go. Ta-ta."

Then he hurried out of the street and to the walking path that led into the bluffs, his legs like rubber.

He couldn't look back to see if Micah was following him because he didn't want to know. Andrew had pulled a goddamn sword out in front of someone he barely knew. It had to look terrifying. All that waiting to run into Micah again, and he'd ruined everything immediately. But he wouldn't go near Lilydale unarmed, and if someone had touched Sam, then he would need the sword. He ran his fingers along the black chain link fence and peered through the thick underbrush as if maybe he could already see Sam's shaggy head. Vivid red columbines and purple phlox kissed the green expanse, but there were no people.

Micah fell into step beside him. Huffing slightly, he remarked, "Where can I get a pair of your gangly long legs? I'd make much better time in the world." When Andrew spared him a tremulous smile, he smiled back and added, "You think you get to ditch me just because you're a little crazy and dangerous?"

Not breaking his stride, Andrew said without looking, "I was giving you permission to ditch *me*."

"I'm not going to ditch you," Micah told him patiently. "I'm going to help you find your friend. And have a word with Cirrus." His gaze slid down over Andrew and he asked, "Any other weapons on you?"

Nodding, Andrew bent and pulled up his pant leg to show the iron dagger strapped to his ankle. "I always wear this one. Partly for the Folk, partly because I never know if I'm about to get hate crimed." They stood near a park bench and at the entrance to the Brickyard Trail. The path underfoot turned from asphalt to loose rocks and wood chips, and the trees bowed overhead, casting them under a soft green shadow.

"Ah. Hate that," said Micah with a sigh. He asked after a moment, "No guns?"

Andrew grunted. "Guns are evil."

"At least we agree on that," said Micah with a thin smile.

Andrew swallowed. He crossed his arms uncomfortably.

"What? You look like there's more you want to say."

"There's a—there's a faerie from Lilydale who's been stalking me." He looked down, silent for a long time. "I know how it sounds, but I swear it's not—it's not psychosis."

Watching Andrew anxiously fix his necklace and push his hair off his brow, Micah's heart wrenched painfully. He wanted to take Andrew's hand, to assure him he knew quite well that fearing the watchful eye of the Folk was exhausting. He also wanted to know who it was, but...

At his prolonged silence, Andrew lifted his umber eyes, unsure.

Micah gave him a gentle smile. He said softly, "I don't think you're crazy."

As he allowed his eyes to go unfocused on the leaves overhead, Andrew rubbed his face and tried to sort through his thoughts. If he was about to go into the bluffs and straight into danger, then he wasn't going to miss his opening. "Micah, can I make a confession?"

Flushing, Micah said with a faintly nervous smile, "Okay."

"I might not have been altogether coherent that night, but...my brain doesn't seem to care. I haven't been able to think about anything besides kissing you since."

Micah's heart climbed in his throat. He could swear—he could hope—that he recognized desire in Andrew's dark gaze, which remained fixed on his face. Micah murmured, "Same here." He lifted his chin as Andrew took a small step closer, a decisive crease appearing between his brows.

Andrew bent slightly, let his eyes slip shut, and brushed their lips together. His cool hand cupped Micah's cheek. Micah inhaled sharply and strung his arms around Andrew's slim waist. It was different than at The Squire. Slower, gentle. Sort of shy. A kiss of strangers.

They separated with a soft sigh. Before he even opened his eyes, Andrew stepped closer so their chests brushed together, brought his other hand to Micah's face, and kissed him again. Micah melted into his touch, clutching Andrew's hips. A faint moan freed itself from his throat before he could trap it, but the sound made Andrew hold him tighter. When they parted, Andrew's lips were bruised with color and his auburn lashes fluttered.

With a shaky laugh, Andrew rubbed his face and said, "Better than the kiss I'd been imagining."

"You'd been imagining us kissing?" asked Micah with a crooked grin.

Chewing his lip, Andrew looked away and muttered, "Never you mind. I, ah...let's...I can't forget why we're out here." He took a step away and then swayed uneasily, letting out a shaky breath.

Micah started to move closer to him and then froze. "You okay?"

"You're just intoxicating," Andrew said with a laugh. "That's the only explanation." He turned to the trail ahead, and then tripped on a protruding rock.

Micah's stomach twisted. "Intoxicating? What do you mean? Do you feel okay?"

Andrew glanced over his shoulder, his eyes crinkling. "Very much so. Do you?"

While the woods absorbed them into its cool shade, Micah ground the inside of his cheek between his teeth. He still felt stuck on the word Andrew had used. *Intoxicating*. It was a little too close. A little too suggestive that maybe Micah was, by nature, like a drug. Like his smell, and his touch, and his breath were imbued with more power than he wished. He clearly wouldn't be able to enjoy himself until he was sure he wasn't going to hurt anyone accidentally. Micah glared into the treetops overhead and considered what to do when he got off the path. At this point, if he liked Andrew at all, if he wanted this to go...anywhere, then he needed more than advice to protect Andrew. He needed some way to guarantee he couldn't hurt Andrew, no matter what. He wasn't knowledgeable enough to determine what to do on his own. But he needed a failsafe. An absolutely surefire way to ensure he wasn't doing anything...magical.

An outcrop of limestone jutted into the greenery, almost a cairn. Andrew went to move past it, but Micah caught the hem of his shirt. "I think we should get off the path here." He was next to an aluminum sign that read HIKING PROHIBITED.

Andrew lifted his face toward the wild bluffs that beckoned him with a sharp, curled finger. He kicked his boot against his ankle knife, adjusted the sachet of berries under his shirt, and swiped stray hairs back from his eyes.

Micah smiled faintly. He climbed into the underbrush and then turned back, holding his hand out to Andrew. "We'll be fine."

Andrew wanted to believe that they would be. But he had a better idea of the danger the bluffs posed now than when he was here last time, and that did not reassure him.

Drawing him back to the present, Micah said softly, "I swear."

Partly out of respect for Micah's sincere expression, Andrew relented. He used Micah's hand as an anchor and climbed off the trail. As soon as they left the Brickyard Trail, the cloud-smeared sky widened above them.

Around them in the groves of black walnut and ash trees, deer watched them cautiously as they passed. Squirrels scampered past with big green walnuts in their mouths. Velvety brown rabbits froze when they were near, but did not scamper out of sight. They kept nibbling the reeds, big black eyes shining. Red-winged blackbirds dove for seeds and then fluttered away, the neon patches on their wings like airplane signals in the dark. A blue jay yelled at them. Cicadas hummed, and the rush of the river below was a constant purr deep from the earth. The air carried on its current the sweet smell of the prairie grasses that could almost be tasted. Micah stole a glance at Andrew over his shoulder.

Andrew's cheeks were bright with concentration but he bent and folded himself to the contours of the land with ease. Rather than treating the life around him like an inconvenience, each footfall was carefully placed to avoid breaking flower stalks and long-stemmed reeds. Andrew moved without causing harm and touched leaves with just his fingertips. He was honoring the natural grace of the land.

Andrew looked up and found Micah staring. His lips twitched and his eyes danced but he kept on without saying anything.

Micah looked away and muttered bemusedly, "I'm in *trouble.*" Especially because, out of context, this felt like a date. The weather was pleasant, the hills were hushed except for the wildlife, and the company was sweet.

But for Andrew, every step took him back five years to when he was looking for his mum. Every step brought his attention back to his shattered sanity. The likelihood he'd run into that scarlet-eyed faerie was way too great. At least this time, he *knew* Sam was out here, closer every minute to having his own deadly encounter with the Folk.

Andrew's ankle buckled. He fell hard on his hip and swore, elbow jamming into mud and clover. On the steep incline of loose earth there wasn't anything to grab to stop himself. His boots scrabbled for purchase as he started to slide. Deafened by his panic, Micah lunged and clasped both hands around Andrew's waist, yanking him to a halt. Andrew gasped, hanging onto Micah's biceps, which bulged to support him. His thigh had come up against a large root crawling with earthworms and beetles and smelling of fresh soil.

Micah stared in confusion at the root. He swore it had emerged out of the ground just to rescue Andrew. He shook off the oddness of it and then looked back at Andrew, whose expression was pained and whose cheeks had turned the bright red of embarrassment.

"You good?" Micah asked, scanning Andrew's foot to see if any angles looked wrong. "Your ankle okay?"

Heart pounding, Andrew held onto him for a few deep
breaths to let his sense of panic abate. Then he nodded
curtly and managed, "Physically, fine. Emotionally, mortified." He used Micah's shoulder and dug his boots into the
silty ground and stood, gingerly testing his weight on his
ankle. It was a bit tender, but didn't give out.

One corner of Micah's lips quirked. "'Physically fine but
emotionally mortified' is the story of my life." He clapped
the mud off his hands and took a step back up the bluffs so
he was equal in height to Andrew. They traversed in silence
for some time, leaving the shelter of trees, the powder-blue
sky swallowing them up.

They were further into the bluffs than Andrew had gotten when he met the scarlet-eyed faerie. The land was
unfamiliar, and growing more fearsome. Ahead, a large
limestone cliff loomed above scraggly brambleberry bushes
and some short crabapple trees. Sparrows roosted in the
branches, chirping, picking at the fruit. The face of the cliff
was scrawled with powdery white graffiti tags and carved
with signatures and profanity, and quite a few crudely
drawn penises.

Micah glared at the defacement, using his thumb to try to
scrape away some of the profanity. "Fucking scoundrels,"
he muttered. He laid both hands on the limestone and
glanced back at Andrew, looking uncertain. "Hey, I have
to—"

"Oh my god. Andrew?"

Under the shadow of the southern edge of the cliff, Sam clambered to his feet, ducking out from under a crabapple branch and slapping at fountain grass like a cat.

Andrew's heart lurched and his stomach dropped, bringing him a nauseating flood of relief as he cried, "Sam! Sam. Sweet mercy, you're all right."

Sam staggered toward him, squeaking as he tripped on a tangle of roots and landed on one knee.

"Hold on, stay right there. Don't slip." Andrew vaulted over a boulder and reached out for his apprentice's arm. When he had a good grip on him, he snatched Sam into a tight embrace and clapped his back. "What a relief." Andrew clutched him by the shoulders and demanded, "Are you hurt?"

Sam shook his head and dashed tears from the corners of his wide eyes. "No. Just very lost. I don't have any cell service. Cirrus ditched me basically right away." He blinked and looked past Andrew. Then up. "Um, holy shit." Sam pointed.

They both turned as Micah reached up and found handholds on the steep crag. After a brief search, he hauled himself off the ground, feet deftly finding purchase. He carried himself straight up the looming cliffside without looking down. Inspect, reach, pull, foothold, repeat. No line, no hesitation, no stumbling. Wearing Vans. Micah clambered out of sight but then his head popped back out, silhouetted against the glare of the rising sun.

"I'll be right back," Micah called. "Don't move, you two."
A handful of limestone pebbles cascaded down from where
he disappeared.

"Wait," said Sam, pointing at the cliff, and then at Andrew.

Hands on his hips, Andrew stood with his head thrown
back, staring, and then barked a small laugh.

"Hold on." Sam's mouth hung open. "Was that Micah?
How did you end up out here with him? I thought you were
at a café!"

"Later. I need to get you out of here."

"Oh my god. I'm so excited for you."

A tendril of frustration flared in Andrew. "Yeah, okay,
but you shouldn't fuck around in Lilydale, Sam."

Sam flinched. "I'm sorry. We were already practically lost
when Cirrus started spouting some gibberish. She thinks
faeries are real, and people think they live out here with
some...some goth Lady in charge—"

Andrew groaned. "She was talking about the Folk? I
knew it."

Blinking, Sam said, "What? Is she right?"

With gritted teeth, Andrew repeated, "Later." He
grabbed Sam's arm and helped him past the jutting cliff
face. It was so steep beyond it, they were practically crawling. "Why did she ditch you?"

"I don't know. She said she wanted to party. I told her I
had to work soon. So she was just like, 'bye, square,' and

then ran into the trees. Bitch."

Andrew growled in annoyance. "Can I get her number from you? I want to rip her a new one."

"It's not—*whoa!*" Sam's free arm pinwheeled. Andrew grabbed the collar of his shirt and hung on until Sam steadied himself. Sam continued, "It's not worth the drama. I'm just lucky you bailed me out." He was just in an oversized tee and biker shorts, and his sneakers were too chunky to be practical. It was impressive he made it out this far into the bluffs without getting hurt.

"You are lucky," said Andrew. "Micah found you right away."

"How?" demanded Sam. "You've been talking about him all month, and then—"

"I kissed him this morning." Andrew bit his lip, ears burning and his stomach doing a flip as he thought about it again. How impulsive could he be?

Sam squealed, "Are you serious?"

"But he's hiding something. I think he—he might be a faerie."

"A what?" Sam grabbed Andrew's elbow and spun him around to face him. "Wait, are you using that as a slur?"

Incredulous, Andrew scoffed, "What? Absolutely not."

"So you mean faeries are real? Like, the magical creatures with the little wings?"

"Why do you think Lilydale is so dangerous?" Andrew said.

Someone stepped out in front of them as if parting an invisible curtain. "Why, indeed?" sang a sweet, high voice.

Sam screamed, and Andrew spun around and drew his sword before he even saw what their threat was. He crossed the blade protectively in front of Sam.

Clutching Andrew's arm with both hands, Sam yelped, "Sword!"

A short, busty woman blocked their way forward. She had a thick rope of silvery-white hair draped over her shoulder, strung with wildflowers and glinting stones. She was in a silky pink bra and white frayed shorts that displayed her ample curves. "I've heard about you, tall one. Where are you two headed in such a hurry?" Her sharp ears protruded horizontally, pierced with delicate golden bars and snug hoops. Her skin was the color of green tea with cream.

"Let us pass," said Andrew.

"I bet you're hungry," said the faerie. She held out a green apple, technicolor-bright.

Dreamily, Sam said, "You're beautiful." He tried to pass Andrew, reaching for the apple.

Andrew stuck Sam with an elbow to his gut. Sam grunted but stayed back. Andrew said coldly, "We do *not* want your food. We're just trying to get back to the park."

The faerie pouted. She said, "You can't leave before you've played with me. How about a riddle?"

Sam whispered, "I like riddles."

Andrew shushed him sharply.

"Chamomile, you little shit!" Micah's voice crashed through the underbrush with him as he jumped onto the path between Andrew and the female faerie. "How did you give me the slip? I'm gonna cut your goddamn hair."

With a dismissive click of her tongue the female rolled bright eyes heavenward and said, "Calm down, Nightshade Boy."

"Nightshade Boy," Andrew repeated under his breath.

"Calm down?" Micah demanded with an incredulous laugh. He stalked toward the female he'd called Chamomile. "You braided my shoelaces into thistle and then hunted my friends!"

Andrew seized the distraction. He lunged at the female, closing the distance between them with two quick strides. His blade arced through the air, the point landing on the hollow of her throat.

Her bright blue eyes widened. She became quite still.

"Oh, whoa, whoa, whoa." Micah straightened. He hooked his arm through the crook of Chamomile's elbow. He held his other hand out toward Andrew. "Andrew, put the sword down," he urged softly.

Andrew kept the blade against her. He said, "She tried to feed us Fae-spelled food. I don't fuck with that. If I hadn't been here and she'd offered it to Sam, then what? He doesn't know any better."

The faerie scoffed and glared at the heavens.

Hesitating, Micah adjusted his hold on her. Then he said gently, "It was an apple from the supermarket. I saw the bag she had. There's a sticker on it."

"Hold on. Huh!" Sam stepped into view holding the green apple. "Look at that. It's from Trader Joe's."

Chamomile's luminous blue gaze shifted to Micah as her white eyebrows arched.

Something wasn't right with that sticker. Andrew's *géas* was tingling as if to tell him it was a lie, but in a trembling whisper and not a scream. Suspicion growing, he looked at Micah and set his jaw.

Micah continued, "Chami is my friend. She wanted to meet you."

Narrowing his eyes, Andrew said to the faerie, "How do you know me?" To Micah, he asked, "And how do you know her?"

Chamomile raised her chin defiantly. She tried to pull free but Micah kept his grip on her elbow, not taking his eyes from Andrew.

"I told her about you," insisted Micah. "I shouldn't have done that and I'm sorry. After The Squire, I needed—well, she's—like Cirrus, it's the music scene..." Micah trailed off at the look on Andrew's face.

Andrew shook his head, once, sharp. He pressed the tip of the sword harder against the faerie's throat. "I'm not buying any of this."

The faerie tilted her head down and gazed at the blade.

Several small red blisters bubbled to the surface of her skin. Lifting hateful, hooded eyes to Andrew, she said flatly, "You have a reputation here."

Andrew froze.

Her pink lips spread in a cruel smile, revealing jagged silver-bright teeth. She traced her thumb across her forehead, in the same spot where the scarlet-eyed faerie had marked him with her blood.

As Micah watched the color drain from Andrew's face, he looked again at the faerie's blistering throat, grabbed her by the elbow, and yanked her back.

Andrew did nothing but allow them to move away from the reach of his sword. His adrenaline and pounding heart locked him in a fighting stance with right foot forward and left foot back at an angle. Andrew's fear made him an animal, hunched down and poised to strike, his umber eyes blank as stone.

After a heavy silence, Micah said, "You guys should get out of here."

"What about you?" Sam asked. "Shouldn't you leave with us?"

Letting his sword arm fall, Andrew said, "He'll be *fine*. Won't you, Nightshade Boy?"

Micah grimaced.

Andrew grabbed Sam by the wrist and strode purposefully past the pair. He stopped beside Micah, their shoulders almost brushing as he faced north toward the park and Micah faced south toward Lilydale. Looking down and locking eyes with Micah, he asked softly, "You've done a lot of lying today. Haven't you?"

By Micah's elbow, Chamomile snickered.

Micah's face turned blotchy red. He searched Andrew's face for a silent moment, lips stretching into a deeper frown. He finally said, "I don't know how to answer that."

Andrew nodded. "You just did."

Chapter Five

The Folk

"Well, that was awkward for you," sang Chamomile.

Micah and Chamomile wound their way up into a cluster of silver birch trees where the humans wouldn't be able to see them. They were in sight of the brick fence marking the faerie compound, and Micah's skin prickled under the watchful gaze of Folk from within. He slumped down at the foot of a tree and cradled his head, eyes closed.

Chamomile touched his arm, making him jump with her silent advance. She crouched beside him, her braid slung over her shoulder and draping down between her knees. Her soft blushing lips were pursed. "I wasn't going to harm them," she said after a moment.

Micah nodded, his forehead on his wrist. "That's good."

"What does he use that little iron seax for?"

"Iron what?"

"The sword. Does he want to kill us?"

Micah shrugged one shoulder, raking his fingers through his tangled and sweaty hair. "I don't know, honestly.

Maybe."

"Be careful with him," warned Chamomile. "You have no-
toriously dangerous taste in partners." She jabbed herself
with her thumb. She hadn't dated Micah for very long. She
got bored rather quickly. She was fascinated with human
life in the same way that humans watched animals at a zoo.
She liked the spectacle and the novelty. She liked to be
entertained by humanity. She was affectionate, and kind,
but Micah knew it was never meant to last.

Evidently a goblin—given her insubstantial height,
and pointed ears that stuck out horizontally from her
head—Chamomile was small, fast, and arguably unhinged.
Even under bright summer sunshine, her skin had a
sage-green tone beneath the creamy white, and under the
moonlight, she was the color of moss.

When Micah was a boy in Washington, he learned of
the Folk by observing—and by figuring out what he needed to know to keep himself alive—but also largely by
lessons from his sister. Among faeries, there were all sorts
of different breeds. The highest-class, such as his sister
and mother, looked like elves from Tolkien. But the other
classes were all colors, shapes, sizes, and temperaments.
Lilydale's residents consisted of winged pixies, waist-tall
sprites with too many bony joints, gnomes like Syabira,
his gardening mentor, some fish-scaled nixies, mild-tem-
pered but mute brownies, and several more goblins like
Chamomile.

In true goblin fashion, Chamomile was also a hoarder. Micah had been in her hut in Lilydale once, and the sheer amount of clutter was enough to make his throat close up and his head swim. She insisted there was order to everything. He insisted he never needed to stay at her place again.

On the hill, listening to Andrew and Sam tramp away through the trees and leave the bluffs, they sat quietly together for some time. Micah stared down into the valley below. Creamy morning sunlight glinted on the surface of Pickerel Lake. Peals of laughter and a jaunty fiddle drifted through the air from the commune; the notes were hypnotic, unreal, nothing you could hear streaming music on your phone.

Chamomile bent a spurt of tiger lilies down toward her and collected the dusty pollen on the pads of her finger. She painted streaks down Micah's arm while he stared out over the river valley.

"He'll probably want nothing to do with me anymore," Micah said bleakly.

"If he still spoke to you after you charmed him into kissing you, clearly he had already figured out a few things," Chamomile said. "Maybe you should be more like me and not lie. He didn't look happy when you lied about my apple."

"What do you think you're doing, offering Fae-spelled foods to humans, anyway?"

Chamomile shrugged. "I knew he would know better."

"How?"

She remained silent, as if he hadn't spoken.

"Chami. What do you mean? How did you know he would avoid foods from Lilydale?"

Chamomile cast her unnervingly bright gaze in his direction. She had a smear of orange pollen on her small nose. "I can't lie, but I *can* decide when to keep my mouth shut."

He scowled. "Fine. What can I do? To keep him safe from me. His *géas* doesn't stop me."

"Don't exert Fae influence over him, obviously."

Micah growled in frustration. "I don't know how. You've got to have other ideas."

Chamomile sighed heavily and fell back into the grass. "You're so much work, Micah."

"Does that mean you'll help me?" Micah asked brightly.

"Only if you agree to see your sister."

Micah yelled, "What? You—that isn't fair!"

"Alas, the asset makes the rules, doesn't she? Come on then. Come and visit Lilydale." Chamomile started to rise.

"No!" Micah yanked on her shoulder. "Tomorrow. I'll meet her at Amore. At noon."

"Micah," groaned Chamomile. "Don't be a coward."

"I haven't been in Lilydale in five years, and I don't miss it. Come back with me and hang out with my dad. He misses you."

She shook her head. "I have supplies to gather if I'm

going to help you. Just know, she won't be happy she has to go meet you somewhere."

Micah climbed to his feet and brushed dirt off his pants. "She'll live," he said.

Arms draped across her knees, Chamomile glared up at him and said after a moment, "It isn't right that you shun her."

He shrugged. "I would do anything for my father."

"She has done everything for *you*."

Micah hesitated. He wetted his lips. "I have to stay away right now, Chami." Shielding his eyes, he scoped out the easiest route back to Cherokee Park. "You can come for dinner. Anything you want Dad to make?"

"Something cheap that comes out of a box," she replied immediately, licking her lips. "Oh, that yellow macaroni and cheese."

"Ew. Gross. What's wrong with you?"

Chamomile showed him her serrated teeth. Then she lay back in the grass; a breeze rose, smelling of honeysuckle, and then she vanished.

"What the fuck?" said Sam in the car on the Smith Avenue bridge.

"What the fuck?" said Sam when he got upstairs to

Andrew's apartment.

"What the fuck?" said Sam as Andrew sat him on his leather couch and put tea in his hands.

"I can answer questions," said Andrew, "but I don't know how to answer that one."

"You have a sword!" Sam exclaimed.

Arwen Undómeow jumped onto the couch and sniffed Andrew's fingers. Her eyes turned into black discs, her tail puffing into a fluffy pipe cleaner that lashed against Sam's arm. Sam stroked her spine until she relaxed and sat on the throw pillow.

"Yes, I have a sword," said Andrew.

"Are you any good with it?"

"Um." Andrew thought. "I mean...I've taken some fencing, and some classes—because you can find a class for anything—and watched a lot of video tutorials. So, no, probably not."

"And faeries are real!" Sam said. His complexion paled as he sagged against the cushions. "I need food."

Andrew nodded, moving to the other side of the island and turning on the oven. He pulled a pizza out of the freezer and unwrapped it from the clingy plastic wrap. "I believe that the proper noun for a group of faeries is the Folk, and the general noun for someone who is a faerie is Fae. So when we talk about food bespelled with magical properties, it is Fae-spelled." It helped to say it aloud, since using the words correctly sometimes gave him a headache.

"How in the hell does serious, tech-savvy, introverted Andrew know about fae—the Folk?" said Sam. "It's all so...whimsical."

"An accident. Remember I've mentioned my mum was an addict?"

Sam cringed. "Yeah."

"She got food from Lilydale. Foods that the Folk make—like the apple that faerie offered you—are highly addictive and dangerous."

"Oh, shit. She was trying to drug me? I thought Micah said it was from the supermarket."

"Micah lied," Andrew said, frowning. "Which is another conundrum. He charmed you, but he can also lie." Andrew's voice dropped; he was talking more to himself than to Sam. "He can't be purely Fae, and he can't be purely human. I wonder if he's even as young as he looks."

"Why would he lie?"

"Good question." Andrew filled the bottom of a whiskey glass with amber Jameson and then leaned over it, releasing a long sigh. Finally, he swigged the liquid from his cup, shuddered, and then said to Sam, "And I don't want to assume that someone was trying to drug you. Fae-spelled foods only affect humans like that, as far as I understand. To her, it was just a pretty green apple."

"From a pretty green girl," sighed Sam.

"Oh, god." Andrew pinched the bridge of his nose.

Sam's phone chimed urgently. He frowned, tapping the

screen as he said, "Cirrus? Where are you?"

Andrew rushed around the counter to see Sam's screen, which showed a video call with the blonde girl from the bar, her makeup pristine, a milk steamer hissing in the background beneath clinking ceramic cups and the chatter of café patrons. Andrew had found Sam dirty and sweaty and distressed—it just wasn't fair that Cirrus looked so...clean and tidy and unbothered.

"Oh, I'm just at Amore," said Cirrus, flipping her shiny, straightened hair over her shoulder. "You just kept texting me, so I figured I'd call."

Sam hummed with displeasure and opened his mouth to reply.

Andrew snapped, "He kept texting you because you *ditched him in the bluffs*." He leaned over the back of the couch to be in the frame of the video. He needed to be sure this girl could see the savage gleam in his eye and his hatefully bared teeth. "What the hell is wrong with you? Don't—"

"Andrew, I got this." Sam reached back and patted his arm. "Where'd you go?" he said to Cirrus. "You just hiked out of there and left me? Kinda lame."

"I mean..." Cirrus glared off to the side. "I stopped by Lilydale, but I just picked up some drugs. The Goth Queen wasn't letting anyone in anyway, and my plug barely gave me my usual stuff 'cause they're apparently *so* scared of her."

Andrew's eyes went round and the color drained from his face in the video as he reached to snatch Sam's phone out of his hand. "Are you an idiot?" he demanded. "Stuff from Lilydale can kill you! What are you thinking?"

"I cannot tell you how much I do not need a crotchety man like you worrying about me," said Cirrus with a sniff. "And what do you know, anyway?" She blinked at the camera and said, "Oh, wait. I don't care."

As Andrew growled and dredged up another poisonous insult, Sam pried his phone back and said calmly, "Hey, Cirrus, that was really lame and it was not fun getting stuck out there alone after you dragged me along with you. You do you, girlypop, but don't talk to me again." Then he ended the call.

Andrew slumped over the back of the couch with a groan. He took down his hair and fought with the snarls as Sam sighed heavily next to him, tossing his phone onto the cushion.

Sam muttered, "She's a psychopath, isn't she?"

"Sam," said Andrew, pushing onto his elbows so he could see his assistant, "if she's eating the foods she gets from Lilydale herself, I can *promise* you that her life is not headed down a good path. If she's giving them to other people, that's not better, because it's going to be horrible for someone else."

Sam nodded, hugging his knees. "I'm getting that." He sighed again. "Sorry I was so stupid."

"You're not stupid," said Andrew softly. "You shouldn't have gotten dragged up there by her."

"Sure," said Sam, "but you got dragged into all this magic stuff a long time ago, didn't you?"

He nodded. "My mum gave me no other choice. I was already involved ages ago. Cirrus didn't give you a choice, either." Andrew straightened and massaged his neck. "Right, then. I need a shower."

With a grimace, Sam shifted on the couch and said after a moment, "I can go and open the shop for a few hours if you want."

"I don't want you leaving my apartment by yourself now that the Folk have seen you," said Andrew. "For me, at least, that put a target on my back."

Sam swallowed. "Oh. Am—am I in danger?"

"Not in here."

Eyes round, Sam silently pushed his glasses up his nose.

Andrew sighed. He came around the couch and sat beside Sam. "Look, plenty of people live near the bluffs and are none the wiser. Everything I've learned is that people only really find trouble when they go looking for it in Lilydale...like I did. And I've done a lot of research to make sure I'm protected from them." He unclasped his *géas* and put it around Sam's neck. "This is a good start. This should negate the effects of Fae charm so they can't trick you or force you to do things." Again to himself, he muttered, "At least it should. But it didn't seem to stop Micah. That must be what happened at The Squire, too. It was trying to ward off Micah's charm, but it was like trying to use insect repellent on a snake."

Sam peered at the sachet of berries, eyebrows going up and lips turning down with barely veiled disgust.

"It isn't for fashion," said Andrew with a beleaguered laugh.

He glared at Andrew from under his bangs. "My look was for your weird analogy."

Andrew picked up the television remote and handed it to Sam. "Perhaps if Micah is involved with Lilydale, I can...maybe he can ensure nobody bothers you. Anyway, why don't you crash here tonight? You can sleep on the couch or on the double in the second bedroom."

Sam nodded slightly. "I don't know if you'll ever convince me to leave here, honestly."

"That's fine."

He blinked his big hazel eyes. "Seriously?"

"Yeah. This is too much space for me, and now that you got sucked into this magic bullshit, I'd be happier having you where I could keep an eye on you. We can go get whatever stuff you need from your place tomorrow. I know I'm probably not the same kind of entertainment as a houseful of queer twentysomethings, but humor me for now at least."

"Aw." Sam's chin quivered. "You're the best chosen brother a guy could ask for."

Andrew paused. "You are, too." He blinked, sniffed, and looked away. "Uh. Anyway. Gonna shower. Throw the pizza in when the oven goes off, will you?"

Micah used his two-mile walk home to try to unspool some of the tension that had coiled between his shoulder blades. He popped in his earbuds and blasted All Time Low, keeping his hands in his pockets and his eyes on his sneakers. He wished desperately to have something else to distract him from thinking about how angry Andrew had looked. Sword drawn, staring at that apple, realizing Micah had lied straight to his face.

All because Micah couldn't avoid this damn Fae nonsense.

Past the long Smith Avenue bridge where the city hung to his right and the lake and the bluffs to his left, Micah took a sharp left to follow the curve of the street through a quieter neighborhood. All human, nothing overgrown or wild to be seen, except for that chihuahua that lived in the corner house. The transition was almost dizzying. All the more reason to stay the fuck out of Lilydale, he thought bitterly.

He sighed as he approached the tall, pale brownstones and went up the outside stairs into his own. He let himself in and followed the mutter of the television up the stairs from the front vestibule. Micah dropped his keys in a decorative floral dish and slid out of his shoes and socks, grimacing, stretching the stiff exhaustion out of his limbs. He hadn't even been out in the bluffs for that long, but it had been a while since he'd scaled that cliff, and it strained unusual muscles.

Julian warily watched him approach as if he could sense the magic of the bluffs still clinging to Micah. Feigning nonchalance, Micah flopped onto the suede couch next to his father and leaned back his head.

"Smells like you cooked," said Micah.

Julian had gym shorts and a plain tee on since the brownstone was muggy with heat. He never let Micah run the air conditioner in the summer, which saved on electricity anyway. Their fluffy orange tom cat, Cinnamon, draped across Julian's knees and peered at Micah through one slitted eye. Micah scratched the cat's forehead and he began to purr.

Julian held out a samosa. "They were fresh for you a few hours ago." When Micah reached for it, Julian caught him by the wrist and inspected the line of pollen on his arm. He brushed it off with a frown. "I thought you weren't going to Lilydale anymore."

Micah popped the spicy samosa in his mouth and licked his fingers clean, stalling. When he swallowed, he said carefully, "I'm afraid I'm going to have a bit more to do with Lilydale than we'd like."

"I don't understand why," said Julian, voice brittle.

Micah hesitated. "It's just gotta happen."

Amber eyes going unfocused, Julian scratched his nails down his neck several times, a little harder each time. Micah grasped his hand, pulling it away from his neck and laying it on his lap. Cinderblocks of dread crushed the air out of the room.

Micah said softly, "You're safe, Dad. I'm not leaving tonight." They sat in silence while Julian's chest rose and fell rapidly. "Let me get you a pill."

"I'm fine," snapped Julian. He leaned his head back on the couch and shut his eyes. "I'm fine," he said more gently. "Sorry, kiddo. I've just been, um...dreaming about *her* again. Your mother."

Fear reared inside Micah's stomach. "Shit. What? That's not good."

"Be careful with them, okay? They're all the same. They're all like her."

Micah remained silent, studying Julian's creased face. He didn't think most men in their sixties looked as old and weary as Julian. The stress showed on his skin. This didn't seem like the kind of day for Julian to know Chamomile would be over. She and Julian typically got along, since she had the tendency to call him "sir" and ask him about his favorite television. But when Julian was jumpy like this, it was best not to aggravate things. Besides, Micah could probably handle a box of mac and cheese himself.

Swallowing, Micah said, "Why don't you take a nap?"

Julian nodded, and Micah helped him scoot the tray back. They both stood, moving behind the couch and up the stairs. Each flight was steep and narrow and doubled back on itself from a short landing where they'd put tall metal bookshelves. He let Julian off on the second story, lingering in the hall where he could see Julian move around his bedroom. Though he'd refused when Micah offered, he picked up the amber bottle of pills on his nightstand and swallowed a pill with a splash of water.

"Love you, Dad."

The black cat Fadil jumped from a shadow on the steps and twined around Micah's ankles as he circled up the last flight and onto the top floor. He followed the striped runner into his bathroom where he flipped on the lights. Fadil jumped on the sink and chirped at Micah.

"Chami is coming over," he told the cat as he turned on the shower, letting it get very hot as he undressed and took off his mulberry leaf necklace. The cat tilted his sleek head and blinked slowly, his cheeks fluffing with pleasure. The only person Fadil liked more than Micah was Chamomile.

Looking up at the vanity mirror over the sink, he glared at his reflection. Why couldn't he have gotten a naturally occurring eye color like Chamomile? Sure, hers were a bit too bright, and a bit uncanny, but still *blue.* Micah's purple eyes could never constitute as naturally occurring. Before he'd known any better, they presented a problem and attracted quite a bit of attention from his classmates in business school. Parties were an integral part of that culture, and having a classmate with eyes the girls swooned over was an excellent party trick. Granted, he usually got along with the girls better than anyone anticipated, and he enjoyed making their spectacle backfire. Before long, he stopped getting invitations to happy hours and house parties, but he never really missed them.

Micah took out the large emerald earrings from his stretched lobes. One of the black rubber rings that held them in place slipped from his fingers and bounced onto the counter. Fadil pounced on it immediately, flipping onto his back and chewing noisily on it so that his fishy breath wafted up to Micah. Sucking his teeth, Micah snatched the ring off Fadil's canine and got several claws through the pad of his fingertip as a result before, fearing inevitable consequence, Fadil jumped off the counter and bounded out of sight. Micah shook out his stinging finger, sending a silent threat after the cat.

After folding more comfortable silicon loops through his ears, Micah stepped into the spray of the shower and let the scalding water burn off the dirt and sweat, and the sickly sweetness from being in close proximity to Chamomile. The tea tree wash he used smelled antiseptic by comparison. He took much longer than necessary, letting the heat clarify him, his thoughts running down the drain and fading into the floorboards, into the soil and the roots and the darkness in the earth.

While he was staring at his feet, rivulets of water stream-ing off his hair and slipping past his parted lips, Andrew's face appeared in his mind. Micah curled his fingers into his palms, embarrassed. As if Andrew would want anything more to do with him after the spectacle with Chamomile. Spinning the squeaky shower knob off, he shook out his hair and fixed a towel around his waist before he left the bathroom. Fadil immediately stretched out at the sight of Micah, pawing at the corner of a fleece blanket on the bed.

The afternoon let only grayish, weak light into his room, so he lit a candle with a cheap lighter. Potted plants of all sizes lined the windowsills and hung from macrame baskets strung on hooks in the plaster ceiling. He'd made some of the pots himself, but you could tell by how crude they looked. His sister was an excellent artist and teacher, but he was fairly hopeless at the arts. His mulberry leaf necklace had been electroformed around a real leaf. He certainly never could have made anything like that.

On top of an antique cedar bookshelf was an altar cir-cling around a juniper bonsai tree that was almost a foot tall now. He also had several pieces of art from his sister, including a small elk antler wrapped in glittering black thread with rough red garnets erupting out of the blunt end. The thread she'd woven herself on a spinning wheel. She'd made him a nightshade blossom out of dyed sticks, silk petals, and gemstone beads. And she'd even made him a circlet of copper vines that nobody else had ever allowed him to wear. That was the worst part of all of this: she was everywhere in his mind, and yet it hurt him to think about her. The last five years had been the longest he'd gone without seeing her in his whole life.

Micah lay across his bed in his towel and thumbed at his phone. Fadil slunk closer and set his butt on Micah's shoulder. Micah grunted in protest, but Fadil closed his eyes and ignored him. The scent of pine was strong now as the wax in the candle melted. He breathed deep and slow, in through his nose, out through his mouth.

Not long past sunset, Andrew switched off the television to the sound of Sam snoring softly on the couch. He unfolded a tartan blanket and draped it over Sam. Then he switched on his bedroom light so he could move in the kitchen without the lights shining in Sam's face.

He poured the boiling water from his electric kettle over a tea ball, which wafted sharp lemon toward him as it bounced in the teacup. Arwen jumped onto the counter to see what he was doing. He started to shoo her, but sighed instead and scratched her between the ears until she purred.

The toneless chime of his landline phone erupted into the

silence. Andrew and Arwen jumped, and Sam snorted and stirred on the couch.

Andrew snatched up the phone and tapped the green ANSWER button before the phone could cause any further disruption. He paused before he lifted it to his ear; Sam settled back on the couch, rolling over to bury his face in the corner of the cushions.

"Magic's Computer Repair," said Andrew softly, picking up his tea and padding into his room in his house moccasins. He waited until Arwen followed him inside and then clicked his door shut with his heel.

"Uh, hi, ah...Andrew?"

Andrew's tea sloshed in his cup and onto his wrist. Hissing, he hurriedly set the cup on his dresser and shook out his hand. "Micah?"

"Yeah. Sorry if this is creepy. I got this number off your business page when I looked it up."

Andrew trapped the phone between his shoulder and his ear so he could wipe his hand dry on his sweatpants. "I mean, it's a bit creepy, but all quite above-board, ultimately. You've already been over here."

"We never exchanged numbers, but I wanted to talk about what happened in Lilydale."

Andrew almost missed his bed, freezing, shifting slightly, then perching on the corner of the mattress with a creak of springs. "That would probably be good."

Micah let out a long breath. "You were right. I lied a

lot today, and I'm not proud of that. I wasn't prepared to deal with any of it, so I took the easy way out and tried to pretend I didn't need to."

"Huh." Andrew combed his fingers through his hair with a waft of his citrus-scented shampoo. He carefully climbed to the head of his bed and leaned back. "Awfully mature of you."

"This is forward," said Micah, "but can I buy you breakfast? I'd like to give you some space if you have more questions. I'm busy at noon, but—"

"I wake up early." Andrew flinched when Arwen stretched out and pawed Andrew's chin with her claws extended. He covered her small face with his palm, and she chirped in protest. "It's what you get," he whispered.

"What?"

"Sorry. I was talking to my cat."

Micah's musical laugh made the hairs on Andrew's forearms stand on end. "Honestly, same."

CHAPTER SIX

THE WARD

HERE," SAID MICAH, REACHING into a small paper bag and hooking his finger through a copper chain. He lifted out a necklace with a vial dangling from it that was a bit shorter than Andrew's pinky. Squinting against the beams of sunlight trying to blind him, he explained, "Chami and I came up with a variant of a *géas* that should work on me."

They sat at a small metal table on a patio which was wedged onto a cordoned off city street between two cafes. The temperature was just a hair above chilly, the sun bringing a blanket of warmth as it rose into a cloudless sky. By all means, it was the kind of day that kept Minnesotans around even through the winters that transformed the Twin Cities into a frozen wasteland.

Micah was wearing a floral button-up rolled to his elbows and fastened to his throat, making Andrew in a striped polo look shabby by comparison. Even if he'd been dressed nicer, though, he was still no match for Micah's striking features and his sun-soaked amethyst eyes. It put to rest any brief notion Andrew had of rejecting Micah after their trip to the bluffs. He simply couldn't entertain the possibility of never seeing him again.

Their skinny waitress set down enormous fluffy pancakes in front of Micah and a vegetable omelet in front of Andrew, and then refilled Micah's coffee cup. Micah gave the waitress a bright smile of gratitude, making her giggle and shove her glasses up her nose. Andrew snorted under his breath. He lifted his own mug and sipped experimentally before making a face and setting it aside.

"Not good tea?" Micah asked as he blew on his coffee and took a sip.

"Most restaurants don't offer good tea," Andrew said. "This place might seem posh, but it's no exception." He cringed at how snooty he sounded.

"Oh. Well, you should come and test mine. My shop has twenty-six loose leaf blends," said Micah, puffing with pride.

"I should warn you," Andrew said, pausing before a bite of omelet, "not even your cute face will make me lie about tea."

Coffee mug in both hands, Micah blinked, grinning crookedly. "You think I'm cute?"

Swallowing, Andrew daintily wiped his lips and cleared his throat. He said, "Anyway. Why would a faerie help you with this? Especially after I stuck a sword in her face. I did less than that last time I was up there and got five years of terror for my trouble."

Micah cocked his head.

Andrew grimaced. "It was all a misunderstanding."

"All right then," said Micah with a raise of one dark eyebrow, "keep your secrets."

"Frodo." Andrew grinned. "Nice."

"Anyway, I've known Chami for ages, and as unhinged as she is, she's never steered me wrong or turned me down when I've asked for help," Micah explained. "So it doesn't matter how she feels about you. Plus, I don't actually think she cares that you stuck a sword in her face. She probably thought it was entertaining."

With a slight nod, Andrew gestured to the necklace that lay on the edge of the table near Micah's arm. "Can I see it?"

Micah picked it up and draped it across Andrew's palm. Burgundy liquid sloshed against a tiny stone and a stained blossom within the small glass tube, which was wrapped in coiled copper and looped onto the chain.

Twisting off the little cork stopper, he wafted the vial under his nostrils. It smelled coppery, a bit like potpourri, and something...wilder, something more like a feeling than an object. Andrew popped the cork back into place. "I suppose it wouldn't hurt."

Micah nodded and explained, "It's made to ward against me and any powers I might use to affect you by using my blood like a blueprint." Micah unfolded a piece of crumpled paper dense with a spidery scrawl that seemed to be a numbered list. "Basically, we did some science fiction shit to my blood with copper and electrodes, and then combined it with some magical shit like a chunk of iron, some tourmaline for protection, and a rowan blossom. It gave me hives when I touched it, so I think that's a good sign?"

Blowing out his cheeks, Andrew raised his brows and said, "Blimey. How long did this take you?"

Micah scratched his cheek. "Oh, I don't know."

Andrew waited, tapping his fingers on his arm.

With a grimace, Micah said, "All right, I mean, I was up all night, but it's really not a big deal. I have plenty of other opportunities to sleep."

"That's sweet." Andrew smiled.

Silent, Micah blushed deeply.

Andrew lifted the necklace, fumbling with the clasp, pricking his short thumbnail as he unhooked it. His fingers tangled with his hair as he tried to put it around his neck. Frustration and embarrassment forced a little growl from him.

"Here." Micah stood and edged around the table. Crouching, he lifted Andrew's hair gently out of the way and draped it over his shoulder. Then he placed his hands over Andrew's and pinched the clasp so the necklace clicked easily into place.

All Andrew would have to do was turn his head for his lips to brush against the muscled column of Micah's neck. The vial bounced against the hollow of his throat as Micah's fingers tickled the nape of his neck, falling beneath the curtain of his hair.

Smelling blooming lilacs and freshly-cut grass, Andrew caught his breath to trap the scent in his lungs while Micah leaned back and fixed him with his concerned violet gaze. "What's wrong?" murmured Micah.

Shaking his head, Andrew curled his fingers into fists to stop himself from reaching for Micah. "You don't need Fae charm to take my breath away."

The corners of Micah's rosy lips curled. He glanced down to where his hands still rested along the slopes of Andrew's shoulders. Andrew was lean, but firm muscles twitched under Micah's palms. Micah caught his lower lip between his teeth and then whispered, "Can I kiss you?" When Andrew gave him a faint nod, honey-stained eyes wide and color on his high cheeks, Micah tilted his head and leaned close, touching their lips together. Micah cupped Andrew's cheek in his palm, holding his breath lest he break the spell that hung between them, sweet and intimate as it was.

Moving away with a sigh, Micah dropped back into his chair, blushing from his neck to his forehead and wearing a silly grin. He took a hurried bite of pancake and then said around it, "I did not come here planning that, just so you know."

"I believe you," Andrew said breathlessly, taking a sip

of his tea and immediately grimacing as the taste soured his tongue and overwhelmed the mulberry sweetness from Micah's lips. "Damn." He set his spoon on the rim of the cup so he wouldn't make the same mistake again.

Micah kept staring at his pancakes, his smile slowly fading. Somber, Micah looked up and said, "It's important that you know that it isn't in my nature to be deceptive. Literally."

Andrew blinked. Then he nodded faintly. "All right."

"I was evasive with you only because I wasn't sure you knew about the Folk. I have a duty to protect Lilydale's residents. And obviously I'm not in the habit of confessing that I'm not human."

"I understand," Andrew said with a nod. "I feel similarly about Sam. He didn't mean to run into a faerie up there. And I want to make sure nobody from Lilydale will bother him like they have me."

Micah shook his head. "Sam will be fine. Chami won't bother him. She hardly ever leaves Lilydale."

Picking at his cuticle, Andrew remained otherwise motionless as he said seriously, "Understand, though, that if anyone tries to charm Sam again, I won't stay my hand."

Micah didn't flinch. "Understood."

"Which leads me to another question," said Andrew.

"Shoot."

Eyes fixed on Micah's handsome face, Andrew wondered where to look to tell if Micah was reacting. If he flinched, or tried to lie. "You did use Fae charm on me at the Squire. Right?"

Looking away, Micah nodded, combing his fingers through his jewel-bright hair.

The confession was...comforting, oddly. A cool breeze on his face. Everything was out in the open now. Andrew asked, "Did you do it on purpose?"

Humorlessly, Micah laughed and shook his head. "I don't know *how* to use magic on purpose."

"Then what happened?" he asked.

"My best hypothesis is that I wanted to kiss you so bad that it turned into a physical influence," Micah said, dropping his head in embarrassment.

Andrew smiled. "Aw."

"Ugh." Micah covered his face.

Chin in hand, grinning, Andrew basked in Micah's bashfulness. It was something to relish following the fear which had woken him after the night at The Squire. Sobering, he observed, "But you can lie. You're not fully Fae."

His face still crimson, Micah picked up his white ceramic mug of coffee, poured a bit more cream in it, and took a long drink. "Yup." He lifted the silver creamer cup. "Half n' half." He made a face like he'd bitten into a lemon. "My dad lives with me. He's Pakistani. And my mother..." Looking down, he set aside the creamer and stirred the coffee in silence.

With a too-bright smile, the waitress stepped up next to

Micah and asked, "How is everything?"

Micah remained as he was, his thoughts elsewhere, staring at the table.

Andrew glanced up at her and said after a moment, "It's all perfect. Thanks." The waitress cast one more look at Micah, disappointed, it seemed, not to catch his eye. As she hurried off, Andrew gazed across the table at Micah, whose fingers curled into a fist on the table, knuckles blanched. Andrew reached over and touched the back of his hand. "I don't want to know."

When Micah looked up, his eyes were stormy and dark as wine. "What?"

"If your mum makes you feel like that, you don't have to talk about her. I get it. I promise."

Micah raked trembling fingers through his hair. He looked back up with a tremulous smile. "I invited you out so you can ask questions. I wasn't supposed to have stuff that was off-limits."

Andrew nodded slowly. "Parental trauma is different."

Micah picked at his pancakes with his fork. "I've never talked about any of it," he admitted.

"You should get a therapist," Andrew said sagely. "Then you can make off-color jokes about how shitty your mental health is, like I do."

"Noted." Micah grinned. "You're really cool with it?"

"Gallows humor? Absolutely."

Snorting, Micah glared at the sky and said, "My Fae half,

you nerd."

"Well, does it make you want to hurt me?"

Incredulous, Micah declared, "No! What?"

"Then why would I care?"

The incredulous look didn't really fade. "I guess...I..."

With a sigh, Andrew explained, "I already knew about the Folk before we met. And I'm a nihilist."

"O—kay...?"

"That means I'm willing to take risks others may not. I'm ambivalent about death. If something is worthwhile to me, that's all I need to know."

"Ah. I see." Micah grinned. "Very romantic, aren't you?"

Andrew looked down. "I don't have any experience with romance," he said quietly, running the pad of his index finger around the rim of his dismal teacup.

Micah held out his hand across the table, palm up with an invitation. "That's okay." Andrew set his hand in Micah's and flushed when he squeezed him. "How can I show you I'm interested in you?"

Andrew's skin tingled. He stammered, "I-I don't really know."

Affection turning his tone sweet as strawberries, Micah said, "Look at that. I was beginning to think you never get nervous."

Embarrassed, Andrew started to pull his hand away, but Micah pressed down with his thumb. Andrew mumbled, "Oh, no. Attention makes me feel all turned around." When

Micah remained silent, Andrew stole a glance at him.

Eyes dancing, Micah searched Andrew's face so carefully it made him squirm. Finally, he asked hopefully, "Can I take you on a real date?"

He nodded. "I'd like that."

Micah's grin made the sunlight seem dim by comparison.

Two curving steps led up to an old red door outside Amore Coffee on the corner of Smith. The sun glared down overhead at high noon, just like always when Micah met with Ingrid within the city limits.

The bell jangled when he pulled open the outer screen door. He went smiling up to the counter, scanning the room past the bar to see if he could catch a glimpse of Ingrid's curls. No such luck. Micah ordered a heart-shaped banana bread and an iced espresso and paid in cash he'd gotten from tips at the tea shop. The shop pulled him further and further in without any sign of his sister until he was around back from the bar where few patrons ventured. Back here, the conversations were hushed; there was no need to compete with the hiss of the milk steamer.

Scarlet eyes tracked him as soon as he came around the corner. His sister sat at a small round table, her blood-red lips curled in a smile as she held her small ceramic mug aloft in her long alabaster fingers. She was draped in a silky black shift that settled low on her chest beneath a necklace she made herself of a chunk of rough garnet set in aged bronze. Her burgundy curls were so tight they almost coiled, settling around her shoulders like a rusty corona that obscured the sharp tips of her ears. She wasn't actually very good at disguising her feelings and was obviously excited to see him, bobbing in her seat and suppressing a smile.

Guiltily, Micah dropped into the seat across from her and stuck his straw in his drink.

She set down her cup with the tiniest *clink.* "So, it takes a bargain with your lover for you to agree to see me?"

"Dude, Chami and I have been over for, like, a decade." Micah bit his banana bread and said with his mouth full, "Keep up, Red."

Ingrid scowled, her shoulders slumping, eyes on the food stuffed in his cheek like she wanted to reprimand his manners. Instead, she said emphatically, "Come back to Lilydale, Nightshade Boy."

Micah took his time responding, chewing slowly until the bread was mush in his mouth. It was mostly to provoke her. She lifted her fingers to fuss with her necklace but caught herself as if remembering when he'd teased her for being fidgety. Finally, Micah said, "I have a job."

"Which you don't need," said Ingrid.

"And my dad," Micah said. She looked away. She didn't

share the same father as Micah, only their mother. Resting his chin in his palm, Micah said, "It would be easier to see you if every conversation didn't result in you demanding that I come to Lilydale. It's a bit tiresome."

"Tiresome?" she repeated, lip curled. "What's tiresome is that you spurn the place where I expected you to be with me when we left Washington together. I did not expect you to try so hard to avoid me. It makes me..." Her voice trailed off, but her expression was transparent, her eyes looking a little too glassy and forlorn, colored the pink of a sunset.

Micah shut his eyes with a sigh. "It's complicated, Ingrid." He looked past her out the windows and watched a couple walk by arm in arm. "But I'm afraid it's more complicated now. I'm...yeah...I'm afraid."

Scarlet eyes snapped back to Micah's face. She asked with dangerous stillness, "Who do I need to kill?"

He grinned. "Thanks, but it's me that I'm worried about. I don't—um, well, last month I met this guy and I charmed him on accident."

She blinked, and then her lips curved in a tight smile. The expression was too familiar, too like their mother. Micah looked away. "You gave me a fright," she said. "I thought something bad happened to you."

Grimacing, he took a swig of his drink. "I'm not excited about it, Ingrid. I never wished for this. I just want to be a normal person."

She scoffed.

"I know, I know. You can't relate. But if I can charm people, what if that's not all?"

Ingrid was quiet, using her canine tooth to scrape her painted lip.

He said after a moment, "Our mother had to know I wouldn't be powerless, but she always treated me like I was. When we left, I was ready to act like she was right."

Ingrid twirled a curl around her finger, frowning, letting it bounce into her cheek before curling it again.

"Is it any surprise that I've been so ready to deny my Fae side?" asked Micah. "When you think about it, *both* my parents wanted me to. Aren't you supposed to believe what your parents tell you?"

"I wish you wouldn't," she said quietly. "It isn't hard to smell the magic on you."

Micah blinked.

"And if your nature is awakening," she went on, fixing him with a pointed stare, "then wouldn't it be safest for you to be among the Folk?"

Sighing heavily, he slumped against the back of his chair and leaned his head back, glaring at the copper plated ceiling. "*Ingrid*, come *on.*"

"No, you 'come on!'" exclaimed Ingrid. "Why must you insulate yourself in the city? After growing up in the Redwoods—"

"This is the exact same argument we had five years ago," Micah snapped, sitting up, leaning across the table. "Why don't you hear me when I talk to you? I *can't* live like you. And also—" He gestured sharply and said with an edge to his voice, "Why exactly would I want to? I know how casually you all hand out Fae-spelled foods. You've got to know that based on how my dad was treated in the Redwoods, I'm not going to take kindly to that. Anything to say about *that*, Lady of the Bluffs?"

Ingrid's gaze cooled, shifting from warm scarlet to deep blood-red. "I am not responsible for the choices of greedy humans."

"That's lazy," Micah told her. Ingrid sat back. Her expression hardened. Sighing, Micah muttered, "Sorry."

"You're not like them," Ingrid said coldly. "Humans."

"I'm not like you, either," Micah said immediately.

"You're right," Ingrid said. "You're a child."

Micah's mouth fell open. "You're petty!"

"What are you so afraid of?" Ingrid pressed. "What is so undesirable about being Fae?"

Picking at the lid on his cup, Micah thought about it. He'd never put it to words. He'd never thought he would have a choice to be more than human. "It's the Queen. What if power makes me as cruel as her?"

They faced each other in silence. Two decades of shared history with their mother crowded between them like an oily cloud of billowing smoke.

Finally, Ingrid said gently, "Hurting isn't the only way to be powerful. It was just our mother's way."

"Was she always like that?" he asked. "Or did the hatred grow in her?"

Ingrid frowned.

Micah shook his head. "I'm sorry. It's just better this way."

Rising with a sigh, she gazed down at him with disappointment. "Come and find me when you quit with the denial." Then she spun around and vanished into a sunbeam.

CHAPTER SEVEN
THE NIGHTSHADE

"FIRST DATE IN A decade," Micah said to Fadil, fixing his hair in his mirror. Then he pointed at his reflection and ordered, "*Don't* do anything *magical*."

Fadil meowed deep in his throat, his sides expanding as he blinked up at Micah from the edge of the sink.

"Ugh." Micah used his forearm and swept the cat off the counter. Fadil landed with a *thunk* by his feet, swishing his tail in irritation. Glaring at him, Micah said, "When you're a jerk, you can't sit on my stuff."

"Micah! Your date is here."

Micah bent and gave Fadil an apologetic back rub before yelling, "I'm coming!"

He crossed through his bedroom door which led to a long flight of stairs, taking them down to the living room two at a time. Julian shuffled past him into the hall to the kitchen, winking at Micah as he passed.

Standing near Micah's painted fireplace, Andrew turned to face him with the anxious smile of someone more accus-

customary kiss on the crown of Julian's head, who reached around and pinched his ear until Micah straightened. Andrew's expression changed, becoming more wistful until he managed a slight smile.

"Where are you boys off to? First date, right?"

"The Night Market in Mears Park," said Micah.

"Is that for humans?" asked Julian.

"Yes," he answered. "Nothing extraordinary about it. Just quaint, ordinary sweetness."

"That's a relief. You'd better not get Andrew all wrapped up in that faerie bullshit."

"Yes, father." He patted Julian's shoulder. "I'll text you when we're on our way back."

Andrew followed Micah down to the foyer where they both stepped into their shoes, Micah's a pair of low-cut forest green chucks, and Andrew's more serious black pennyloafers.

When he locked the front door behind them, Micah said with a sigh, "Sorry about my dad. He's not well-socialized."

Andrew snorted. "Neither am I. But, uh—is he always so..." He thought of Julian spitting the words *faerie bullshit* and tried to find the right way to say it.

"Hostile?" Micah provided.

"About the Folk," Andrew said quickly. "'Faerie bullshit'," he repeated in air quotes.

Micah smiled weakly. "Afraid so. He's got every right to be, with what he's been through." Andrew had more questions, but the smile faded so quickly from Micah's lips that it made him hold his tongue. Micah gripped the railing, glancing up at Andrew, worry creasing his brow. "Hey, uh, you okay? About my age."

Andrew thought for a moment, standing one step down and gazing at the row of linden trees lining the curb. The breeze played with strands of his hair loose from his half-ponytail. "Could be worse than being eight years my senior," he said. "Would you still look like this if you were two hundred?"

The iron railing under Micah's palms chilled his skin in a way that helped him keep his composure. "Don't know," he said softly.

Andrew leaned next to him, arms crossed, patiently waiting and urging Micah on with his silence.

"There's no rulebook for me to consult," Micah said. "I stopped aging like a human when I was twenty-five or something. But that isn't a guarantee that I'm immortal, like the Folk." He gazed into the bushes below, frowning. "A foot in each world, and a stranger to both."

The linden trees rustled over their heads, dappling early evening sunlight across Micah's arms. He looked up when the leaves kept rustling with no voice joining them and found Andrew's honey-flecked eyes fixed on his face.

"That sounds lonely," murmured Andrew.

Micah's throat tightened. Andrew gently turned his chin, leaning toward him and brushing their lips together.

Micah strung an arm around Andrew's neck, slipping out of his body and into the space they made together, where nothing hurt and there was no fear.

Salt stained Micah's taste buds from his tears, distracting him. Pulling back, he pressed the heel of his hand into his eyes. "Sorry. Crying. I cry a lot," Micah rasped.

"That's all right," Andrew said in a whisper. "Men ought to cry more." He caught a teardrop on Micah's lash with his thumb.

"Listen, um, why don't we get going?" Micah said, drying his face and taking an unsteady breath. "If you keep me going on all this...depressing shit, I'm gonna be a puddle by the end of the night."

"Yes. Of course." Andrew offered him his hand, and they clanged down the steps together as he beeped his keys and unlocked his Saturn. "I was planning to drive, if you'd like."

Micah beeped his own set of keys, making the taillights on a handsome Prius flash. With a sidelong grin, he said, "You sure? It's a hybrid."

Andrew eyed the much nicer car and scoffed, "Fancy old man. What, are you a business executive or something?"

"As a matter of fact, I did get my MBA from Carlson School of Management." Micah tugged Andrew toward his car and opened the passenger door for him. "Presumably, without Fae influence. Though now I have to wonder a bit."

Andrew settled into the passenger seat. "Huh. I should hire you as a business consultant."

"With your cute face? I'd do it for free." Micah pecked his cheek and then shut the door, but lingered so he could see Andrew's ears redden. They were both grinning as Micah pulled away from the curb and joined the slow, dense flow of traffic into the heart of the city where Mears Park was situated. As the car crept through pedestrians and Micah started to look for an open street parking spot, he said, "So, I've been wondering—shit, that's too small, isn't it?"

"My Saturn could have fit."

"Wow." Micah laughed. After one more trip around the block, he snagged a spot just as someone left it. They climbed out onto a wide sidewalk outside the park, which was a small curated plot of nature among the modest sky-scrapers in downtown Saint Paul. It was hemmed in by tall black lamp posts with frosted bubble lights. Geometric cobblestones were paved wide enough for clusters of people to meander with no rush or claustrophobia, with wood-en benches and slabs of limestone used for more seating. Tonight, for the night market, vendors lined the cobble-stone walkway and spilled into the grove of trees. Their generators vibrated the air and made the park sound like it was in a much bigger city than it was.

"What were you wondering?" asked Andrew. They me-andered among the stalls, peering at taco trucks next to pottery vendors next to a face-painter. At the opposite end of the park, there was a large bandshell with a jazz band playing a dizzying tune.

"You said you've only been up to Lilydale once. Did you just stumble upon it?" Micah asked.

"Sort of," said Andrew. "I was looking for my mum."

Micah stifled a giggle with his wrist.

"What?"

"'Mum.' You're so cute."

Rolling his eyes, Andrew continued, "I left her when I was eighteen. Kind of distracted myself through university. Also at the U of M."

"Go Gophers," said Micah dryly.

"Indeed. It wasn't before I got settled at Magic's that I started to wonder what became of her. Ah, tofu dogs. I love those."

"So does my dad. He's not even vegetarian."

"Neither am I," said Andrew with a laugh. He jumped into the line with Micah ambling after him, his violet eyes roaming over the crowd as he shamelessly people-watched. Andrew selected a hot dog and two lemonades, and Micah held out a bill to pay the vendor. Andrew slapped his hand away and paid for it himself.

"Ow. Why would your mom—your mum be up in Lilydale? Unless...ah. Shit." Micah's voice dropped to a whisper. "Fae-spelled foods."

Andrew nodded, handing Micah one of the cups and then tapping the rims together in a toast. They moved out of the line and scanned the park for open seating. Micah took him by the elbow and led them to a slab of limestone near a foot bridge that ran over an artificial creek. The creek was lined with bowing birchwood trees, their bark silvery in the twilight. Micah rested his hand against the smooth trunk of the nearest birch, which seemed to breathe under his palm as if it was a slumbering wyrm. Such an illusion was a common experience for Micah, especially back in the Redwoods.

Andrew sat next to him, pressing his bony knees together to hold the checkered paper tray. "My mum and I left my dad when I was twelve. He was prone to...violent temper tantrums. His worst tantrum was when he found out I'm gay."

"What!" Micah exclaimed. "Ugh. Are you serious? How primitive."

"Mm, he was." Andrew's expression remained neutral as he took a bite of his hot dog, following it with a sip of lemonade. He went on, still blank-faced, "He gave my mum chronic migraines since she took most of his hits. So when we came here after that, she got hooked on painkillers. We ended up homeless a few times."

"Oh, man. I'm sorry."

"Someone at Catholic Charities sold her something from Lilydale when her pills ran out. That was when I was almost seventeen, I believe. Things got much worse for her after that. One time she turned on all the gas burners on the stove because she thought they smelled like roses. I came home to her about to light a cigarette."

"Oh, shit, no," Micah said, gripping his leaf necklace. "Do you know how often shit like that happened where I grew up? I saw someone die at least every week. From a heart attack, or...or worse, dangerous shit like that they thought was fun. People stabbed themselves or walked into a river and drowned, laughing. It was grotesque and terrifying, and...and here, the Folk up in Lilydale just shrug about it."

Andrew nodded. "I met a faerie, when I was up there. She was ambivalent at best. About people misusing their food."

"They all are," said Micah with a groan. "It's made it much easier to stay away. I'm resentful of their indifference."

"Yeah," Andrew said thoughtfully, "but why should they care? We make terrible, destructive choices all the time. Unfortunately, not even my mum is an exception. Nobody forced her to abuse substances like that."

Micah cocked his head. "I'm sorry, you're really justifying the Folk? I'm so confused. I've literally never heard a human do that."

Andrew shrugged. "I'm not saying it's what I wanted. But humans aren't always innocent. We're not always just victims."

"Huh." Micah took a long drink from his lemonade, puckering his lips. "Lawfully neutral, aren't you?"

"Yes," he agreed, his eyes lingering on Micah's lips. "Generally speaking." He set aside his food, curling his fingers closed, gazing at the trickling creek near them. "But I'm not so sure that's what happened to me. I'm not sure what I did to that faerie in the bluffs warranted what she's been doing to me since then. I—I only pulled a knife because she was a stranger lunging at me in the bluffs!" The scene started flashing behind his eyes, doubling his heartrate, his blood slamming in his ears. He curled in on himself, ducking his head so his hair veiled his features. "It was fair that I defended myself. Her cruelty hasn't been. She's always watching me. Stalking me. Terrorizing me." Andrew sniffed, swiping at his face. "I'm going mad." He was silent for a moment before giving a breathless little laugh. "Sorry. Do people usually do this much crying on first dates?" He lifted his head to give Micah a pained grin, his eyes red-rimmed.

Micah frowned, brushing his fingers against Andrew's knee. "I'm sorry. I've had that same feeling myself, that tingly someone's-watching you thing, honestly." Andrew looked at Micah's hand, touching the *Ingwaz* mark on his index finger. Micah turned his palm up and gently laced their fingers together. He met Andrew's eyes and said softly, "But I can promise you one thing. As long as you're with me, nobody from Lilydale would dare to trifle with you."

Andrew scoffed. "Yeah, right." But the hunch of his shoulders relaxed; hope lit in his eyes. "Micah, you can't—you can't tease me with that. She has been a curse on my life for five years. How can you just...take it away?"

"Just give me a chance," Micah said with an unwavering smile. "Chami isn't my only connection up there."

"I can't get my hopes up," Andrew whispered. He shook

his head. "Nothing's worked so far."

Micah kissed his knuckles. "Okay. Don't get your hopes up, then. That isn't going to stop me."

Andrew's eyes burned. "That's my limit," he warbled. "Too much emotion. Why...why don't we take a turn around the park?"

Cupping Andrew's face in his hands, Micah nodded and leaned in to kiss him.

Smack.

They both yelped. A honeysuckle blossom fell onto Micah's knee; he rubbed his stinging cheek.

"What in the—?" asked Andrew, picking up the flower.

"Nightshade Boy," crooned a voice like a mourning dove over Micah's shoulder. He swiveled on the limestone to face a small woman with skin the color of acorns, and a cloud of soil-black hair.

"Oh my god! Syabira!" Micah exclaimed. He leaned down to plant a kiss on both of the woman's cheeks. "I didn't know you had a stall here." Over her shoulder was her display bearing a wall of flowers of all colors exploding from glass vials, crates of flowers below them, interspersed with gleaming glass light bulbs radiating buttery light. "Oh, it's beautiful."

"Come over," she said, her inky eyes sliding over to Andrew. "I must make you an arrangement." Her eyes stayed on Andrew.

"Me?" Andrew touched his chest. "Why? You're..." His

voice dropped. "You're from Lilydale? You called him—"

Syabira nodded slightly, her lips like rose petals as she curled them in a smile. She wore a wide silk wrap around her forehead, her ears tucked inside; her dress was frothy white and fell like a waterfall to her ankles. "I saw you earlier this week, confronting our archer."

Andrew raised his brows.

"Chami's an archer," Micah supplied softly.

"I didn't realize I had an audience," Andrew said.

"We're always watching," said Syabira. She reached between her breasts and withdrew a nightshade blossom, indigo petals circling a vivid yellow stamen, the stem also deep purple in hue. "Especially where the Nightshade Boy is concerned."

"Syabira, you just happen to have a nightshade blossom nestled in your bosom?" Micah hissed, snatching it out of her hands.

"I felt you would be here tonight," she said coyly. Then she crooked a bony finger toward Andrew. Her fingertip was powdery green. "Come, noble knight."

"Noble knight?" repeated Andrew. "What is happening?"

"Don't tell my dad that things got folksy," muttered Micah. They rose off the limestone slab, Andrew skirting off to throw away their food waste in a bin marked for compost. Syabira returned to her stall to help a handful of customers that had gathered when she was away talking to them. She was perhaps waist-height, small like a child but built like a grown woman. When she spoke with customers, she had a lilting, musical voice that soothed like a lullaby, so people went from buying one small bouquet to an armful of blossoms without realizing.

"I'm so sorry," Micah said while they waited their turn. "Syabira does a lot of flower vending around the city, and she's taught me an absolute ton about gardening. I owe her a lot. My house thrives because of her."

"It's all right," Andrew said with a gentle smile. "She seems nice. But why are you the Nightshade Boy?"

Micah scoffed, swiping a hand through his hair. "It's a title that followed me to Minnesota," he answered. "Something about beauty and unassuming danger. And my eyes, I guess." He held the blossom near his indigo gaze, which almost perfectly matched the petals of the nightshade. "Should I eat this?" He opened his mouth.

Andrew slapped his hand down, scowling. "Gallows humor doesn't suit you."

Syabira grabbed Micah's wrist and yanked him up to the stall. Thoughtfully tapping her chin, she inspected Andrew as he stepped up by Micah's shoulder. Under her scrutiny, Andrew awkwardly smoothed his hair and chewed on his nail. He felt he was sitting for a portrait.

It was odd, and not altogether unpleasant, meeting a faerie among humans that wasn't being hostile. She moved among her fragrant blossoms with confident grace, glancing up at Andrew as she picked each flower and set it across a large square of newspaper. Micah curled his fingers around Andrew's elbow, silently watching Syabira work. When she had amassed twenty or so flowers and wrapped them delicately in the paper, she held it out for Andrew.

"Wow," he breathed, overwhelmed by the heady, wild scent. The spray of white, purple, and yellow among the deep green leaves was like an impressionist painting.

Micah held a twenty dollar bill out toward her, but Syabira curled her lip and spat on the ground. "It's a gift, Nightshade Boy. Don't insult me."

"Come on!" he exclaimed.

"Pay me back by coming up to Lilydale," said Syabira tersely.

"Ugh. Have you been talking to the Lady of the Bluffs?"

Syabira sniffed. "It's what we all want."

Micah scowled and glanced up at Andrew. "This happens every time. No matter who I'm talking to."

Andrew bowed slightly at his waist to the small vendor. "I cherish your gift, madame. But we have more of the market to explore. If you'll excuse us."

Surprised, Micah's lips parted in a faint, but very appreciative smile. With a glint in her eye, Syabira inclined her head. Then she turned toward another couple bending over blossoms and beamed at them, neatly ending her interaction with Andrew and Micah.

Sighing, hands in his pockets, Micah left the flower stall

and gazed distantly at the other vendors for several silent minutes. Wanting to bring Micah back to him, Andrew brushed his fingertips against Micah's wrist, gently drawing out his hand and twining their fingers together. Micah's attention returned from wherever it had roamed, and he looked up at Andrew, the faerie lights reflecting like constellations across his eyes.

"Shall I test my knowledge?" asked Andrew, leaning over the bouquet, the ambrosia making his head spin. "Spiderwort, oxeye, aster, coneflower...what's this little four-petal one?"

His forehead touching Andrew's, Micah murmured, "Mayapple. Why do you know these?"

"Don't want to get poisoned." Andrew grinned.

Micah laughed, the sound trailing off into something more humorless. "You jest, but if anyone in Lilydale would do that, it would be Syabira."

"Yes, well. So far so good." He slid the pink honeysuckle blossom into the center of the bouquet. Micah slipped the nightshade next to it. Andrew said, "Less so now."

Micah snickered.

"I think you need something to eat," said Andrew.

"Oh, yeah? I saw some cotton candy by the bandshell."

"Micah, that is not food."

"Yeah, well, you know what? 'Candy floss' makes less sense than cotton candy."

"You just had to make this personal."

Though the Night Market was small and easy to scour, Andrew and Micah passed several hours without noticing. The concert ended, but the cicadas picked up when the music fell silent. The crowds might have thinned, but truthfully neither of them noticed. Eventually Andrew stifled a yawn, and Micah with his arm around Andrew's slender waist led them back to his car. The silence on the drive back was comfortable, Micah feeling surprisingly little pressure to speak, and Andrew grateful for that.

The windows of Micah's brownstone were all dark, which hopefully meant it was a successful night where Julian had gone to bed without issue. Micah cut the engine and glanced over at Andrew, who slid his seatbelt over his chest so it folded up his lapel when it retracted.

After all the places they'd met—The Squire, and the co-op, out in Lilydale, even at breakfast—Micah was glad to notice Andrew seemed different now. His forehead was smooth and unlined, and his lips curled at the corners with a coquettish smile. He hooked his fingers through the door handle, ready to get out onto the curb without a second thought. But Micah caught his wrist.

Andrew started, warmth lighting in the pit of his stomach as he settled back into his seat and turned to Micah, whose eyes were a luminous lavender under the streetlight's golden glow. Paler somehow than Andrew remembered them, it seemed their hue had shifted with some thought or feeling. Micah made no attempt to hide his feelings, though, as he reached over and slid his hand along Andrew's neck, thumbing his pronounced jaw, drawing Andrew toward him with his fingers curled against the nape of his neck.

They met over the center console, light glinting through the windshield and staining syrupy gold across their lips as they kissed. Heat seared the air around them; Andrew gripped Micah's collar, opening his mouth so their tongues could meet for the first time, curious and eager. Micah's fingers teased Andrew's hair, tracing a shiver down his spine. Micah left the kiss to brush his lips over the lean column of Andrew's neck, eliciting a breathless moan of pleasure that made Micah's toes curl. Andrew dipped his head, finding Micah's lips again, his tongue quick to follow as they leaned against the console and into each other, arms twining, desire surging.

Micah forced himself away, catching his breath and holding it, his cheeks hot enough to burn.

Andrew's eyes stayed closed, his lips bright and glistening, his hair mussed. One umber eye slit open with displeasure. He tugged on Micah's collar, trying to bring him back.

"Let's do this again," Micah said hoarsely. "Another date. Please?"

Headlights flashed through the car, dazzling them both into squinting. The darkness became velvet after the light faded, cooling the cabin of the car as they both drifted back to earth like pebbles sinking into the shallows.

Andrew leaned on his elbow, head lowered, fingers touching his mouth and his cheek and his neck as if in disbelief. His chin flicked down in a nod as his eyes darted back up to meet Micah's elderberry gaze. "Mm." He shifted to rest his chin on his hand, smiling again in that cheeky way that made Micah fight to resist kissing him again. "More dates?" Andrew said softly. "Obviously."

They climbed out into the cooling night, wobbly as if they'd just learned to walk. Andrew pulled the keys to his Saturn out of his jeans, balancing on the curb as he made his way back down to the older beige car. Micah trailed after him in the grass, clasping his wrist behind his back, admiring Andrew's slender hips and lean legs as his weight kept shifting to keep his balance, the bouquet dangling prettily from his delicate hand.

"Got your sword in there, just in case?" Micah asked as he leaned against the back door on the driver's side. "I want to make sure you get home safe. Should I ride with you? I can walk home."

Andrew dropped into the driver's seat. As he turned the ignition and the engine growled into life, he grinned up at Micah. "I know how to use the sword. It'll be okay."

"I don't know," said Micah. "If anything happens to you, I might go feral." Gripping the hood of the car, he leaned down toward Andrew and said softly, "Who knows what I could do then." He winked, a dimple appearing in his cheek. Then he looked down at the bouquet laying across Andrew's legs. "Put that nightshade blossom on your windowsill, how about? Wrap some twine around the stem and hang it from a nail, to make sure your cat doesn't get it. And make sure you wash your hands after handling it." Micah shrugged. "It'll just send a little message to the Folk up there. They'll know what it means."

"Ah." Andrew glanced at the bouquet. "I can do that. Cool."

"Send me a photo of it when you do," Micah insisted. "I'm not letting you off the hook."

"Trust me," Andrew said, one slender brow rising, "I am more than happy to accept any and all relief from this haunting." His lips curled. "I'm really grateful for you, Micah."

Micah shook his head. "Don't. I'm still making up for charming you. And for lying."

"How do you feel about sushi?"

"It's amazing." Micah grinned.

"All right. Make it up to me with sushi. Let's go, whenever you have your next day off."

Grin widening, Micah nodded, leaning down into the car and giving Andrew one final kiss before he sent him away.

Micah strung his fingers behind his head as he watched Andrew's taillights fade into the distance down Saint Claire. It was a comfort knowing Andrew was quite literally just out of sight, just on the other side of West Seventh, and that he'd amassed enough ways to protect himself from Folk meddling with him.

Micah felt a niggling fear that it was Ingrid that Andrew had run into in the bluffs. But if she'd been caught off guard by Andrew, Micah thought there would have been little stopping her from just slaughtering him on the spot. She'd often been sent on human hunts for the Queen; she was more than capable of killing.

Regardless of who it was, Micah hoped the nightshade would be enough to ward off the Folk for now. If it wasn't, and Andrew reported any additional harassment, that would be more than enough to summon Micah back to the bluffs.

Chapter Eight
The Eyes

THREE MORE WEEKS, FOUR more dates, twenty-one nights of staying up late on the phone with each other. Despite their difficulties with Micah's Fae side, everything with each other felt...right. Intimate. Easy.

"Any trouble with the Folk?" Micah asked, every day.

"Just you," Andrew answered every time.

By the third week, every night they greeted the dawn as it spilled periwinkle across a navy watercolor sky, sitting on Micah's front steps or in the park across from Magic's. Talking, or sometimes not even talking, they were simply learning the shapes of the spaces they each took up.

The fifth date was the wettest so far. It was raining, and their shoes were soaked. The movie theater parking lot had been bursting with cars, necessitating a long walk in growing puddles to and from the theater. The movie was fine, mostly uninteresting to both of them, given that the main incentive was to make out in the dark like they were high schoolers.

"What do people call it?" remarked Micah, scratching his cheek. The Saturn idled in front of his brownstone on Saint Claire, headlights cutting into the shadows. Through the static of the rain, the windows on the row of tall houses glowed with buttery light or were already dark with the oncoming night.

"Call what?" Andrew couldn't help but notice his heart do a little somersault.

"Oh yeah. Want to come in for a nightcap?" Micah faked a very poor British accent.

"Sure. If you never do that accent again. It's worse than Sam's." He shut off the Saturn and they got out together, not really minding the rain since they were already damp.

Micah said smugly, "I'm going to perfect it. Just you watch."

When Micah unlocked the front door and it swung inward, a crash resounded from up the stairs. His eyes widened. He dropped his keys on the landing and tore up the stairs, slipping on the top step, but recovering and disappearing just as fast.

Andrew hurried in after him, throwing the lock shut on the front door as yelling echoed down from the level above him. Tripping out of his shoes, he staggered into the living room, but nobody was there. Andrew followed the clanging and yelling down the hall and came to an open kitchen on his left.

Baking sheets laid across the floor like corpses, the flour

coating the tiles like blood. A fire alarm was screaming as smoke streamed from an oven door hanging open. Julian knelt in the mess with shoulders hunched and tears streaming down his face. He yelled, "It's not the same! It's not right. I can't get it. I'm gonna die."

After throwing open a window over the dining table and twisting the knob on the oven off, Micah crouched near his father. Hands up, focused on Julian with desperate intensity, Micah said only just loud enough to be heard over the smoke alarm, "Dad. Dad, hey. You're safe. You're not alone. It's okay that you can't get it right. That wasn't good for you."

Julian screamed, "I don't care! I want to go back." He picked up a spatula and cast it aside so it cracked into the refrigerator. Then he leapt to his feet and lunged at the knife block near the sink. "If I can't—" Micah was on him in a heartbeat, pinning his wrist to his stomach, turning him away from the counter. The knife clattered to the ground.

"Dad! Dad. Take a breath. Come back. You're safe here. I know it's not the same, but it's safe."

Julian gave a guttural wail and hunched down to try to free his hand from Micah's grasp, clawing at his wrist.

Micah glanced furtively at Andrew and said through gritted teeth, "Can you help me get him out of this room?"

Andrew stepped in and Micah directed him to grab a hand and an elbow, and together they hauled the crying man from the kitchen and into the living room. Micah dropped Julian onto the couch and came around and knelt in front of him, forcing his father to hold both his hands.

"Dad. What do you smell? Soil, from the plants next to you. You keep them alive," said Micah, crooning as if to an infant. Julian groaned, dropping his head. Micah continued, "What do you hear? I'm turning on your favorite music. It's that old John Denver stuff." Micah had his phone in one hand and he tapped at it without looking. Heavy, slow guitar began and Julian shuddered violently. "Do you feel my hand on yours? Do you feel the couch under you? The springs are old, they're probably poking you." Julian went still, chin to his chest, breathing raggedly. "It's late," said Micah softly. "You should be in bed."

The man lifted his head. He looked at Micah and screamed, flailing an arm that connected with Micah's chin and sent him crashing into the coffee table. "The eyes!" screamed Julian. "Her eyes. No! Don't touch me."

Dazed, Micah tried to shake his head clear and rubbed his chin, groaning. Before he collected himself, Julian jumped off the couch and grabbed Micah by the collar, shaking him. "How could you do this to me?" he demanded.

Andrew sprang onto Julian. He hooked the man from behind by his elbows and hauled him off his son, pulling him back and calling over Julian's protests and sobs, "Where's his room?"

"Next floor up," Micah managed, shielding his eyes, knees pulled up to his chest.

The first few steps, Andrew had to drag Julian. Twice, he lost his footing and almost sent them both falling down the stairs.

Then, once Micah was out of sight, the fight left Julian. He grew quiet, sagging against Andrew as he dragged his feet up the stairs. When they got to the landing above, Julian tugged him toward an open door where a large bed was visible. Andrew wasn't ready to release him, but he let him lead them.

When Julian reached the bed, he picked up a prescription bottle on his nightstand, threw back a pill with a swallow from a mostly empty cup of water, and then kicked off his slippers. Julian climbed into the bed and curled up like a child, eyes closed, hands tucked up under his chin. He was still audibly panting, but he was motionless. Andrew lingered near the foot of the bed. He knew all too well how these kinds of meltdowns went. Sometimes there was a second wind.

The stairs creaked, and Micah padded onto the landing in the hall. Arms crossed, he stepped into the doorway, watching his father with a furrowed brow and a deep frown. Andrew backed up, hands in his pockets, until he stood next to the doorframe to wait with Micah. For several minutes, heavy silence blanketed the three of them like muffled winter air. A fluffy orange cat crept out from under the bed, its minty green eyes finding Micah and staring at him for several beats. Micah rubbed his chin, which seemed to break the cat from its paralysis. It jumped on the end of the bed and sat there, eyes on Julian's still form.

Finally tearing his gaze off his father, Micah turned back toward the stairs. Without looking, he said quietly, "Hey, uh, if you have any extra time, you wanna stick around?" His voice started strong, but faded into something soft that quavered like a leaf.

"Yes," whispered Andrew. "Of course."

Micah led them up another flight of stairs to the top floor of the brownstone. There was a door in the far corner cracked open to a bathroom lit dimly by a nightlight plugged in next to the sink. The rest of the floor was wide open with a tall beveled ceiling. A large open wardrobe displayed a somewhat unkempt collection of garments. An L-shaped desk sat in the far corner with a desktop computer on one end and paint supplies on the other. Plants were everywhere. A black cat edged into sight and acknowledged them with its tail down and thrashing.

Micah dropped down on his bed. His face crumpled, and he pressed the heels of his hands to his eyes and began to cry. Sitting so their thighs touched, Andrew pulled Micah into his side and held him in silence.

"I'm so sorry you had to see that," Micah said wetly, using his shirt to wipe his cheeks. "It hasn't happened in like, a month."

"That happens regularly?" Andrew balked. "I'm so sorry for you guys."

Micah said through his tears, "I stopped bringing him to the hospital. They only make it worse, asking nosy questions, trying to call him delusional, but it's trauma from a place nobody thinks exists. He relives what she did to him and he craves the Redwoods and it's—" He covered his face, hardly intelligible as he moaned, "That fucking *bitch*."

Andrew asked tentatively, "What happened to him?"

Micah got up and began to pace over the rugs on his floor, tangling his hands in his hair, breathing more raggedly. "He was just a...a tool, so she could make me," Micah said, quaking beneath the rage and the injustice of it all. "Can you imagine?" Eyes narrowing, teeth bared, he said, "An eighteen-year-old oblivious kid, probably a virgin, on his first solo trip with his friends—she killed all of them, by the way, because that's the type of crazy shit she does—and he's snatched from the woods on a hike and...that's it!" He gestured violently. "That...that...that's it! His whole life. Just fucking...ripped away from him. And now he's that." He swung an arm in the direction of the stairs. "God, every time this happens, every time he struggles, it...it...it just makes me want to *kill* her!" He lashed out, kicking over his desk chair, which clattered into the floor and bounced several times with its wheels spinning.

Andrew jumped. For a second, he was twelve years old, hearing his mum's lawn chair crash from the force of his father's violence. He dug his fingers into the soft fleece blanket under him, focusing on the way the fibers caught on his skin, the small rustling noise they made. He inhaled, smelling sandalwood and vanilla, counting to five in his head before he exhaled.

Micah snapped free of his rage, freezing. He listened to the silence in the house, face toward the stairwell like a cat listening for someone at the door. The silence remained undisturbed, the two of them the only conscious people in the house.

"Oh my god," groaned Micah, leaning over his desk, head between his shoulders. "I'm sorry."

"No," Andrew managed to whisper. "It's okay."

"No, I saw you jump, and I..."

"It's just old baggage."

"I shouldn't have lost my shit," Micah murmured. He rubbed his eyes with his fingers and sighed. "My dad...there's...there's been so much of this since we came here. He doesn't even know what his name used to be, before the Redwoods. I'm all he has. I...I have to care for him. But it's *so* triggering for me too."

The way Micah's voice broke brought Andrew fully back to the present. He leaned toward the desk and said softly, "Yes, I see that. Please tell me about it. I can handle it."

"I'm not sure," said Micah. "I don't want you to..."

"Keep talking," Andrew insisted.

Micah shook his head slightly. "I don't even know. It's...it's unrelentingly cruel, that rather than let him go after I was born, she...she kept him high on her fucking little cakes, year after year after year, displayed for everyone to see next to her throne. I think she did it to keep me docile." He blinked. Tears dropped onto his hands. "So I was."

"How awful," Andrew said quietly.

"I was twenty when we got out of there." He slowly straightened, hugging his arms across his chest. "I was brand new to living around humans. I worked at two coffee shops and went to community college so I could try to figure out what the fuck I was supposed to do to survive here alone. I had to learn fast. My dad was...way worse than this back then. None of the meds the hospitals put him on did anything."

Andrew nodded grimly. "He's not psychotic. Those kinds of meds won't work. I've tried them."

As he tore a paper towel off a roll on his desk and wiped his face, Micah flashed Andrew a quick smile. "Now you see why I didn't question you." The smile faded almost at once. "The only thing that ended up working? Pretending like we were a happy little human family. Going to school, getting the tea shop, cooking meals together. Giving him the kind of mundane little life he was supposed to have. Eventually, most days out of the month he felt okay. Burying that shit kept him safe." Sniffing, his breathing still unsteady, Micah glanced at Andrew and concluded, "Until I met you, I was able to deny that the Nightshade Boy really existed. And when I charmed you, it made all my worst fears come true."

Andrew paused. "Which are?"

Leaning against the windowsill a safe distance from him, Micah looked overhead at his hanging plants, chewing on his words. "I...don't know what I am. What I could be. I'm not just a guy, like I was supposed to be."

"I imagine that would disappoint you," Andrew said.

Micah nodded. On the pothos above him, he turned over a leaf with a crispy brown edge, using his nail and thumb to clip off the dead part. "I wish it made me feel more ready to retreat and give you up." He brushed his fingers over the other leaves, looking for blemishes. "But I still want to be with you, even though I'm a liability."

Andrew snorted. "Shit, I am too. I'm very unstable."

"I respect your opinion," said Micah wearily, crossing his arms, "but you're not the one with the dangerous magical potential."

"That we *know* of."

Micah frowned.

"I just..." Andrew laughed, a humorless puff of air lodged between the ridiculousness of their argument and the fear that Micah was actually going to push him away. "I'm sorry, Micah, but it's my risk to take. I'm an adult. And so are you. Of course, I can't make you get involved with me if you're constantly going to be worried that you'll go off like a firework or something."

"No..." Micah slumped against the window. "No. You're right." He glanced over at Andrew, unsticking his still-damp shirt from his chest. "You can always change your mind, okay?"

"Lovely. Same to you."

Micah rolled his eyes, but he grinned a little, covering his face with hands.

"C'mere. Quit cowering by the window. Or do I smell? Is it the wet socks?"

Pushing off the window, Micah glanced down and muttered, "God, yeah. Everything's soggy." He unlaced his sneakers and pulled them off.

"Do you need an ice pack? Your dad really clocked you."

"I'm okay." Peeling off his jeans with an admirable amount of self-assurance, Micah walked lightly over to the bed. The mattress shifted as he climbed on, tipping Andrew so he bumped into Micah's thigh. Soft curly leg hairs tickled Andrew's arm, making goosebumps rise on his skin. He stole a glance and confirmed that even the hairs on Micah's legs were faintly green. Andrew started to sit up, but changed his mind, flopping onto his back instead and gazing up at Micah.

Sitting back on his knees, Micah looked down at him and said with a faint smile, "So, are you staying?"

Faint light from the rain-doused street lamps turned the

bare curve of Andrew's shoulder milk-white. He slept soundly among Micah's blankets, hair draped over his cheek, lips slightly parted. Micah climbed back into bed as gingerly as he could, the chill of the air sharper near the warmth rising from Andrew's skin. Outside, the rain was still trickling down in a whispered cadence, but evidently Micah still made too much noise—maybe it was the little creak of the mattress—since Andrew's eyes flickered open.

"Sorry," Micah whispered.

Brushing his hair off his cheek, Andrew mumbled, "You apologize too much. Everything okay?"

"Just went down to check on my dad." Micah tugged up the blankets and then tucked them under Andrew's chin after he'd pulled them loose getting settled.

Andrew made a soft noise of understanding followed by a sigh like he'd never been more comfortable in his life. His eyes slipped shut for a moment and then blinked back open. "Do you not sleep well?"

Micah paused, rubbing his cheek on his pillow. "Never," he finally said.

Andrew's cool, soft fingers found Micah's elbow under the covers and then trailed up to his wrist. "That sucks," he said, drawing Micah's hand to his lips so his breath coasted across his knuckles. He left Micah's hand draped against his face, which was faintly coarse with stubble.

Unable to resist, Micah shifted his thumb slightly and brushed Andrew's lower lip. The flesh curved softly under his touch as Andrew smiled, eyes still closed.

"Sorry," Micah murmured again. "I'm just really excited to have you in my bed."

Andrew's smile widened. "The pleasure's all mine," he said against Micah's mouth, lazily joining their lips. His palm grazed Micah's cheek, his neck, and came to rest on his chest, fingers pressing firmly. Spurred onward, Micah slipped his arm around Andrew and his tongue into his mouth. As their breathing stuttered faster, Micah pushed Andrew lightly onto his back, propping himself on his forearms and leaning over him. His mouth left Andrew's to explore elsewhere, sucking lightly on his sharp clavicle, on his pectoral, then his nipple. It was salty and warm and dragged out the most delicious gasp from Andrew's throat. Andrew's hands slid down and gripped Micah's rear. Growling softly, Micah unclasped from Andrew's chest and ran his hand along his firm stomach, which quivered beneath his touch. When his fingers reached Andrew's waistband, Micah paused.

Andrew's cheeks and eyes shone with desire, and when Micah stopped, his brow crinkled. "What's wrong?"

"I want to have sex with you," Micah told him.

Andrew raised an eyebrow. "But...?"

"But not because I just got carried away." Micah lay back onto his side next to Andrew, who frowned at the ceiling as he scraped his fingers through his hair.

"I'm confused," said Andrew, panting, a note of desperation in his voice.

"I had a lot of reckless trysts in the Redwoods," Micah explained. "And...a few here. Ages ago. But you're not like any of them. Will you be patient with me?"

Andrew groaned. "Seriously?" He covered his face. "Ugh. Yes, of course. I respect your intentions." He peeked through his fingers at Micah, the beam of a street lamp glimmering in his eye, turning it topaz. "But I'm *frustrated.*"

Micah clasped Andrew's face between his hands, laughing and pressing a kiss to the tip of his nose, his chin, and each of his cheekbones. "I swear I'll make sure it's worth your while."

"That's the trouble," murmured Andrew. "I very much believe you."

Andrew woke up to a cell phone chime he didn't recognize. Laying on his stomach, he peered through the veil of his hair. A large black cat crouched on the windowsill, which slitted its pale green eyes and glared at him. Andrew blinked slowly at the cat. Put off by his challenge, the cat flattened its ears. It stretched out its neck to the sharp leaf of a spider plant and opened its mouth of fangs, which glinted ivory in the morning light.

"Fadil," Micah called in warning.

The cat clamped its mouth shut. Its tail uncurled from its body and thumped against the wall under the window. It shot Andrew a look that suggested this was all his fault. Then it turned to glare sullenly out the window. Andrew couldn't resist a little grin of satisfaction before he rolled over.

Micah lay on his back beside him, frowning at his phone over his head. His thumbs tapped furiously, briefly, and then he dropped his phone on his chest and sighed.

"Everything good?" Andrew murmured to him.

Micah jumped. Scraping a hand through his hair—he seemed to do that when he was anxious—he looked over and managed a smile that almost passed as convincing. He reached behind him and let his phone clatter onto the milk carton he used as a nightstand. "Yeah," he said, nestling closer. "Yeah. Dad's gone out. I was checking in with him."

"Mm."

"And hey," Micah added, "thanks for staying over."

Andrew smiled faintly, slipping his arm under Micah's neck and drawing him into his side, where they lay together bathing in the warm morning light. He glanced down at Micah's closed eyes and then reached over and brushed his fingertip over his eyebrow. "Your eyebrows are turquoise."

"Oh." Micah touched them absently, eyes still closed. "Yeah. I usually put pomade on them. Draws less attention."

"I wish you wouldn't hide. It's unfair to you, masking your beauty."

Micah's eyes blinked open, gleaming lavender in the sunlight. "Beauty?"

"Of course." Andrew nuzzled his face into Micah's soft hair, toying with the heavy glass earring in his stretched lobe. "You're stunning." He inhaled deeply. "And you smell like summer. It isn't fair that you look the way you do *and* you are the most compassionate person I've ever met."

"You give me too much credit," Micah said against Andrew's throat.

"I'm not in the habit of that," Andrew said, hugging Micah tighter. "If I am, then it's because you've got me so smitten."

Micah moved back to scrutinize Andrew, who peered down at him with a sly and unapologetic curve of his slender peach lips. Snaking his hand out from under the covers, Micah tucked Andrew's hair behind the shell of his ear. "You too, huh?"

As realization brightened Andrew's features, sunlight glanced off the depths of his dark eyes. He cupped Micah's face between his hands and pressed a kiss to his brow, each cheekbone, his nose, and finally his lips.

In the kitchen, barefoot and wearing only track shorts, Micah poured boiling water into a coffee press and stirred around the grounds inside. He breathed deeply the rich, earthy smell of the beans to brace himself. Then he slowly began to pick up the pans and spatulas and dish rags his father had thrown around. He reached into the oven and pulled out the charred contents on the cookie sheet, frowning at the foul smell. It looked like they were supposed to be little cakes. Julian was trying to replicate the Fae-spelled cakes from the Redwoods. Those wretched little sweets.

Micah used a spatula to scrape them loose and into the garbage under the edge of the counter. Wiping the bottoms of his feet free of flour, he pulled out a cordless vacuum and powered it on to suck up the rest of the fine layer of powder on the tiles. With a sigh, he returned to his coffee and used the palm of his hand to slowly send the plunger down to the bottom.

When it was almost ready, Andrew appeared in the doorway. He'd rummaged through Micah's clothes to find a pair of black jersey shorts, tied tightly Micah noted, and thrown on a striped tee that was baggy in a way that made Andrew look unwittingly street chic.

"Hey, handsome," said Micah, smiling automatically at the sight of him. "You look adorable in my clothes."

Andrew tugged at his collar. "I don't think Fadil liked that I borrowed from you."

"He's very protective," laughed Micah.

Crossing the kitchen tiles to reach him, Andrew thumbed Micah's cheek and asked, "Flour?"

"I had to clean up." He pulled two mugs down from a hook. "Do you drink coffee, or just tea?"

"Coffee's fine if a cute guy is making it for me."

Micah puckered his lips at him, making Andrew giggle. He poured the steaming drink in both cups and picked up a sugar dish shaped like a house. Andrew shook his head when he held it out. Micah frowned at him and added a generous scoop of sugar to his own cup. Then he led them out through the living room and nudged open a door to the balcony.

The balcony was maybe ten paces long in perimeter, its triangular shape making it feel cramped. But to compensate, Micah had strung twinkling lights from the rafters overhead and put down bright yellow rugs on the planks underfoot. He had a hanging bench against one of the railings with throw pillows tossed across the wooden seat. There were plants sitting on the floor, plants hanging from the rafters, and planters on the railing.

Micah folded up on the cushioned bench and patted the space beside him for Andrew before taking a long sip of coffee. Behind his head, white violets twined through a small lattice he'd secured between the chains holding up the bench.

Andrew sat beside him with one knee tucked under and the other brushing Micah's. He blew gently on the steaming cup and then took a drink. "Where's your dad?"

"He usually avoids me the day after a meltdown." He pulled his phone out to check the Family app that let him track his dad. Micah's frown deepened. "But this feels...worse than usual. He's pretty far away. Like, over in Chaska. We don't know anyone out there...too far...west." Micah typed up a text to him asking where he was going and then set his phone aside. He held his mug in both hands and drank the coffee down quickly, its warmth filling his belly fast enough to make him feel nauseous. Staring distantly, he gazed at the tree-speckled space behind the brownstones, and the children's toys that splashed bright colors on the grass below them. Micah's phone dinged. *I'm fine,* was all Julian wrote. He groaned. "Wonderfully vague." He tried to start a call to him, but it was sent to voicemail after two rings. He texted instead, *Why are you in Chaska?? Please call.*

Tapping his thumbs together, he stared at his phone and waited. Ellipses bobbed over Julian's side of the screen.

Dont worry a bout me kiddo

Dad, I already am. I know it was a bad night but we should really talk about it.

Please come home.

Ellipses. They bobbed. And bobbed. Then they disappeared. Micah groaned again and tossed his phone onto the bench.

Andrew reached for it. When Micah didn't object, he thumbed through the exchange, and then frowned. He fished out his own phone, tapped in Julian's number, and dialed it. His lips pressed into a thin line.

"What?" Micah demanded.

Andrew looked between the two phones before his frown deepened. "Says his number isn't in service."

Micah snatched his phone back. He dialed his dad again, but Andrew was right. He hung up and pulled back up the Family app. Julian's icon was gone.

"What the fuck?" Micah muttered. A chill spread from his shoulders, turning his stomach and his legs numb, a buzzing sound rising between his ears. The Family app let Micah track Julian even if his phone was shut down. If Julian's icon had completely vanished...

He glanced up at Andrew, who was silent and watchful, a faint furrow in his brow. It was apparent that Micah didn't need to say aloud what he feared the most. Micah pulled up Chamomile's contact information and dialed her. The first time, it didn't make any noise. He dialed Chamomile again. A click.

"Who is this?" She slurred her words.

"Add my goddamn number to your phone," snapped Micah.

"Micah?"

"Obviously."

"What do you want? I'm still drunk."

"Chami, listen. Please. It's my dad."

"It always is." The lilt of her voice held a sigh of dismay and tenderness. "What's wrong with Jules?"

"I think it's serious."

The line went flat.

Micah swore and pitched his phone. Andrew flinched. It bounced away and lay screen-down on the rug. Then Chamomile stepped out of thin air onto the balcony, yawning and stretching her shoulders. She was completely naked.

Micah and Andrew screamed. Micah's full coffee cup tipped into his lap and his scream of surprise turned into a yell of pain. He jumped to his feet and swiped at his lap. Leaping up, Andrew pulled off his shirt and used it to mop up the coffee on Micah, sliding the fabric under the hem of his shorts to keep the heat off him.

Chamomile's eyes were half-closed as she looked around like she wasn't sure where she was. She wiped her arm across her eyes and shook her head as if to gather her senses. Her thigh-length hair was loose and bedraggled, her cheeks rosy, the tips of her ears and the contoured muscles of her belly sage-colored. She had smears of gold on her face and shoulders and a crown of flowers on her head.

"What the *hell,* Chami!" cried Micah. "You scared the shit out of us."

"Phones make my ears ring," she answered with a shrug. There were prominent golden kiss prints trailing down from behind her ear toward her chest. "What's wrong with you?"

Micah sagged back onto the bench. Andrew followed him, reluctant, eyeing Chamomile with mild contempt.

A scrabbling at the door made Chamomile turn around. She popped open the door inside and a black shadow streaked onto the balcony. "Fadil!" Chamomile squatted and scooped up the cat, whose purr rattled his body. Then she turned back, incidentally covering her chest with the cat, and raised her almost invisible eyebrows at them. "Well? What is it?"

"How did you do that?" Andrew demanded. "Just appear here."

"I folded some shadows," Chamomile said dismissively.

Ignoring their aside, Micah told her, "My dad fell off the grid. He was talking about my mother last night and then left on his own this morning. I have a bad feeling about it."

Chamomile frowned. "What am I..."

Micah interrupted, "I need you to tell Ingrid. I need her help. If he's trying to get back to my mother, I don't trust her to keep him alive."

"Why would Ingrid help you with that? She has better things to concern herself with than one human desperate for the Redwoods."

His expression darkened. "She'll help me."

"Then I will take you back with me so you can ask her yourself." Chamomile jutted out her chin.

"Chami—"

"You act as if you haven't spent the last twenty years rejecting your status and avoiding Lilydale," she added, not with as much cruelty as Andrew expected. "And also, you know I care about you, but I am not at your beck and call."

Micah blinked his stinging eyes, looking away with a nod.

Andrew let out an audible sigh. "I'll go with you," he said to Chamomile, standing up.

"No! Why would you do that?" Micah pulled Andrew back down to the bench, making its chain ropes grind.

"Because you don't want to," said Andrew, shrugging.

"That's insane. You're human. Don't recklessly go in and fuck with the Folk," said Micah.

"Ah." Andrew gave a humorless smile and wagged a finger. "Important thing to know about me. I am actually incredibly reckless."

"Hey, hello. Loverboys." Chamomile waved, annoyed. "I don't care who tells her, just not me. Can I go now?"

"Maybe I'm overreacting about my dad." Micah looked at his hands and said halfheartedly, "He keeps telling me I'm babysitting him."

Andrew and Chamomile didn't speak for a moment, the plants on the balcony whispering among themselves.

"Ingrid learned how to scry," Chamomile said helpfully.

Micah's heart leapt. He stood up, his mind racing. "So she can check where my dad is."

Andrew held his hand out to the faerie. "Let's go."

After blowing Micah a kiss, Chamomile clasped Andrew's fingers. As Micah yelled and jumped to his feet, the two of them vanished.

CHAPTER NINE

THE SIBLINGS

FOLDING INTO THE SHADOWS sent Andrew's brain into somersaults. Chamomile's grasp on him burned like fire but she dragged him along with her like the tail of a comet. The power plant, and then the river, and then the little road that snaked along the foot of the bluffs blurred beneath him as vaguely recognizable streaks of color. Then everything slammed to a halt. Andrew fell head over heels. Landing with a thump on his stomach, he groaned, clutching his head.

"Sacrilege," Andrew said, peering through one slitted eye. "Did I already throw up?"

"Come on, it's not so bad. Really, traveling in the shadows is a privilege not many humans get." Her hot hands wrapped around his upper arm as she sat him upright.

When he climbed to his feet, his world spun. Doubling over, he dry heaved and spat out the acidic taste of coffee. "Fucking coffee."

"I'm telling Micah you said that."

He squinted against bright morning sunlight cast through the trees from a clearing just ahead. He was so unprepared for the dazzling light that it pressed into his skull like a vise and forced his eyes closed for a moment. He pressed the heels of his hands into his eye sockets, grunting. There was no more time to fuss about the light though. Andrew blinked and blinked until finally his vision regained equilibrium.

The underbrush surrounding them was tall and, Andrew thought dismally, likely rife with deer ticks. He made a mental note to check his skin when he got home. Chamomile gave him an impatient glare and started off. As he hurried after her and out of the cover of the grove of cottonwood and silver maples, the crumbling structure of the Lilydale brickyard unfolded before him. He'd seen photos in the history books, but they paled in comparison. The Folk took the wreckage of the failed brickyards and helped nature reclaim it, and what had once looked decrepit now thrived, wiped clean of the greasy thumbprints of humanity. The bricks had crumbled and fauna sprouted back up where the foundations had been laid. The limestone bluffs grew around the cobbled fence like a moat.

"Shit." This had...probably been a bad idea. Unarmed, barefoot, without a plan, all he wore to protect himself was Micah's blood ward. It had some leaves and berries in the vial, but it wasn't made of iron. Who knew if it would even work on other Folk. After as much effort as Andrew had put into standing a fighting chance against the Folk, he'd just walked defenseless into Lilydale simply to spare Micah the pain of it.

Chamomile was two steps away, half turned toward him as she eyed him through hooded lids. "Nervous?" she asked with a flash of her jagged teeth.

"Obviously, yes," said Andrew, annoyed. "I have no need for bravado." But then his eyes accidentally drifted down to her pert nipples; she saw, and she cackled with cruelty.

The air just behind Andrew split with the sound of canvas tearing. He jumped and spun around. And then Micah stumbled and fell into his upheld arms.

"Whoa," gasped Micah.

"Whoa," exclaimed Andrew, kicking his back foot behind him for support as Micah worked to regain his balance.

Chamomile said thoughtfully, "Interesting."

With a hysterical giggle, Micah straightened and fixed his hair as he said, "Well, that's new."

"What's new?" Andrew asked.

"He's never done that before," said Chamomile. To Micah, she said, "Looks like someone must be accepting his Fae nature, at last."

Micah ignored her. Clutched in both hands was the sheathed black sword from Andrew's Saturn. "Here." He thrust it into Andrew's hands and forced his fingers to curl around the hilt.

"What are you doing?" Andrew demanded. "You didn't need to come."

Micah scoffed, "Yeah, okay. You wanna go talk to my sister without me?"

"Sister," Andrew repeated. "Ah."

Chamomile cackled as she wandered away from them.

"Here, let's sit for a minute before we go in there," said Micah.

"That's probably a good idea. I think my recklessness is catching up to me."

Micah led him to a limestone boulder ringed in by orange tiger lilies. The stone dug into his bony pelvis as Andrew laid his sheathed sword across his knees and stared at Lilydale.

He tilted his head. "So that's it, huh? It's kind of...small."

"There's only like, two dozen Folk in there," agreed Micah. "Such a huge, nasty reputation for such a modest estate."

"So, um...is your sister from Lilydale?"

Micah shook his head. "No. She came with me and my dad from Washington. She's full Fae; we only share our mother."

"Which is...the Redwood Queen," Andrew guessed.

Micah nodded slightly. Facing the river, Micah stood over him, anxiously flexing his shoulders, sending tawny muscles rippling down his back. "I wouldn't be going in there if not for my dad. I haven't been in Lilydale for, like, five years. My sister is too much for me to deal with." He glanced down, head tilted as he searched Andrew's face with a bewildered frown. "Why do you want to help me?"

Gazing out at the marshy floodplains below them, Andrew rolled the sword across his thighs and wetted his lips. "Your dad reminds me of my mum," he said. "She slipped out of my reach. But your dad hasn't yet." Andrew drew Micah closer so he could slide a hand around his bare waist. "I came here trying to get her back and couldn't. If I can help you get your dad back, it seems only fitting it's by coming to this place."

Micah remained motionless, his eyes glistening, shifting to indigo as he blinked tears loose from his lashes.

Past him, the silver-haired faerie reappeared in the gap in the cobbled fence. "Micah!" she yelled. "Hurry the fuck up!"

Though he didn't turn around, Micah's hands closed into fists.

Standing up, hands on his hips, Andrew said in warning, "All right."

She hissed at him and ducked out of sight.

"She gets like that when she's hungover," Micah said.

Andrew gave him a look. "You know her *really* well."

Squeezing his eyes closed, Micah blurted, "Yeah. She's my ex."

Andrew groaned. "Seriously?"

"Yeah, I'm not altogether gay," Micah said, peeking at

Andrew through one eye, bracing himself. But Andrew had to find all this out eventually. Telling him in Lilydale was less than ideal, but here they were.

Andrew dropped back onto the boulder and let a breath out through his teeth. "That's interesting," he managed. "Lots to unpack, eh? All right." He combed his fingers through his hair, inhaled, and held the breath. When he looked up, worry creased Micah's brow as he twirled the string of his shorts busily between his fingers.

Pushing back to his feet, Andrew asked quietly, "But you said you like me, right? You're smitten." With disbelief Andrew touched his own chest and added, "With me."

"Yes." Micah caught Andrew's wrist, sincere, unsmiling, his eyes boring into Andrew's like their souls were brushing together. "Completely."

"All right then." He trailed his palm over Micah's warm cheek until the lines of concern faded from his skin. "Are they going to team up and drown me in the river? Your ex and your sister?"

Micah took Andrew's face between his hands. "Andrew, I swear I won't let anyone in Lilydale cause you harm, or so help me, they will rue the day for all time."

His cheeks heating up, Andrew sniffed, "Well, now, there's no need to go overboard."

"I'm nothing if not dramatic," Micah remarked, tilting Andrew's chin down and touching their lips together.

"Right then." Andrew clasped their hands together.

"We'd better go in before I come to my senses."

Tall grasses rustled against their legs as Micah led them to the short cobblestone fence. They made slow and tedious progress, being mindful of their bare feet and what might be lurking under the veil of the grass, including loose stones ready to send them rolling down toward the river.

"I looked right at her boobs," Andrew said with a shudder.

Micah snickered. "It was hard not to."

There was a big enough gap in the sepia-toned stones to constitute a rough gate. Micah knew the gate would push back against those not welcome inside, not enough to bar the way, but enough to create vertigo or a sour stomach. For Micah, passing through the gap felt like going through a curtain of warm water.

Inside the gate, there was a small grove of trees up the slope to the left, shielding most of the eastern edge of the compound from Highway 13 over the bluffs in the distance. The trees were oak, maple, ash, and poplar, as well as a handful of pine. Their lush leaves whispered in the breeze as the branches reached up into the powder blue sky. Hammocks and large wicker baskets were strung far off the ground between branches. Dangling down from them on lengths of braided twine were small bones, glinting crystals, and dried bundles of flowers. The bones clattered softly in the breeze, but the effect was pleasing, not macabre. Between the trees were large white toadstools, flat-topped boulders, and explosions of colorful wildflowers.

Though the trees looked uninhabited, Andrew's skin prickled in a way that left him certain that Folk were watching him among the branches. He followed Micah down a small cobbled path that seemed like it had been laid a hundred years ago, faded and smooth, with clover growing up between the chinks. The path branched off into limestone stairs climbing westward. Each of the steps were painted with colorful swirls, flowers, and strange but beautiful symbols. Shallow amphitheater steps curved around an enormous fire pit, currently black and cold. Near it, one side of a great fallen tree was sanded into a flat tabletop, laden with trays of diced fruit, freshly baked bread, and pitchers of golden honey mead. All perfectly provincial to the Folk, and wildly dangerous for human consumption. The sight of it made Andrew's limbs tingle with anxiety, how easily he could divert the course of his life with just one bite of the addictive spelled foods.

Andrew tucked his sword under his arm. Not that he looked very threatening at the moment, but there was no reason to antagonize anyone...yet. His body was ready to catch a glimpse of scarlet eyes and marble-white skin. His body didn't understand that he wasn't alone this time, that Micah had made a crazy promise to keep him safe, that maybe such a thing could be true.

About a dozen Folk mingled in the clearing, lounging on the trunks of fallen trees, dancing in lazy circles hand in hand, or crafting with flowers. When Micah appeared, gasps and whispers rippled around them.

"Micah's back," cried a female with pink dragonfly wings flashing between her shoulders. She held a half-finished crown of leaves on her lap and excitement in her small round face. Beside her, a man with furred hooves for feet sat up with a tuft of half-braided green hair falling over one eye.

The small flower vendor from the night market ran up to them. She blinked her large liquid eyes at Andrew and then held out a curling lupine to Micah. It matched his eyes. "This is better," she said. "Much sooner than last time."

Fingers trembling, Micah smiled and accepted it from her without speaking.

Above the crescent of steps was a massive brick kiln the height of two men and three times as wide, arching toward the heavens. Roots dangled down from the bushes and small trees growing above. Several faeries, mostly child-sized and winged, sat on the crest of the kiln holding jars of mead or bouquets of flowers. One of them with a pair of cream-streaked moth wings jeered at Andrew when he approached the steps. A quick glare from Micah, though, and the sound cut short in the faerie's throat. It quickly looked down, and its companion socked its shoulder with a fist. Andrew cast Micah a strange look.

In the shadow of the kiln spread an ornate Persian rug beneath piles of multicolored throw pillows. A misty smudge of a person sat on a small throne of bronze fashioned as if melting like a candle. Creamy alabaster legs crossed on the seat, veiled by a skirt and bandeau of gauzy black, with mahogany curls cascading over sloping shoulders.

And when Andrew met her scarlet eyes, they both gasped. The faerie was on her feet with a dagger in hand just as Andrew unsheathed his sword, the scabbard clattering back down the steps. The point of her gleaming blade was against the apple of his throat before he even caught his breath. But he'd landed his sword flush on the curve of her shoulder, the edge pressing against her neck. The iron reacted with her ivory skin; she hissed through her teeth. A slender curl of smoke rose from her shoulder.

Eye to eye with the tall woman, he said to her with a snarl in his throat, "You have robbed me of my peace every single day." All that latent indignation, all the crazed energy that brought insomnia and paranoia since he met his scarlet-eyed specter—it all blazed into a furious inferno. "Haven't you had enough?" His voice trembled, and a single tear flicked onto his cheek. "When will we be even?"

Eyes flashing like molten rubies, the woman bared her teeth and sneered. "Your misery delights me."

The Folk of Lilydale gathered around the kiln, pressing their angular, predatory bodies together and creating a living barrier. Andrew was a clay pot caged within the kiln, about to explode under the fiery gaze of the Lady.

Bravely, Micah wedged himself between them, jostling both of them with his shoulders like a child budging into a line at school. "Andrew, Ingrid! Please don't hurt each other!" Micah exclaimed. He pushed at the faerie's bare midriff, moving her away from Andrew.

The female hissed at Micah, slapping his hand off her. "You brought me this fearful fox as an apology gift, didn't you, Nightshade Boy?"

"Apology gift!" Micah repeated, incredulous.

"Fearful!" spat Andrew, his muscles turning to magma as his heart pumped his fury through his veins. "You created my nightmare! You invaded my dreams! You...waited in the shadows and watched me on the streets! My fear is *your* masterpiece!"

"Cruel, Ingrid," Micah said hoarsely.

"I never touched you," she said with a smug raise of her eyebrow.

"Don't *toy* with me now!" Andrew said, voice rising frantically. His mind played a very vivid fantasy where he got to lob off her head with the sword that she'd forced him to learn how to use. He curled his other hand around the sword hilt, his palms sticky with sweat and potential.

"Ingrid," Micah said as he pushed her again and laid his hand on Andrew's hip. "You'd better back off *right* now."

"Or *what?*" sneered the scarlet-eyed faerie.

Micah said with a tremble in his voice like a stone warning of an earthquake, "Or you will never see me again."

Sighing, Ingrid glared at the bricks over them. "You're a bore, Micah."

He shot back, "You're a stalker."

"You wouldn't care were you not entangled with my prey," Ingrid remarked.

"Wanna bet?" Micah said.

"I knew that's what I was to you!" said Andrew. He'd been right all these years. All those times he felt like a frightened animal in the forest, it was precisely by design.

"Look," Ingrid said to Micah. She spun her dagger, slipping it into the waistband of her skirt. Hooking her finger through her glinting bandeau, she pulled it down to reveal a raised pink scar between her small breasts. "He provoked me."

"Ooh, a wittle scar," taunted Micah.

Glowering at him, Ingrid fixed her top and obscured the scar once again. "Petulant whelp."

Micah stuck his tongue out at her.

Eyes flashing like chips of ice, Chamomile approached Ingrid wearing a pink gossamer robe, with a longbow slung over one shoulder and a quiver of arrows over her other. She nudged Ingrid's thigh with her elbow and said, "The fox slept over at Micah's last night, too."

"Chami, mind your business!" Micah exclaimed.

Ingrid groaned, "Of all the humans!"

Still glaring at Chamomile, Micah said in exasperation, "Ingrid, we all know you probably would have killed Andrew if he hadn't defended himself. Better you have a scar than he be dead."

Chamomile let out a dubious laugh.

Ignoring her with obvious effort, Micah continued, "It's not his fault if he caught you unawares. You're the one who passed out in the middle of nowhere."

"If he'd harmed me in the Redwoods..." she began.

Micah interrupted harshly, "We're not *in* the Redwoods. That's the whole fucking point."

Before they could keep arguing, Andrew decided to interrupt. He dropped his blade and let it clatter to the ground. He lifted both hands, palms up. "Truce. All right? Truce. For Micah."

Micah and the scarlet-eyed faerie both froze, effectively

distracted by his demonstration.

The scarlet-eyed faerie curled her lip, contemptuous and mocking. "Why?"

Andrew swallowed. He let his hands fall. The sneer on her face brought him instant regret over dropping his sword. "You and I both know I hoped to never see you again. I didn't come here for you. I came here to help your brother."

"I should have guessed when you put that nightshade in your window," spat the scarlet-eyed faerie.

"Wait," said Andrew, exchanging a glance with Micah.

Eyebrows raising, jaw dropping, Micah looked back at Ingrid and said, "Ingrid, you literally just proved you've been stalking him within the last *month*. While I've been dating him."

She sent a sharp puff of air out her nostrils. "You have no right to judge me."

"Yes, I do. I'm pissed at you."

"I'm 'pissed' at you too," she retorted.

While the siblings squabbled, Andrew felt his sword against his foot, planning the movement he would need to make in order to pick it back up. Just in case.

Micah nodded to the ring of Folk, still and watchful. "Call them off. We need to talk."

Ingrid scowled.

Micah glared back.

Rolling her eyes, Ingrid waved a preternaturally long

hand at the Folk gathered behind them. When only them
and Chamomile remained under the shadow of the kiln,
Ingrid sat down on the bronze seat and crossed her elegant
legs so her black skirts fluttered like curtains of darkness.
Chamomile sat on a pink cushion beside her, arms crossed,
eyes narrowed at Andrew. Returning the same narrowed
eyes at her, he used his foot to scoot his sword closer.

"What could you possibly need that made you finally step
foot in here, Nightshade Boy?" asked Ingrid with hooded
eyes.

Micah said, "It's my dad."

A blue-skinned male faerie wearing silver trunks ran up
to Micah. He held out a crystal glass filled and sloshing
with golden liquid. A pair of minty green wings vibrated between his shoulder blades, delicate and pale as an
aphid. Micah declined the drink. The faerie's cerulean gaze
dropped; he looked vaguely wounded.

Ingrid touched her chin contemplatively. She looked at
the beverage the blue faerie held. "Take a drink, and we
can talk."

Micah blinked, incredulity creasing his features. "Are
you shitting me? Don't be childish."

Ingrid gestured with two fingers toward the cup.

"Why do you care what he does?" demanded Andrew.

Darkly, Ingrid stared down at Andrew. She growled,
"He's one of us." To Micah, she said with not a trace of
aggression, "Chamomile said you folded shadows to follow

her here. That means you have another ability you didn't know about."

Micah grunted wordlessly.

"You need to stay here until you understand what you can do."

"I most certainly do not." Micah crossed his arms.

"You want to be among humans and accidentally turn a car into a pumpkin? Or wither a plant at a café just because you're in a bad mood? Do you think they would still accept you if you frighten them like that? Humans cannot even accept other humans not like them."

Ingrid wasn't wrong, but Andrew wouldn't even have agreed with her at knifepoint. Hushed, he told him firmly, "We can go look for your dad ourselves."

"Likely to fail," said Ingrid.

Eyes narrowing at her, Micah grabbed the drink and slammed it back in a single swallow. He smeared gold from his lips and snapped, "You happy now, your royal dryness?"

Ingrid took a goblet of deep red wine from the same blue faerie. She swilled the cup in a bejeweled hand, her familiar black nails setting Andrew's teeth on edge. She caught his eye and smirked, tapping her nail against the rim of the cup and eliciting an involuntary shudder from him.

Micah exclaimed, "Hey! What're you doing? Trying to scare him, right in front of me?" He snatched Andrew's hand and started to turn them to leave.

"Stop, stop," said Ingrid. "Fine."

Andrew pulled back on Micah's hand, keeping him in front of the scarlet-eyed faerie's kiln throne. It was true that his blood was pounding noisily in his ears, and he would love to sprint out of here as fast as he could. But if something was wrong with Julian, that didn't seem to matter.

Micah glanced up at Andrew, uncertain, searching Andrew's face. He tried to determine the implication of Andrew's quavering smile, drenched in unease, forced and stiff. Ingrid turned him into someone almost unrecognizable, a skittish wild animal Micah only saw in that first time or two they met and never again. Not when Andrew had carried Julian up the stairs last night to spare him from Micah. Not when they were laughing over bad lines in movies or falling asleep together after staying up too late talking. This twitchy, ghostly pale man had been torn apart with his gnawed-upon bones left to decay among the detritus...all because of Micah's sister. And yet Andrew wasn't letting them leave, hung onto Micah to ensure they could do what they came here for.

Ingrid cleared her throat and said, "What do you expect me to do about your father?"

Micah paused. The warmth of the honey mead he'd swallowed turned gravelly in the pit of his stomach.

"Go on then," Andrew murmured to him, squeezing his palm.

He wetted his lips. "My dad was acting weird and then

fell off the grid. I need to figure out where he went and get him home. Chamomile said you can scry now. Can you find out where he is?"

Ingrid looked away, her chest puffing proudly. Then she stood and smoothed down her skirts. "Fine."

Micah's shoulders relaxed. Crouching, he picked up the sword and scabbard, sheathed it, and handed it back to Andrew. "You're entitled to be armed. But she won't do anything to you now," he said.

"Why not?" Andrew asked skeptically.

"There's nothing she wants more than to have me back," said Micah softly. His eyes were stormy as he stared at the molten bronze seat.

The noisy bray of a pheasant reached them from somewhere nearby in the bluffs.

Andrew said after a moment, "She doesn't deserve you."

Micah didn't say anything. His throat bobbed as he swallowed. Then he grasped Andrew's hand and they left the kiln throne. Ingrid's hut was behind the throne closer to the southeast corner of the commune; the fastest path was not very direct from the throne, requiring some climbing through vivid orange tiger lily patches and using a root to haul themselves up a small wall of limestone. Having gotten up to her door much faster than them, she waited with her back against the hammered bronze, arms crossed.

"You're not coming in," Ingrid said to Andrew, her lip curled. "Your smell would be impossible to get out."

Andrew held up his hands. "Fine. Though the commentary was unnecessary."

"Quite," she said blandly.

He glanced at Micah. "Scream if you need me."

Micah grinned halfheartedly. "Same to you."

Grabbing his bicep, Ingrid opened her door and pulled Micah inside. He pinwheeled his arms to keep his balance as she said brashly, "Why are you giving so much trust to someone you hardly know?"

He righted himself, frowning. "Better than not trusting anyone."

"I trust several people," Ingrid said defensively.

His eyes began to paint in the details of Ingrid's hut as he adjusted to the dimness. Micah hadn't been in here for years. It was...very easy to feel comfortable as he slid down to his knees on a large floor pillow. Maybe it was the smell of warm mulberries rising with a spiral of smoke from a golden incense jar. But every inch of the hut had his sister's flair.

Woven tapestries depicting star charts and woodland life hung over her brick walls. There was an old yellowing map of Minnesota with all its lakes touched with a shining deep blue that made them look like thumbprints of real water. Candles were everywhere, flickering merrily in a ring along the walls.

Leaning his arms on her glossy, low table, he returned his gaze to his sister. "I've been alone for a long time. I haven't so much as held hands with anyone since Chamomile. I know you're comfortable with that, but I get lonely."

She nodded slightly. "So you're... interested in him? Um...romantically?"

"Very. I started seeing him—" When she frowned, he clarified, "Spending time with him, last month. He practically knows everything already."

"Doubtful."

"Well, he's done a ton of research on the Folk. Know why, Ingrid? Go on. Guess."

Ingrid *tsked* and glared at the wall over his head.

"Yes, that's right. What delightful irony that I got involved with someone you've been tormenting for literally no reason." He clipped each word to a sharp point. When she opened her mouth to object, he lifted a hand and said hastily, "Oh. Right. Right. He had the gall to wound you *in self-defense* and bruised your ego, since humans aren't supposed to be formidable. Right?" Micah sniffed, eyes narrowing. "Mother would be so proud."

"Are you finished lecturing me?" Ingrid grumbled.

"I'm not sure. Have I made you feel dumb for it yet?"

Silent, she looked away, candlelight flickering brightly against the guilty downward curve of her lips.

"Great. Then yes. I'm done. So anyway, I think he's a wise choice for a partner, actually, and I hope you'll come around to that idea for me."

Outside the hut, Andrew sat down on a wide limestone

step next to a brilliantly fuchsia hydrangea bush. He kept both hands on his sword, sliding it absently in and out of the sheath, watching the colored specks of traffic fly over the interstate bridge in the distance. His blood pounded in his ears, and his shoulders tingled like usual, but that was his only indication that he was still uneasy. It was serene inside Lilydale; voices and music drifted like rustling reeds. And the view over the river basin was spectacular, with the skyline of the city northwards past a mirror-bright lake below them.

"Do you know any riddles?"

Andrew jumped, looking sharply away from the scenery and down to his elbow. The woman from the Night Market sat right behind him. With her hair unwrapped, Andrew saw she had two small ivory horns on her brow at the edge of her hairline. Her ears were small and protruded like a doe's.

"Syabira, right?"

She nodded. "Riddles?"

While she gazed up at him expectantly, Andrew wetted his lips and smiled faintly. "Yeah, I know heaps. Let me think."

Back inside the hut, Ingrid and Micah gazed at one another in scrutinous silence. Ingrid kept her eyes on him as she lowered herself to a cushion opposite Micah. Slowly, she removed the antler crown from her head and set it on a stand of lashed together branches that was clearly made for it. With her fingers, she combed out her curls. All the while, her attention remained fast on him. He seemed to know she was still assessing, and he remained quite still, unblinking, expression open and hopeful.

Ingrid stretched across the table and poked his nose. "Whatever you say, Nightshade Boy."

Micah let out his breath.

"Maybe if I say I support you, you'll come around more often," she muttered.

Sighing, Micah picked at a cuticle and said, "Yeah. Maybe."

She eyed him for a moment longer, her wine-red irises swirling into a softer rose hue when Micah looked up and gave her a faint smile. Her lips didn't move, but the tiniest crinkles appeared beneath her painted eyes.

Ingrid lifted something heavy off the shelves beside them and set it in front of her on an ornate silver stand. She pulled back a cloth that flowed like water to reveal a sphere clear as a bubble. The candles reflected in its iridescent surface like starlight.

"Holy shit," whispered Micah. "It's beautiful."

Nodding, Ingrid picked a fleck of dust off the glass. "I had to go down to New Orleans in order to find someone I believed truly had the Sight—a *swamp faerie*," Ingrid added with disdain. "I brought them gifts for a week before they agreed to teach me their craft."

"It's awesome," Micah said.

"I agree." She grazed the globe with her fingertips and then tucked a dark curl behind her ear, which came to an elegant point and was lined with tarnished gold hoops. Then she looked down at Micah. "Is there more that you want? From me."

He hesitated. "Honestly, it depends on where he is."

She dropped her gaze. "Micah, if your father is in the Redwoods..."

Micah rubbed his temple. Hearing Ingrid say the word triggered too much in him. Too many images. Too many feelings.

Rainy gray sky, deep red wood chips, dark leaves obscuring the land beyond, ferns taller even than the Folk. Branches dripping with moss. Velvety, thick green undergrowth. Elk treading cautiously in the distance, maybe ordinary animals, or maybe cursed humans. Lilydale was beautiful, but the Folk's Redwoods took his breath away.

But it wasn't just the scenery. He'd have stayed for the scenery.

The Redwood Queen put on great hunts like nobility hunting foxes, with her two red hounds flanking her. Only she wasn't hunting foxes, she was hunting humans. Even when she couldn't bother to go catch humans herself, she would send her underlings—often including Ingrid—to the perimeter of her domain to set traps for hikers.

Hikers like Micah's father.

Once captured, they would be teased and tormented and

pleasured until they wept for the Redwoods. Until the lives they left behind were just a dream, and all they desired was just as unreal.

Julian was a special capture, as the Redwood Queen had chosen him to be her sire. Faeries had a difficult time reproducing biologically, so she expected to keep him for as long as it took. As far as Micah understood it, Julian's relationship with the Redwood Queen was never consensual.

Swallowing sickly sweet bile, he nodded again. "Then I'm going to the Redwoods."

Nonplussed, Ingrid nodded silently. She turned her attention to her scrying glass. Her striking eyes grew distant, unfocused, concentrating. She bit her lip with a bright white canine and stroked the orb with her fingers. She spoke soft words that sounded like a rushing stream.

The orb flickered, dim at first and then blindingly bright, blinking a few times as if a projector bulb was firing up an image. Ingrid's breathing quickened. The strange sounding words she continued whispering made Micah's ears ring.

Micah leaned forward. Within the orb, a misty lens showed cars rushing past, out of focus. Treetops. Gray sky, then a glimpse of sunlight, as if the vision was going so fast the weather had shifted. Then the vision pulled back to show his father, sitting with his back to something, hands folded on his knees. His eyes were glassy and his lips curled with pleasure.

The image went dark.

"W-we need to see more!" Micah exclaimed. He stared at his own face reflected back at him, curved, distorted, contorted with dread.

Ingrid asked expressionlessly, "Do we?" She draped the cloth over the orb. "You didn't recognize that vessel?"

Micah began to shake his head and then stopped short. He dropped his forehead into his hands. "*Fuck,*" he said with a groan. "Her chariot."

She released a sigh through her nose. "The Redwood Queen is baiting you, Micah."

Hugging himself, he curled up as fog burned all rational thoughts from his brain. He never knew the name of his own mother. Nobody did, so they said. He only called her Your Majesty, even when he was as tall as her knee. She'd kept Micah's father in a gilt cage beside her on the dais. When she bore Micah and he'd lived, Julian was no longer needed, but she wouldn't set him free. Micah understood when he was older that there was a good chance he wouldn't survive infancy, and the Redwood Queen wanted to be able to pick Julian back up like a toy she'd discarded. Even after that, he still believed that Julian's continued imprisonment was used to manipulate Micah.

Julian's quarters had been—not inhumane. Not a concrete cell. But small and barred from the outside. He had books and food and a washroom, but no electronics. Micah was allowed to visit him one day per week. They spent the whole day in his chambers, as Julian was not permitted to leave the manor grounds. Micah remembered every single visit from the time he turned five and on. There were over seven hundred days spent in that little room, but each one burned like its own bonfire in his mind. All his dad had gotten to do for him was teach, and encourage, and try to hide his pain. He made Micah play mahjong and chess with him, and they would read a novel or a philosophy book per week while Micah was away and talk about it when he came to visit. Julian taught him long division and chemistry, slow and stalled of course, but tirelessly. It was Julian who made sure Micah had some grasp of human history. Micah collected the newspapers from the Lake Sylvia State Park building each week and went through them with Julian. They would analyze politics, talk about the stock market, and make up imaginary plots for the movies that were showing in theaters.

Once, when he was about fourteen, Micah rushed into his dad's chamber with a bouquet of ferns and cinqfoils. As a teen, he was a bit eccentric, trying to find his fashion sense among a court of beautiful creatures who dressed in nature and gossamer and silk. He ended up with hot pink jeans, a crushed velvet vest, jewelry Ingrid made, and flowers in his hair. He was lucky cameras didn't work in the Redwoods.

"Dad," he exclaimed, sliding into his cedar chair by the window. The walls in Julian's chamber were deep orange, as he was housed in the heart of the Queen's massive Red-wood tree, about four hundred feet off the ground. "The cinqfoils remind me of your eyes. Super amber." He slid the bouquet into a vase Julian kept on his table, as Micah always brought flowers.

Julian said hoarsely, "Beautiful, as always." He wiped his nose and sniffed, and then wiped his eyes as he turned away from the window to face Micah. He managed a smile.

Micah stilled. "Dad?"

"Sorry, bud." He took a drink from a goblet filled with green wine the Folk fermented themselves.

"Are you okay? What can I do?" Micah clambered off his chair—he was very clumsy at fourteen—and knelt beside his father's seat. Julian was only in his thirties, but the lines in his face were that of a much older man. The Queen kept him dressed like a thrall, in a tattered brown tee and jeans he'd worn probably for the last decade. He needed glasses, but the Queen wouldn't let him wear them.

"N-nothing. I'm sorry, son. I don't want you to worry." Julian looked away, swiping at his nose again with fingers that trembled.

"Dad," said Micah more firmly. "Talk to me."

Julian's expression crumpled. His hazelnut complexion was washed out from being kept indoors, making him look sickly. Tears pricked at the corners of his eyes, but he kept wiping them away before they fell. "Sometimes I-I get in my head. This...this is not the life I imagined for myself,

kiddo. I wanted to be an architect, and now I live in a tree."
He choked on a laugh.

Micah didn't smile. "Dad," he whispered sadly. "You can
talk to me about this stuff."

"Why bother? There's nothing we can do about it," said
Julian. "Maybe if one of my..." he trailed off.

"What?"

"Maybe if Her Majesty hadn't killed all my friends," Julian choked. "But I'm it. The lucky survivor." He smiled,
bitter.

Guilt burned in Micah's chest as he held his dad's hands,
realizing he'd never thought how miserable Julian must
be, imprisoned by a faerie queen who pretended he didn't
exist.

"You don't have to call her 'Her Majesty,'" Micah said.
"She's a bitch."

Julian gazed out the window, smiling faintly, dreamily.
"Don't talk about your mother like that."

After this conversation with his father, Micah's feelings
about Julian's circumstances shifted violently. He was com-
placent about it before then, but for the rest of his teens,
he became increasingly protective of his father. He tried
to sneak him in a cell phone he'd picked up at Montesano,
but it didn't work in the Redwoods. When the phone was
discovered by Sivarthis, a member of the Queen's guard,
the Queen ordered Julian to be beaten. She made Micah
watch.

Micah petitioned Ingrid for her help, but she had been around the Redwood Queen for enough decades that she was reluctant to get involved. Her best way to interact with her mother was to not interact with her. But Micah's restlessness just kept getting worse, and so did his attitude. Ingrid worried he'd get himself in trouble, and he had little enough to his credit as the Queen's half-breed son to lose any more esteem.

Then Micah turned twenty. He'd seen enough, and worried enough for his dad, and realized how dangerous everything really was in the Redwoods. Though she was reluctant, Micah got Ingrid to agree to get Julian out of the Redwoods. She charmed a group of humans from Montesano into wandering near the perimeter of the Queen's domain, and effectively lured the Queen out on a hunt.

With Julian sober, alert, and determined to get out even if it killed him, he and Micah escaped the Redwoods during heavy rain, covered in mud and moss so they could disappear if a faerie looked twice at them. Julian seemed surprised, as if it shouldn't have been as easy for him and Micah to escape without being seen. Micah credited his desperation and assumed it gave him extra stealth. It just seemed easier to find mossy trees to hide within when they crossed paths with a Redwood guard. It seemed Folk looked right through them, like the trees came to their aid.

When they reached the edge of Lake Sylvia State Park, Ingrid appeared out of the shadow of a cedar tree.

"I'm leaving with you," she told him. For the first time since he'd known her, she wasn't wearing her crown of bronze branches. Instead, her curls were restrained in tight French braids.

Micah's jaw dropped. "You're what?"

She shook her head. "Don't ask questions. But I'm done with the Redwoods, too. Now. I know where we should go. It's in Minnesota. Are you ready?"

"Micah," said Ingrid evenly. He snapped back to the present. "Look at me, Micah." It sounded like she'd said his name more times than he'd heard. He lifted his head from his knees and stared listlessly at her. She crouched close to him, taking his hand. "You said yourself your father cannot let go of the Redwoods. He's a prisoner to what it made him feel. Why not let him live out his days where he wants to be?"

"No!" Micah said. He shoved her back by the shoulders. She limply allowed this, too stunned to be angry. "You don't understand! He doesn't love it. He's addicted to it. On his good days he says that it's like a craving in his bones. If you think that's good for someone, you're delusional." Micah climbed to his feet. "I will *not* give him to her. I will die trying to get him out if that's what it takes."

"You're an idiot," remarked Ingrid, still crouched, chin on her palm.

Micah set his jaw. "Fine." Moving back toward her doorway, he added more gently, "Thank you for your help."

Ramming his shoulder into her heavy door, he pushed himself back into daylight.

Andrew jumped up at once as Micah emerged and let the door swing closed behind him.

Covering his face, Micah dropped into a crouch. He made himself small, childlike, half concealed by the fat hydrangea blossoms growing against Ingrid's hut.

Andrew knelt beside him and slung his arm around Micah's shuddering shoulders. "Hey, what is it? What happened to your dad?"

Before Micah calmed himself enough to answer, the bronze door creaked open. Ingrid stepped out beside Micah, her hand spread on the door, her eyes downcast and glinting like blood as she glared at Andrew.

She said, "The Redwood Queen took Julian back."

Chapter Ten
The Choice

Above Magic's Repair, Andrew showered hastily, tied back his hair, and dressed in dark ripped jeans and a maroon tee. He packed slowly and methodically, hoping it would stop his hands from shaking. All his dangerous possessions were on his bed and a black Jan-Sport slouched open as he rolled up several changes of clothes.

Sam watched him from the doorway, holding Arwen and stroking the cat's head. When Andrew pulled down the crossbow from his closet, Sam finally exclaimed, "Holy fucking shit, man. Who are you?"

Andrew extended the crossbow to Sam. "Wanna hold it?"

"No!" Sam cried, flinching back. "Are you gonna need to use that?"

"I don't know. Maybe." He took down a pack filled with extra iron bolts and jammed it into the backpack.

Sam stared at Andrew with a crease on his brow. He narrowed his eyes and said, "You know, you seem weirdly comfortable with the idea of running off with a bunch of faeries who have been trying to kill you for years."

"Ingrid never tried to kill me." Andrew zipped up the backpack. "She could have if that's what she was going for." He paused. "I mean, not to discredit the fact that she made me fucking crazy. And anyway, I think I'm just going with Micah." When Sam didn't respond, Andrew glanced warily at his assistant.

As soon as their eyes met, Sam blurted, "Dude, what if you die? Why the hell are you doing this?"

Sighing heavily, Andrew shouldered the bag and turned back to Sam. He put both hands on his shoulders and leaned down to see his hazel eyes behind his glasses. "Sam, I'm not gonna die. And I'm doing this because..." He thought for a moment. "Because I care about the situation Micah is in, about him, and about his father. Lord knows if my mother got kidnapped by my father, I would be showing up to murder him in a heartbeat."

Tears swimming in his eyes, Sam ground his teeth and then said, "Doesn't this queen eat humans for breakfast?" As Andrew opened his mouth, Sam hurried on, "Metaphorically. I'm just saying, how do you *know* this isn't gonna kill you?"

Andrew straightened. He smoothed his hand over his hair and then leaned against the doorway. Looking down at Sam, he shrugged and said slowly, "You're right. I don't know."

A tear raced down his cheek as Sam dropped his gaze.

Putting his arm around Sam, Andrew led his assistant into the living room and sat them both down on the couch. Keeping his arm in place, Andrew went on, "The thing is...I've had no control over any of the bad shit that's happened in my life. It's happened to me, despite me."

Sam sniffled, not interrupting.

"For the first time, I have the choice between running toward danger or not. Sure, the smart choice would be to stay home. To let Micah go by himself on a fool's errand to rescue his dad from an evil faerie kingdom. But what if he dies? And I'm just dicking around here, pointlessly existing?" Andrew shook his head slowly and said, "I wouldn't be able to live with myself, knowing I could have helped and didn't. And then what's the point? I'm dead either way."

Sam pushed his glasses onto his forehead, wiped his eyes, and sniffed again. Andrew handed him a box of tissues from the side table.

"And look at us now," Andrew added gently. "Remember my fun joke at your interview? You're the person who'll know if I die. And I value that."

"Andrew, that's incredibly depressing," Sam said with a choked laugh.

Arwen went running a second before there was a knock at the door. Andrew got up as Sam blew his nose several times. He slid back the chain on his door and unbolted it.

Micah stood on the top of the stairs, serious, unsmiling, anxious. His hair was damp and combed slightly back, and he'd put on a purple tee with a wide collar that framed his clavicle. The mulberry leaf hung from his neck, and his large earlobes stretched around wooden earrings carved to look like trees. His eyes flicked toward Sam and a frown deepened on his lips.

Then Chamomile stepped out from behind him. She held Micah's large black cat in her arms, which blinked impassively at Andrew and swished its tail. Chamomile grinned up at Andrew, the smile unfriendly, offset strangely by her rosy apple-shaped cheeks. The cat, Fadil, jumped from her arms and padded confidently into Andrew's apartment. He watched the cat pass with a blank stare and one raised eyebrow, but how could he not let his boyfriend's cat into his apartment?

Chamomile, meanwhile...she whipped her silver ponytail and heaved up her breasts in the extremely short sundress she wore, which very easily could have been a child's camisole. "What do you say, tall one? Shall we 'hit the road,' so to speak?"

"What?" Andrew stared at her. "You aren't—"

But Micah's eyes slid shut and his lips pressed into a thin line, and that told Andrew that it was already decided.

"Let's see," said a new voice, the low timbre making Andrew's knees weak. "You've been oh so protective of this home, little fox, so it must be truly splendid." The scarlet-eyed faerie moved near Micah's shoulder; she leaned into the doorway as if Andrew's nightmares were finally coming true.

"Ingrid," Micah said through gritted teeth. "Knock it off." He shoved his elbow into her stomach, buying Andrew some space and allowing him to finally release the breath he'd been holding.

Chamomile scampered past Andrew and into his apartment as she said, "The wards you've set up are...fine." She peered at the hawthorn shag over his door. "But they would never have kept the Lady of the Bluffs out if she wanted in."

"Why can you get past them now?" asked Andrew.

Breasts bouncing as she danced around him, Chamomile sang, "I'm not trying to hurt you. Intentions matter, you tall oaf."

"*That* hurts," Andrew remarked, hand on his chest.

She shrugged dismissively. "Just your feelings." Prancing away, she scrambled onto his stool and stuck her fingers in the soil of his bromeliad. With a frown, she disappeared past the counter, a sage-colored hand darting up to snatch a glass with a bit of water in the bottom. Then she clambered back onto the stool and watered the bromeliad. Andrew watched her with his hands on his hips. He was dying to ask her about her name, which evoked the soothing fragrance of a cup of tea before bed, and not...this jagged-toothed, voluptuous, chaotic goblin. Even if she was watering his plant unprompted.

"I understand if they're a deal-breaker for you," said Micah, still standing in his doorway. "And you don't have to come."

"We'll be just fine without you," Ingrid said beside him, arms crossed. She had put on a silky black shirt dress and tightly braided her mahogany hair. At least with her hair back, she looked a bit less like she did in her hauntings.

"I wasn't going with because I think I'll be critical to the rescue mission," Andrew snapped.

He turned away from the door. Across from him, sitting in the hall outside Andrew's bedroom, Chamomile let Arwen sniff her fingers with an enormous smile on her face and nothing but warmth in her large eyes.

Ingrid and Micah argued in whispers in the doorway. Micah waved his hand at her and hurried into the flat, stepping out of his sneakers. He reached for Andrew's arm but stopped just before he touched him.

"She's really just a prissy princess," Micah said, jerking his chin toward the scarlet-eyed faerie. Ingrid rolled her eyes with a scoff, leaning cross-armed against the door.

Chamomile swiped the television remote from a couch cushion and started tapping buttons with her eyes round as saucers, glancing up with childlike delight every time the television did something.

"Chami, quit getting into all his stuff!" Micah exclaimed. Sam giggled.

Going back into his bedroom, Andrew zipped up his backpack and picked up his sheathed seax, the short Viking-era sword he'd picked up from eBay early in the days when Ingrid started stalking him. He weighed the well-balanced blade in his hand, letting out a long sigh through his teeth. Then he flopped onto the edge of his bed, forearms on his thighs, head drooping between his shoulders.

A dangerous rescue mission with just Micah was one thing. But trying to imagine sharing space with the scarlet-eyed faerie...his chest tightened even at the thought. She was *outside his door*. She...she'd done all this torment on purpose. Delighted in it.

"It smells like you in here," said that meadow breeze of a voice. "Almonds and tea."

Andrew lifted his head to look at Micah, dragged up from the muck of his rumination. He said with a faint smile, "Don't lie. It smells like old carpeting and bad wallpaper glue."

Micah grinned, glancing around the room with his arms crossed. "There's no wallpaper."

"I know. It's weird."

Looking down, Micah said with a sigh, "Andrew, I hate to say it, but I could probably use Ingrid and Chami with me in the Redwoods."

Andrew remained silent, folding his hands, digging his fingertips into his knuckles. He glanced at Micah, who quickly looked away. Andrew finally said, "I understand that. And that does probably mean it would be wiser if I didn't go. If the Redwood Queen is anything like Ingrid—"

"Which she is."

"—Then I can't imagine I'd enjoy being around her."

Micah nodded. "I understand."

Picking up his crossbow from the bed, Andrew scrubbed its scope with the hem of his shirt, silent.

"Well," said Micah, his voice too nonchalant, light and strained like he was playing off an injury, "sorry for the change of plans. I should be back in a few days if I can pull everything off. Then maybe we can take an actual road trip. To Duluth or something. Um. See ya." He awkwardly saluted and then left the room.

Andrew loosed a heavy sigh, propping his forehead on the butt of the bow as it rested on his knee. He flexed his toes into the carpet, rolling his shoulders back.

"Wow! Andy, c'mere!" called Sam from the living room.

Still wearing his backpack, he hefted the bow onto his shoulder and stood up with grimace. When he came around the corner, Ingrid still lurked impassively in his doorway, her eyes melting a metaphorical hole in the stairwell, pointedly not engaging with anything in his flat.

On the couch, Chamomile sat with a black cat on each of her knees. Sam scratched Fadil under the chin, looking up as Andrew entered and pointing at Chamomile and Arwen.

"Look, Andy! She loves her!"

Micah crouched in front of the cats. "Who's this pretty girl? Arwen, huh? Aren't you lovely?"

Andrew blinked. "I've never told you her name."

Micah looked up sharply. "Uh."

"Holy shit," said Sam. "Can you talk to cats?"

"Er." Micah's face turned bright red. "Not exactly. But kinda."

Depositing Arwen in Micah's arms and Fadil in Sam's arms, Chamomile pranced over to Andrew, snatching his crossbow out of his hand. "This is cute. Look, Ingrid." She closed an eye and swung the crossbow around the room.

"Careful!" cried Ingrid. "Those bolts are iron, I can smell it."

"Hm." Chamomile hauled it up and aimed it at Andrew. "That's nasty of you."

Scowling, Andrew yanked on the bridge of the bow, but she didn't fight him. She let it go and ran off cackling, hiding behind Ingrid by the door.

"It's time to go," said Ingrid, frowning. "This place is giving me a headache."

Sam stood up from the couch, fidgeting with his sweat-shirt strings with a wary eye on Ingrid. "Cirrus told me about her," he whispered.

"Who?" said Andrew. "Micah's sister?"

"Yeah. She called her the Goth Queen of Lilydale," he said, reverent.

Over Sam's shoulder, Micah burst out laughing, whooping with delight. He ruffled Sam's hair before he set Arwen delicately on the couch.

"All hail," sang Chamomile, crossing a closed fist over

her chest. Ingrid glared sidelong at her, stoic.

First looking at Sam, and then glancing quickly toward and away from Andrew, Micah said, "Hey, uh, I wanted to leave my house keys here. And this." He had a folded half sheet of paper in his hand and a keyring dangling from his pinky. "In the event my dad and I don't make it home, you can do whatever you want with my house. This has the information you'd need." Micah set them on the counter.

Andrew's knees wobbled.

Sam blinked a few times and then pushed up his glasses. "Are you serious? Do you think you're gonna die?"

Micah shrugged. "Don't know." He went to the door, stepping into his shoes and sticking his finger into the heels to unroll the canvas. He started to lose his balance, but Ingrid's white hand shot out and pushed back on his shoulder to steady him. He didn't acknowledge her intervention except to lightly pat her hand. Then he looked into the kitchen and glared. "Chami, put his tablet down. You have your own. Let's get out of here."

Andrew hesitated, bearing crossbow, sword, and backpack, watching as Ingrid and Chamomile answered easily to Micah, even if Andrew's tablet ended up in the sink. Silently, Sam watched Andrew from the couch, chewing on his lip.

Andrew said, "Micah, could we...?" He gestured toward his bedroom.

"Oh." Micah straightened, hand on the open door, Ingrid

and Chamomile freezing on either side of him as if his sentry. "Sure."

Andrew shrugged off his backpack and set down his crossbow on the kitchen island. He moved out of the kitchen, hands curled into fists. Micah followed him in silence, and once inside his room, Andrew closed the door behind them.

"Here's the thing," Andrew said quietly, leaning over Micah, reaching to touch his face but pausing just before. "It would be much wiser for me to stay home—"

Micah's expression didn't even shift. But his irises darkened, swirling from powdery lupine into deep merlot, as if the yellow light from the fixture in the ceiling had suddenly gone dim.

"—But I don't think I can do that."

Micah's irises flowed back into lavender. Andrew wondered if he knew how revealing his color shifting was.

Andrew continued, "I'm very frightened of Ingrid. Literal nightmare fuel. Because of the nightmares I've had. Of her. For years."

Knuckling his eyes, Micah sighed, "Andrew, you don't have to..."

"I know, I know. I'm getting off track. Because I'm also thinking about your father. And I can't stand what's being done to him after how many years you've sacrificed for him to make his life better." Andrew took Micah's hand. "And you both deserve to come back. To be normal again. So.

I'm going to help. As long as Ingrid doesn't scoop out my eyeballs or French-braid my intestines."

"Jeeze!" Micah exclaimed.

"I had that nightmare a few times." Andrew scratched his chin. "She must be an artist type."

Silent, Micah shook his head, sighing through his nostrils and staring at the ceiling.

"Is she?" asked Andrew.

"An artist type? Yeah, kinda."

"Hurt me. Is the scarlet-eyed faerie going to hurt me now?"

"You call her the scarlet-eyed faerie?" Micah grinned, just for a moment.

"Yes. Your sister. Ingrid. Such a pretty name for...that unhinged woman," remarked Andrew, more to himself, looking down. "Is she a woman?"

"No, not really." Micah shrugged. "Anyway, absolutely not, no, she will not hurt you. You can take my word for it, but also, you can wield iron against her, and if she tries anything, use it."

Andrew raised an eyebrow.

Micah said, "It'd be a natural consequence."

"Okay." Andrew nodded. He put his hand on the doorknob. "I trust you."

Micah gazed up at him for several beats, unsure, scrutinizing. But when Andrew stared back, starting to turn the doorknob, clearing his throat, Micah rubbed his neck with a sigh. "I'm becoming more and more sure that if I blow it with you, that's it. Forever alone. I'm doomed."

Andrew snickered, his ears warming, touching the turquoise fringe of Micah's hair where it fell over his brow. "Well, I was kinda hoping you'd be my boyfriend."

Micah straightened. He came a bit closer, tilting back his chin as he asked, "Oh, yeah?"

"If you're interested," Andrew mumbled, flushing.

Micah grinned. "I am."

"Then let's not waste another moment," Andrew declared. He put his arms around Micah's shoulders and squeezed him tightly. Micah grasped Andrew's chin and brought him closer to steal a kiss, pulling Andrew against him with an arm around his waist as he teased open Andrew's mouth with his tongue. They bumped into the bedroom wall, tongues dancing, gripping each other with a ferocity that suggested that the bed was beckoning them and would drag them down like a siren song if only the moment were a bit different. Andrew pressed his palms into the wall over Micah's shoulders and tore himself away, lips shining, cheeks flushed. He leaned their foreheads and their hips together and gave them a minute to come back to themselves, to cool their burning skin, to allow Micah's fingers to dig back out of where they'd burrowed into the small of Andrew's back.

"I have a boyfriend." Micah's hand slid down to cup Andrew's rear before giving it a pinch. Andrew turned crimson, biting his lip, gesturing to the door, but not before he twined his arm around Micah's neck and kissed him again. Once, twice, three times, hot enough to melt skin down to bone. Micah reached for the doorknob, grazing his lips against Andrew's neck as he did. Andrew groaned in protest that the moment had to end as he pushed himself upright on shaky legs before clasping Micah's hand.

They left the bedroom together, and when they emerged, Sam was by himself standing awkwardly by the empty doorway, arms crossed. Micah slipped past him and disappeared down the stairs.

Andrew dropped onto the floor to pull on his black Docs, lacing them tightly. He glanced up at Sam, who watched him with red cheeks and tears in his eyes. With a pinch to Sam's knee as he climbed back to his feet, Andrew fixed his ponytail and gazed at Sam with a sardonic curl to his lips.

"Please be careful," Sam warbled. He threw his arms around Andrew and mashed his face into Andrew's chest. "Please don't die."

Patting his head, Andrew said, "Wear the *géas* while I'm gone. Don't worry. I'll text you as much as I can. And I'll be back before you know it. Do as much or as little for the store as you want, and order food with the company card. It's in my desk drawer, the locked one."

Sam nodded. He said wetly, "Andy, you're a badass."

Andrew grinned and ruffled his hair. "Balderdash."

Locking the door behind him, Andrew clambered down

the steps and out into the parking lot. The sight outside did not particularly instill him with courage. Micah and Chamomile were screaming at each other, how seriously Andrew couldn't tell, but Chamomile was cradling both Fadil and Arwen like twin babies in her arms. She was leaping out of Micah's reach like a grasshopper every time he lunged at her. Brooding under the ash tree in the lot was Ingrid, arms crossed, eyes closed.

"Chami, you don't understand how important he is to me! He's barely still coming with as it is! You can't kidnap his cat!"

Andrew noticed one of Ingrid's eyes peel open to a slit; she peered at him across the lot with the slightest twitch of her lips.

When he looked away from Ingrid, Chamomile was standing in front of him, craning her neck to peer up at him with the sky gleaming in her large, bright eyes. "You don't care, right?" she said. Arwen purred loudly against Chamomile's neck.

"Um, I mean, that's probably an over-simplification," Andrew answered.

Chamomile stuck out her cherubic lower lip. "You aren't going to say no to me though, are you?"

"Probably not," Andrew said.

Jaw dropping, Micah put his hands on his hips.

With a shrug and a smile, Andrew said to him, "I trust the will of cats and wild girls."

Under the tree, Ingrid said, "We have to take your car. It isn't made of as much iron."

Andrew blinked. "It isn't?" She remained with her arms crossed, not elaborating. He pulled out his phone, curiosity too strong, and searched the make and model of the Saturn. "Huh."

"What?" asked Micah.

"This year of Saturn was made with a plastic body." He glanced up at Micah's hopeful face and shrugged. "That's fine. But it might die on the trip." He unlocked the car and then popped open the trunk, setting his bag and crossbow inside.

Ingrid shrugged. "A worthy death." She followed Andrew, elbowing him out of her way and setting a handsome sheathed blade inside. After depositing the cats in the backseat, Chamomile appeared on his other side and put a different, shorter bow inside with her quiver. When Andrew glanced down at the goblin, she leaned toward his arm and tried to bite him.

Micah grabbed her by the back of her neck and hauled her away so she stumbled, her blue eyes wide. She spun around to swipe at him, but Micah blocked her wrist and glared down at her until she relented.

Micah said with a growl, "I swear that if either of you harm so much as a glorious ginger hair on Andrew on this trip, I will spend the rest of my days and all of my energy getting even with you." He crossed his arms. "He told me first he's coming with me, and he's the one I *want* with me. His safety is non-negotiable. If you two have any care for me, which you obviously do since you're coming on this trip, then you will respect this wish and swear not to harm him."

Chamomile wailed mournfully, "You're an absolute bore!"

"Agree," said Micah, shoulders squared, glowering up at his sister.

"Fine," snapped Ingrid. "I swear we won't try to harm him." Her eyes glinted.

"Physically or emotionally," Micah added.

Ingrid's shoulders sagged slightly. "Physically or emotionally."

"Milady!" cried Chamomile. "Must I?"

"Yes," said Ingrid.

Andrew snaked past the arguing Folk and climbed down into the driver's seat as Micah lectured his sister on needing more from her than a ceasefire. "Metaphors don't work on me. There have been no weapons fired," she was saying.

He glanced at the apartment and wondered if Sam was right, if going on this trip was insanity.

"It probably is," he muttered. He stuck the key in the ignition and turned over the engine, making a point about the delay being caused by the two faerie women.

Shortly after him, Micah dropped into the passenger seat, unsmiling, a vein visible in his temple. "I'll pay for everything for the car," he said, not looking at him. "Gas, a tune up when we're back, any emergency repairs from the wear and tear. And I'll also go bring your cat upstairs if you want. But when she's with me and Chami, she won't get spooked very easily. They'll both probably be fine." Micah stared at the seedlings from the ash tree on the windshield.

Andrew answered him with silence, watching in the rearview mirror as the faeries climbed onto the bench behind him. Chamomile helped Fadil into the shelf behind the seat against the rear windshield. He promptly began bathing himself. Arwen climbed onto the armrest between the front seats, sniffing Andrew's elbow, mewing softly. He glanced in question at Micah.

Micah looked up from the cat and then shrugged. "She just wants pets." He scratched her between the ears, down the neck and between her shoulder blades.

"All right." Andrew buckled himself in, shifted into reverse, and glanced at Micah and the women behind him. With a faint smile at Micah, Andrew said quietly, "Let's go save your dad."

Andrew was told to get on 35-E Northbound, and soon they were speeding along in the leftmost lane leaving the cities behind, bound for North Dakota. Chamomile was braiding small sections of her hair, while Arwen furiously chewed on a silvery blonde strand. In the slanting, dim light of the car, the sage-green undertones of Chamomile's skin were more apparent. Fadil was asleep with his head on Arwen's back. Next to her, Ingrid was still as a marble statue, staring out her window with an unreadable expression.

"By the way," Andrew said, "where are we going?"

"Oh," said Micah. "Sorry. It's just a vague answer so I've been avoiding it. It's my Fae side, I guess."

"Or you're just lazy," said Chamomile, kicking the back of his chair.

Ignoring her, Micah said, "We're going pretty close to the coast of Washington. It's in the Hoh rainforest. We get into her domain through Lake Sylvia State Park."

"Washington has a rainforest?"

"Yeah. But technically, the Fae territory there doesn't exist. Not since she sealed off the Redwoods that grew there so humans couldn't cut them down for lumber. She allied with the Native Quileute population out there—albeit briefly—and their shamans lent her some magic to help with the ritual."

"For such a seemingly wicked ruler," said Andrew, "that's certainly no small conservationist feat."

"I think it actually created a lot of the resentment that the Redwood Queen has toward humans, though," said Chamomile. "She turned her back on compassion or mercy for bitterness and cruelty because she was angry at what humans have done to the planet."

Andrew glanced in the mirror as the goblin pulled Arwen up against her shoulder and nuzzled the cat with her cheek. He asked, "You've heard of the Redwood Queen?"

Chamomile raised a white eyebrow. "Everyone's heard of the Redwood Queen."

"Huh. She wasn't in any of my books."

"She destroys the texts that mention her," said Ingrid. "As well as their authors."

"The historian in me weeps," Andrew remarked.

"That's what tyrants do," Ingrid said. "That's always what tyrants do. Lest the better rulers turn on them and end the cruel practices that serve them. Like her human hunts." She twitched, her neck and shoulder folding toward each other as she said with a darkened eye, "I was there when we captured Julian. I saw the moment he realized all his friends were dead. That he was about to die a different kind of death."

Micah's fingers curled around his knee hard enough that his knuckles blanched.

"She's not just apathetic," Ingrid finished. "She's sadistic."

"I didn't realize you dislike her as well," said Andrew.

"I have decades of reasons to hate her," admitted Ingrid.

"Is that why you left and came to Lilydale?"

Ingrid was silent for a moment. "No. I left for Micah."

Micah smiled, but the expression was bittersweet.

Chamomile had been right, when she'd said last month that Ingrid would do anything for him. He'd *known* that, but in a way that he took it for granted, treated it like a given. Now that seemed selfish of him. She dropped everything to come with him even though she didn't think going back to the Redwoods was a good idea. She was even *sort of* obliging him about Andrew, and had stopped actively antagonizing him.

"Wait, wouldn't that make you two a prince and a princess?" Andrew asked.

Ingrid scoffed. "I was called the Ruby Daughter."

"More lately, the Goth Queen of Lilydale," giggled Chamomile.

"I don't even know what a goth is."

"You don't need to," said Chamomile, poking Ingrid's cheek. "You're living it."

Andrew glanced at Micah. "What was your title?"

He stared out the windshield as if Andrew hadn't spoken. The silence was thick and awkward for a few breaths and bumps of the car over potholes in the road. Andrew tapped his thumb on the wheel, regretting the question.

Softly, Ingrid answered for him, "The Redwood Queen didn't allow the use of any titles for Micah. If anything, people called him halfling."

Andrew shook his head. "But she had you intentionally. Why would she then dishonor you like that?"

Micah remained silent and frozen but for a very faint

shrug of one shoulder.

"That's why he's my Nightshade Boy," said Ingrid. Her white hand snaked around the back of Micah's seat and tugged on his earlobe. The gesture shook him loose; he pulled his head out of her reach and managed a faint smile. Ingrid explained, "People overlook him, but at their own peril."

CHAPTER ELEVEN
THE MOUNTAINS

"HEY," MICAH SAID, PUTTING his phone down and tapping Andrew's elbow, "we need to stop. It's after midnight. Let's rest."

Hugging the foot of Montana mountains, the Saturn chugged along in the dark. Its gas tank had emptied twice so far, but the party inside had managed to need no other stops than that. Still, Andrew's eyes were rimmed with the red of exhaustion, and he couldn't stop yawning.

Andrew said something back but it was unintelligible through another hearty yawn. He nodded. "Fine. All right. Tell me where to go."

They left the interstate and wound away from city lights and other traffic and to more rustic roads until tall spruce and fir trunks surrounded them like a ribcage stretching toward the heavens. Micah pointed them down a barely marked gravel park road until the only lights anywhere but the sky were from them.

Knees tucked up on the bucket of the seat, Chamomile

was asleep with the cats against her chest. Her breathing was soft, so slow it was barely there. Ingrid had spent hours braiding in eucalyptus leaves and flower buds to Chamomile's silvery tresses, and still toyed with it now.

The jostling of the cruder road roused Chamomile until she sat up, squinting blearily, looking down in confusion as her hair stayed twined in Ingrid's fingers. Ingrid struggled to untangle herself, but Chamomile giggled.

"Park by the butte," said Micah. He pointed off to the right.

"By...by the what?" said Andrew.

"That thing. It's the big rock hill."

"Oh. Why didn't you say hill?"

"Because it's called a butte."

Andrew snickered.

"You're a child," scoffed Micah.

"That's not how it's pronounced," said Ingrid.

"Yeah, okay." Micah sniffed.

Andrew eased the Saturn as far off the trail as he could risk it without fearing he'd get them stuck. The four of them unloaded and stretched.

On Micah's side of the car, Chamomile and both cats jumped out.

"Wait a second," Andrew protested.

"They want dinner," Chamomile said with a glare in his direction. "Speaking of..." Out of the backseat she pulled her bow and quiver. It was a beautiful instrument, the bow polished to a shine that glinted with starlight, and the quiver made from supple leather. The arrows protruding were tipped with feathers from a red-tailed hawk she and Micah had recovered after it had been hit by a car. Chamomile dipped in a half-bow toward Ingrid. "Shall we?"

Ingrid nodded. The two females melted into the shadows and were gone.

"What are they going to hunt?" asked Andrew cautiously.

"It's better that you don't know," he told him. When Andrew paled, Micah laughed, "I'm kidding. Probably hare or pheasant. Maybe a hart if they get lucky."

"A hart?"

"A deer."

"Who says hart?"

Micah gave him a look.

"Oh. Right. Someone raised in faerieland. My mistake."

Grinning, Micah bent and picked up short sticks near his feet, snapping off thinner branches and stripping off leaves. "I'll get a fire going."

"Do you just call fire into being?" asked Andrew.

Micah looked confused. "No. I use a flint stick and a knife. Silly city boy."

Unbothered thanks to Micah's affectionate tone, Andrew tilted back his head at the treetops far above them. The stars glinted bright as daylight, pinpricks in an inky black shroud. The clearing near the butte was hardly large enough to fit the Saturn. A thick canopy of trees bowed around them with underbrush heavy enough to feel oppressive. Though it was nothing like the hum of the city, of electricity and engines and the crowd of humanity, the forest was *loud*.

"On that note, this looks, uh...*very* wild. What lives around here?"

Micah rested his chin on his hand with his arms braced on the roof of the Saturn. He closed his eyes, focusing on the feeling of the ground under his feet. The crisp air, free of car exhaust, sewage, litter, garbage dumps. Peat moss and rich fertile soil, the distant chill of mountain air, animals and their droppings, the sting of spruce. Animals rustling as they settled back into the quiet after being disturbed by the Saturn, the wind in the trees, the crickets and cicadas. A great-horned owl crying mournfully. A pheasant screaming in reply.

He smiled, releasing a long breath. "Name it," he said, eyes still closed, "and it's probably nearby."

Andrew's heart dropped through his feet. He tried to fortify himself, but the truth was that Lilydale was the wildest wilderness he'd ever been in, and it was hemmed in by people within a few miles. But Micah looked so peaceful. At home. Even though the underbrush was thick and ominous. Even if creatures called through the darkness, and he felt eyes on him all around.

Smiling, Micah opened his eyes, which glowed like opals under the half-moon. Andrew pretended like he wasn't wearing the blood ward, like Micah's gaze could inject him with courage, like the look in his eyes made his fear melt away. Weirdly, it worked a little.

Micah pushed off from the car and unwound the flannel from Andrew's waist. He helped Andrew into it and then held him by the waist as he murmured, "I'm really fortunate that I met you." He looked away. "I probably shouldn't have let you come with me though."

"You probably couldn't have stopped me." Andrew grinned. "I'm very hard-headed."

"Whatever's in there," said Micah, smoothing Andrew's hair, "it's very, very good."

Dismissively rolling his eyes, Andrew slung his arms around Micah's shoulders and leaned his cheek on the crown of his head. Their body heat smelted them together like they were made from precious metals as the night enveloped them.

After they let each other go, Andrew rummaged through the trunk. He always had a pair of sleeping bags in his car as well as a flashlight and a first aid kit. Micah picked up the sleeping bags but blocked Andrew's hand when he reached for the flashlight.

"It's better we use the stars, or the fire," he explained. "Your eyes will adjust."

They gathered more than enough wood—sticks, downed

branches, and even a few logs—in just a few minutes from around the car. Andrew stayed out of his way while Micah got a fire going. He did it with such ease Andrew started to think there was some magic to it after all.

As if reading his mind, Micah said with his face aglow with flickering light, "It's really not magic." He flashed him a grin. "And before you get any ideas for future outings, no, I'm not the camping type." Micah's smile faded. Using a long dry stick, he prodded the kindling around in the flames. Sparks flew up toward the expanse of the heavens. "This is all just...in my nature."

Andrew sat down in the dirt beside him, clasping his hands over his knees. "You take no pleasure in it?"

"I don't know if it's that," Micah said, staring thoughtfully into the flames. "I love...adore the natural world. But it scares me, too. I feel like I'm part of it." He held his fingers up to the tongues of fire, wincing slightly, but not withdrawing. "Like it's just waiting until I give up on humanity so it can reclaim me."

Andrew gently lowered Micah's hand away from the heat. "You can do that if you want. Or don't. But it's your choice. That's what being human means."

Micah blinked a few times, then nodded. "Yeah," he said softly.

Leaves rustled and a twig snapped very, *very* close to them. Andrew tensed and grabbed the hilt of the dagger on his ankle. Micah covered Andrew's hand with his own.

On the opposite side of the fire, two sets of emerald eyes caught the firelight and glinted bright as gemstones, blinking once or twice, bobbing closer very slowly.

Clutching Micah's arm, Andrew whispered, "Is it bobcats?"

"Maybe," Micah said, but Andrew shot him another look at the playful note in his voice.

Arwen and Fadil padded into the firelight. Arwen chirped deep in her throat and nosed Andrew's leg, dropping a dead sparrow at his feet. Feathers on the tip of its wing twitched twice. Arwen tilted back her head and blinked cheerfully at Andrew. She nudged the bird with her front paw, and then turned away. She followed Fadil toward the boot of the car and the pair of them jumped into the open trunk. Tails flicked up and blocked out the stars for a sliver of time before the cats disappeared. The shocks of the car squeaked softly.

Heart thundering in his chest, Andrew stared at the bird.

"A gift from the bobcat," Micah said.

The fire was almost embers now. Micah lay on his back on top of a sleeping bag and stared at the heavens. The stars were so bright and clear he could see the band of the Milky Way, speckled overhead like titanium white flicked over a painter's canvas. Orion was not only the belt here but the whole warrior, with his shining silver weapon and his shield outstretched.

Micah thought of his mother—he'd thought of little else since they'd gotten on the road—and how she acted like she was capable of overthrowing the natural order of the world and just chose not to, simply couldn't be bothered. But the stars ruled over her, too. Even she was just a speck in their solar system, in the swirl of the galaxy.

A branch crackled and swung to the side over his head with no pretense of being subtle. Upside-down, a smudge of white caught firelight. A thigh, then another, then a narrow ghostly face with rubies for eyes. It was no wonder Ingrid had so thoroughly terrified Andrew. She emerged from the darkness like a predator, and Micah felt lucky he was not in her diet. He rolled over and propped himself up on his elbow.

Ingrid folded her long legs into a crouch. She said in a voice like wind slipping through fissures in a cliffside, "Chamomile and I made camp elsewhere. We'll be back at sunrise."

"Aw, you know how I worry," said Micah, grinning. "Thanks for letting me know, Red."

Ingrid blinked at him, eyes like pools of wine in the faint light from the embers. She patted his head, and then she melted back into the darkness.

Resting his chin on his palm, still grinning bemusedly,

he looked beside him where Andrew slumbered, tucked into his green nylon sleeping bag, fingers curled under his cheek. He'd taken mere moments to fall to sleep. Sighing wistfully, Micah reflected on his own consistently awful sleep. For him, the only nights he never remembered were the ones when he'd pinched one of his dad's sleeping pills. And that kind of dark and dreamless sleep frightened him too much to keep him coming back.

He wondered if that's what made his father so miserable. That every instinct to rest was thwarted, overtaken by darkness and anxiety. That it was all just endless weariness. That the Redwoods lived in Julian like a tapeworm, making him forever hungry.

"Maybe Ingrid was right," he said to the stars. Maybe the Redwoods were Julian's only relief from misery.

Micah sat up and pulled his knees to his chest. He nudged the fire with the toe of his sneaker. A column of sparks rose heavenward, transforming the embers back into small licking flames. He picked up a stick burning like a match and turned it in his hand, transfixed by the heat and the raw fury of the flame. All his emotions fled before the impending injury, which was his favorite part. He brought the tooth of the flame up to his skin and let it flicker against flesh, hungry, more than capable of melting skin down to bone. The pain was hot and slow and he sucked a breath in through his teeth. The soft skin over his tendons began to blister angrily.

A hand slapped the stick out of his grip. It tumbled back into the fire. Micah frowned with annoyance, glancing at Andrew.

"What the hell are you doing?" Andrew demanded, hair sticking skyward from its elastic band. Red finger marks were imprinted on his cheek. His eyes were wild, sparking with fury.

Shaking out his wrist, Micah looked down and said blankly, "Sorry. It's a bad habit."

"You have a habit of self-harming?"

"It's not—"

"Oh yes it is." Andrew drew Micah closer to inspect his wrist. Twisting awkwardly when Andrew pulled him, Micah ended up with his legs tangled in Andrew's and their shoulders pushed together.

Andrew looked up sharply. "There's a ton of scars here."

Shame gripped the pit of Micah's stomach. He pulled at his arm, but Andrew held him fast. They were both silent, the fire crackling angrily. Andrew blinked, shaking his head slightly. His dark gaze shined with tears.

"Don't cry," begged Micah.

Releasing his wrist, Andrew dropped his head against his chest. He swiped his hand across his nose and then across his eyes. "I tried to kill myself when I was fourteen," he said. "I fucked it up; I didn't take enough pills. I just vomited a ton for a few days." He paused. "My mum never even knew. I didn't have the heart to tell her."

"Oh, Andrew, I—"

Hardly hearing him, Andrew said, "I just felt so alone then. I'm over twice that age now and, possibly for the first time, I'm glad it didn't work." Andrew met Micah's gaze with a tear trailing down his cheek like a shooting star. "I hope you don't feel like this forever. That you have to hurt yourself. I hope I can prove to you you're not alone either."

Frozen, Micah blinked disbelievingly at Andrew, lips slightly parted. It had only ever been Ingrid who caught him harming himself once, in his teens, and since then not even Julian knew. Back then, she'd reprimanded him, called him foolish, told him never to do it again. Understandably. That's what he would expect from someone. It hadn't stopped him from continuing to find ways to cause himself pain when things were too stressful, even as an adult, but he'd learned enough not to get caught. But now this? His *boyfriend* had woken up to find him trying to burn himself and...empathy? Andrew had reacted with empathy? The shared knowledge of the kind of solitary suffering that made it feel as though pain was the only option? It didn't seem right. There had to be a catch.

Andrew stood and went to the trunk of his car, pulling out a little red canvas bag before returning to the sleeping bags and sitting cross-legged, facing Micah. The bag was a First-Aid kit emblazoned with that universal white plus sign, which flashed in the firelight as Andrew unzipped and opened the pack. He unscrewed the top on a white tube and peeled the paper off a latex bandage. As it settled in that Andrew was about to dress this stupid little burn, tears sprang into Micah's eyes again.

Andrew paused. "Hey." He raised Micah's chin with his finger and held his tearful gaze for several seconds before he said softly, "There's nothing to be ashamed of."

Micah began, "I'm a grown man that—"

"Hush." Andrew squeezed a spot of ointment onto his pinky and spread it gently on the small burn on Micah's arm. "That doesn't change anything, being a grown-up. Pain is pain. Mental health can suck at all ages." He stuck the bandage loosely over the burn. "And secrecy certainly doesn't lessen any of it."

"How do you do this?" Micah rasped through his tears. "How do you stay unbothered by all my biggest secrets? I'm a fucking disaster."

Andrew shrugged, kissing Micah's soaked cheek. "I like imperfection," he said, wrapping his arm around his waist as he gently drew him into his lap, laying Micah's head on his shoulder and kissing his brow. Before long, Andrew noticed Micah's breathing change, feeling him sink against his chest, limp and heavy. Micah's arm dropped, his fingertips twitching where they curled slightly on the sleeping bag. Caressing the bristly hair over the nape of Micah's neck, Andrew felt his heart swell. Maybe it was a lot of work, keeping everyone under the impression you were carefree and cheerful all the time. Maybe being caught in a darker mood was a relief to him.

Tilting his chin back, he gazed overhead at Cassiopeia shining amidst the creamy band of the Milky Way. Judging by how much the fire had shrunk, it had been hours since they'd made camp and laid down. Andrew watched the stars for some uncertain passage of time, slipping in and out of a meditative state, thoughts coming and going from his mind. Each time a worry clawed at his thoughts, he released it and let it blink away like a shooting star. This was the time to focus on what was constant. The earth cradled him beneath the blanket of the heavens while the flames snapped and hissed, singing words in a forgotten language, an ancient balm to all his unspeakable wounds. Micah's slumbering breath was a whispered harmony, his body soft and warm in Andrew's lap. If it were possible, he would have slept just this way, as he could want for nothing else. But slowly, the chill of the night crept into his bones, and his legs pinned beneath another body began to lose feeling. Such was the difficulty with meditation. Eventually, the corporeal body complained.

As slowly and minutely as he could, Andrew scooted onto his back until his shoulder blades settled onto the sleeping bag. For a moment, he thought he'd adjusted successfully, but then Micah's weight shifted, his forehead bumped into Andrew's chin, and his breathing stuttered.

Andrew winced. "Sorry. I tried not to wake you."

Micah rubbed his temple and said, "Oh, god. No. Sorry.

I zonked out." He let his hip slide to the ground and leaned on his forearm so less of his weight was on Andrew's chest. "You were really gonna let me sleep on top of you all night? You saint."

"It seemed like you needed it," Andrew said. Micah leaned over him, firelight painting a sharp orange brush stroke along his square jaw. His collar billowed off his chest and Andrew's eyes were drawn to the exposed pectoral muscles underneath.

Micah saw his gaze drift and felt his cheeks grow warm. He said after a moment, "I did." He reached out and twisted a loose strand of Andrew's auburn hair. "Amazing you can be so lanky and yet so soft."

Like a spasm, Andrew's fingers clenched around Micah's waist, his thumbs catching bare skin between shirt and waistband. Micah swallowed, his smile forming into something more serious as he noticed the heat which ignited in Andrew's ochre gaze.

Micah leaned down, closer to Andrew's lips, his lashes fluttering as he tried to keep his eyes on Andrew's face. But Andrew's eyes slid closed, and Micah didn't want to keep his slightly parted lips waiting. Micah pushed up on his arm, brushing their lips together briefly, pulling back so Andrew had to peer through slitted eyes with an unspoken question in the rising color of his cheeks.

When Andrew realized he was being teased, he clutched Micah's face between his hands and brought him down again to meet him for another kiss, blazing from within with heat and hunger. He flicked his tongue past Micah's lips and into his mouth. Then he let his face go and slid his hands beneath Micah's shirt, roaming along the muscles of his back and the contours of his firm stomach, realizing very quickly that this wasn't going to be enough for him.

Andrew tipped his head to the side so he could say, "Sorry, but if you want to stop..."

"I don't." Micah's voice was deep and hoarse, like a tree creaking during a storm. "I don't want to stop, that is. Do you?"

In answer, Andrew pulled Micah's shirt over his head and set it aside. Micah's hair was mussed over his forehead, sticking to his long moss-green lashes when he blinked and grinned devilishly down at Andrew.

He slipped an arm around Andrew's waist to lift him off the canvas under them enough to strip him of his flannel and shirt, accidentally freeing his long hair. Micah's heart flipped over the sight of Andrew's fiery locks cascading over his sharp brow, the ends brushing his shoulders like licks of flame.

Micah touched his knuckle quickly against the blood ward under Andrew's throat to confirm for his own peace that it was still cool, his delay long enough to prompt Andrew to grab him by the belt and uncinch him from it.

Delighted by his eagerness, Micah straddled Andrew and lightly pinched his nipple, which made Andrew's back arch off the ground. He planted a kiss on Andrew's sternum, then on the hollow of his throat, and then on his chin. He said against Andrew's lips, "I won't stop, but I want you to know that I'm going to savor this. So breathe." Micah undid the button on Andrew's jeans, slipping his hand inside the fabric. "Let me savor you."

Hotter color rose on Andrew's high cheekbones visible even in the corner of Micah's eye. Micah's exploration elicited a breathless little moan from Andrew, who twined his trembling fingers through Micah's free hand as they kissed again.

It was shockingly cold in their afterglow, their bodies practically steaming next to the dying fire. Goosebumps raced along Andrew's bare thighs and up over his stomach as he leaned on Micah's chest. Micah stretched over him, grabbing the corner of the second sleeping bag and fumbling with it until Andrew realized what he was doing. They unzipped it together and draped it over themselves before settling back down beneath the stars.

"I hope you won't be miserable in the car all day tomorrow 'cause of this," Micah said softly.

Andrew grinned. "Miserable is not what I will feel about this." He tugged on Micah's wooden earring.

"I meant—"

"I won't even notice any pain," Andrew said, twisting to plant a kiss against Micah's cheekbone. "But it's sweet of you to be concerned."

"I was worried I got a little carried away."

"You did. And it was great."

Micah grinned up at the heavens, pulling the sleeping bag up to Andrew's chin and tucking him in. "It certainly was."

"So," said Andrew, settling back into Micah's warmth like he'd known it his whole life. "We've established you're concerned about me. But are you concerned about the Redwoods?"

"Ah," Micah huffed. "You could say that." He glanced at Andrew with eyes that flashed wine-red. "Are you regretting coming with me?"

"Oh, yes. Nothing but regrets. How I wish I could be watching reruns with my cat talking to the zero people who give a shit about me."

"Okay," said Micah with a gasping laugh. "Jeeze."

Andrew snickered. He poked his pinky finger near the corner of Micah's eye. "They were silver, when we were...in the middle of things. But they turned red when you mentioned your mother."

"Oh. Yeah. I know they change color, but I don't keep track of the specifics. I think they're stupid."

"All right, seems like an odd opinion to hold about one's

eyes."

"Says the guy with the lovely, nonmagical brown eyes," Micah muttered.

"Anyway. It makes me curious. I can obviously surmise what silver indicates..."

"You'd be right." Micah grinned.

"But what about the red?" Andrew ran the pad of his finger along the fan of Micah's lashes, smiling slightly since it tickled when he blinked. "Typically, red means danger or, you know, blood. Overall, bad. Bad feelings."

"That would accurately describe my feelings about the monster who bore me," agreed Micah. "I'm terrified of her. And furious at her. And I wish, desperately, that I could exist without her. Suffice it to say, there is no love there."

"It must be overwhelming, then, having to go back there." Andrew cupped Micah's cheek.

"If there was any conceivable way to save my father without ever having to step foot in that godforsaken kingdom, you'd better believe I'd already be doing it." Micah pulled Andrew's hand off his cheek so he could plant a kiss in his palm. "But my father's suffered there enough, and I've worked so hard to keep him safe in Minnesota. I can't abandon him there, even if she only did this to get me back."

"Do you think so?" Andrew asked, watching the goosebumps race up his arm at the feeling of Micah's lips in his hand. "That's why Julian disappeared?"

"I don't think he chose to go back there. I can't pretend to understand what motivates the Queen. But I doubt it had to do with him. She never had any regard for him. I'm sure it's me."

"So you're walking into a trap?" Andrew clarified.

"Probably." Micah shrugged. "But it's better than doing nothing."

Andrew trailed his finger along Micah's smooth sternum. "Maybe I should be more like you."

"I would not advise that," Micah said with a grin. "Why do you say that?"

Andrew was thinking about his mother, left behind when he turned eighteen. But he shook his head slightly. "Maybe I want your cool green hair."

Chapter Twelve
The Bobcat

Micah woke to red hair tickling his cheek as Andrew shifted and burrowed his face into the flannel sleeping bag with a sigh. His eyes adjusted sluggishly to the unsaturated light easing away from the velvety night as he stroked the frizzy halo of Andrew's hair. He wanted to roam further, underneath the sleeping bag which obscured their nudity—full of potential, but not the time.

Snaking his hands out of the bag, Micah rolled onto his back with a sigh. The sky was unblemished by clouds, powdery blue with a glow of gold rising from the horizon. The sun was just beginning to rise; it couldn't be later than five in the morning, based on how low the light shafted through the slender trunks of aspen, fir, and pine, turning them gold as pillars in a temple. Rearing in the southern sky was a mountain range of mostly velvety greens save for the highest snow-dusted peaks. White asters and the biggest lupine he'd ever seen dotted the underbrush like morning stars. A doe, muscular and silky, blinked at him when he climbed to his feet.

Micah smiled at her, stretching mightily, digging his bare toes into the grass beside the campfire embers. Then as a chill snaked up his spine, he hugged his elbows and hurried past the Saturn. A woodpecker yelled at him in a fir tree over his head, furiously tapping at the trunk of the tree. He found an unassuming spot a yard or two away from the Saturn and took care of himself. When he was about to go back to the clearing, he paused. His shoulders tingled strangely. Micah rubbed his goosebumped arms as his gaze roamed to identify what caused the feeling.

Then he gasped, "No way!"

Out of the leafy underbrush cloaking Micah's ankles rose a cluster of indigo five-petaled nightshade, neon yellow stamen trembling slightly like an eye blinking up at him. He crouched to study the alien flower with a slight shake of his head and a grin tugging at his lips.

"Serendipitous," he murmured.

When he looked up, a large pair of amber eyes round as full moons blinked at him. Micah yelped and lost his balance, toppling onto his hip and elbow, taking a mouthful of leaves on his way down. He spat them out as quietly as he could, freezing, his heart beating so fast it made his head spin.

A cat the size of a Labrador crept silently through the bushes toward him, its tawny, spotted fur rippling over muscled shoulders. Black tips twitched on its ears as its pink lips peeled back to issue a small chirp.

"Bobcat!" Micah whispered as he saw its stubby striped tail. "I'm locking eyes with a bobcat. Uh. Hey, pretty baby." He swallowed a hysterical giggle.

Micah held his breath as the bobcat stretched out and sniffed his chin, then his mouth. Then the bobcat butted its silky forehead against his. They remained face to face for a moment and Micah felt, rather than heard, the cat's deep rumbling purr.

When the cat moved back, Micah remained with his head bowed. Its sandpaper tongue kissed his forehead, coarse enough to feel like rugburn. The contact sparked a vision: twining green vines, a birchwood tree, an ice wall sprouting ivy. Feelings of courage and purpose. It took his breath away and he gasped, lifting his head. The bobcat blinked its amber eyes and kneaded the earth with knife-sharp claws.

Movement caught his eye and he looked to his left, back toward the Saturn. Andrew crouched past a sprig of juniper in the clearing, a silent portrait of terror, his hands clamped over his mouth.

Crashing past Andrew, Fadil bounded into the bushes toward the bobcat, tail straight up and puffed like a pipe cleaner. The bobcat's wedge-shaped head swung towards Fadil. Its white jowls split to show all its fangs as it hissed at the housecat. Fadil froze, dropping down to his haunches, eyes turning round and black.

Satisfied, the bobcat looked back at Micah, meeting his

eyes once more and blinking slowly. Then it twisted, turned away, and padded into the bushes past the nightshade. In a moment, it had vanished into the woods.

Andrew crashed into the undergrowth and said, "Alright! Okay! What the *fuck?*"

Shaking, Micah climbed to his feet in mute wonder. His knees buckled once and he bent over with his head down. Andrew caught him by the elbow and steadied him. Without letting Andrew go, Micah scooped Fadil into the crook of his arm. When they got back to the Saturn, Micah hiccupped and then collapsed against the back door, dropping Fadil into the open trunk, diaphragm spasming with manic laughter interspersed with thin gasps.

"That was so amazing!" Micah said. "I...I saw stuff when it licked me! Visions!"

"I thought it was gonna claw your face off!" said Andrew. "I almost peed myself. I...I...I think you just got blessed." Andrew shook Micah's elbow. "That wouldn't happen if you were just going to fail in the Redwoods! My mum would say that was a goddamn *omen*, and a *good* one."

"Okay, settle down," Micah laughed, but he was thinking the same thing.

Andrew turned in a circle and braced his hands on the roof of the Saturn. "Look at this place!" he cried. "This is—ooh, a lake. Come on, then." They rounded the car to get a better look southward.

Down a steep slope, the trees grew sparser, obscured as

they were by a veil of mist. A small mirror-bright lake reflected the peaks of the mountains, which were outlined with golden light as if kintsugi stitched together the mountains and the sky. The surface was still as glass except for where a great blue heron stalked through the shallows, searching for fish with ancient golden eyes.

Clasping hands, they gingerly picked their way down to the lakeside, unclothed and barefoot and covered in goosebumps. The underbrush hindered their progress a few times, but Micah always found a smoother course and ways to avoid the worst of the thistles and sharp branches. Then the ground cleared and turned to heavy, dark soil, and then coarse sand at the edge of the lake. The heron eyed them skeptically, shuffling its wings before it resumed hunting.

They stepped into the water. Andrew swore, hugging himself, dancing back onto shore to catch his breath. He tried again, a few times, but he kept gasping as soon as the water reached his chest.

Micah splashed in and belly-flopped. He opened his eyes under the welcoming swirl; there were colorful pebbles underfoot, nothing of the silty algae in Minnesota lakes. Yellow and green fish darted away from them, hopefully into the beak of the hunting heron.

When Micah emerged, shivering, he slicked back his emerald hair with both hands and spat a mouthful of water with a lopsided grin. He grabbed Andrew's hand and pulled him into a silly teeth-chattering waltz up to their shoulders in the lake.

They looked up just as something flashed through the air. The blue heron squawked in anger and spread its wings, taking off in a flurry as someone cannonballed into the lake. The wave caught Andrew on the back of his head, dunking him underneath. Coughing and wiping his eyes when he surfaced, he spluttered, "What the hell?"

"It's Chami," Micah told him with a wan smile.

Near them, Chamomile cackled as she wiped her eyes and swiped a stray silver-white hair back into the pile of a braided crown on her head. "This w-w-water is ice cold!"

Andrew sniffed and asked, "Does she ever make less dramatic entrances?"

"No. No she does not."

She swam over to them, water beading off her round chin. "Well, well, well. I have a suspicion you two got *closer* overnight."

"Mind your business," warned Micah.

Andrew wanted to say he had similar suspicions about the absence of the female faeries, but he kept his mouth shut.

Straight-faced, Chamomile used both hands to slap Micah with an enormous splash. Spluttering, he shoved her away, but she snapped at his hand and almost got his finger.

Past her, on the shoreline, Ingrid stepped into the shallows, naked and covered in dirt and blood.

Startled, Andrew yelled, "Whoa! Are you hurt?"

Hands on her mahogany curls, Ingrid blinked at him. "What? No. Why?"

"Blood," he said.

Ingrid paused. "Oh. We hunted," she said.

Andrew blushed. "Duh."

Ingrid paddled into the depths of the water near them, but she kept her curls dry, tied on top of her head. Clusters of yellow buttercups and small violets dappled her hair. She splashed her face clean even as she sharply inhaled through her nostrils.

Chamomile exploded to the surface at their elbows with a battle cry, breasts bouncing, climbing Micah's shoulders till she sent them both beneath the water with a gurgle and a splash. Andrew opted not to interfere, drifting away and dropping to his knees so the water lapped at his chin. He'd adjusted, or gone numb enough, to the temperature of the lake so he realized how silky the water felt. As long as he ignored the sensation of tiny fish lips poking at his ankles.

As she pulled herself onto a protruding boulder, Ingrid sighed, "Those two might have been lovers, but they act like children together."

Andrew glanced at her like he was looking at a work of art—flawless alabaster skin, soft muscles, and small breasts. She rolled her slender shoulders and looked at him with an eyebrow raised, her lips curling down in a frown.

"Sorry," he told her, combing his fingers through his

heavy wet hair. "I don't suppose you're the Venere di Milo."

"I'm not *that* old."

"Just thought I'd ask."

"I'm not interested in a sexual relationship with you," she said, faintly apologetic.

Andrew snorted. "Likewise, madame. Fear does not arouse me, and neither do females." He paused. "I just like art."

Ingrid said nothing. The look on her face hadn't changed. She still seemed a bit penitent. Or maybe Andrew just hoped she did. Not because she didn't want to fuck him, obviously. But because she was forced to spend time around him, to consider him more than just her prey now that he was involved with Micah.

Micah and Chamomile had reached the other side of the lake and were standing on the shore skipping rocks. Chamomile's rocks bounced across the water a dozen times, each time disappearing with a *plunk* within an arm's reach of Andrew, and he was pretty sure that was on purpose.

He looked back at Ingrid. "I think you need a hobby."

She glared down at him, hugging her knees. "What do you know?"

"You put a lot of work and creativity into driving me insane," he told her.

"Hm, yes, and yet it seems to have failed," she said with a regretful shake of her head.

"How do you know? Maybe I just internalize everything. Don't be too hard on yourself. There's lots of different kinds of crazy."

"I think you're making fun of me."

"That would be ballsy of me," he said, looking away with his lips quirked.

"If that means foolish, then yes." Andrew glanced back up at her to see her eyes dancing. "Just like coming on this trip."

Ignoring that, he said, "Okay, but you know how often I was armed. Couldn't you have justified my training and fought me instead of doing all that haunting and stalking? Like, yeah, sure, I'm glad you weren't hurting me, but your methods were so much more fucked up."

"I didn't care to fight you. That wasn't really the point."

"Oh, I'm sorry, then what exactly was?" Frustration colored his tone, but at this point, he didn't think that expressing himself would get him hurt.

"Micah would say I was being 'petty.'"

Andrew snorted. It was ridiculous, but it did explain things. "Joke's on you, I liked when you turned my tea into flowers. I pressed them in a textbook."

Ingrid looked bewildered, blinking several times. "You're an odd man."

"Yes, thank you, I'm aware." Then he tilted his head and asked, "Why *didn't* you just draw blood for blood?"

Her eyes shined like stained glass lit from within. "I

would have then and there, but it surprised me when you immediately threw a medical kit at me. I was intrigued."

"Intrigued enough to put all that effort into stalking me for the next five years."

"Correct."

"So sweet."

Ingrid hesitated, scrutinizing his face. "Oh. That's sarcasm."

"I wouldn't dare."

Ingrid made a very undignified noise and looked away, but the corners of her lips curled in a faint smirk as she let the morning sunlight dry the beads of water on her skin. She closed her eyes and lifted her face to the rising sun. Behind her, the last of the mists clinging to the foot of the mountains began to dissolve.

Across the lake, Micah threw Chamomile in and then dove in after her with a whoop.

"But how *did* I manage to do it?" he asked. "How did I sneak up on you? You're...you."

She sighed, her cheeks turning slightly pink. "You showed up the day that Micah had last been in the bluffs. We argued. I was angry. And...sad." She pieced apart two curls with her nails and tucked them behind her long ear. "I got very intoxicated and wandered off for a nap."

Andrew started to laugh and then caught himself, clamping his hand over his mouth.

Narrowing her eyes, she stared at him in silence while he

collected himself.

"So our encounter is what I like to call a natural consequence," said Andrew with a snort.

"Hm," she grunted, and then cast her gaze away from
him, watching Chamomile climb onto Micah's shoulders
with a war cry.

Andrew said after a bit, "Micah met a bobcat."

Ingrid's red lips rounded in surprise.

"He was taking a piss one second and then the next
second I look, it just came right up to him—"

She stared up at the mountains in the distance, the
smooth skin between her thin brows crinkling just slightly.

"Why don't you look surprised?"

She shifted her garnet-hued gaze toward him and
smiled. "Come with me."

"Are you going to do something bad to me?"

"I swore I wouldn't. That's binding."

He paused. "Do you still want to?"

"Not particularly," she said with a shrug. "Do you want
to hurt me?"

"Not particularly," he echoed with a shrug.

"Okay, then *move*."

Andrew followed the tall, naked faerie from the lake as if
he was an unwitting hunter in a fairytale. He climbed back
up the hill and into the trees. Going much faster than him,
Ingrid vanished between two spruce and a sunbeam. Andrew took his time, listening to the birdsongs, soaking in

the forest, sinking his toes into a patch of velvety moss and touching a puff of pollen in a marigold. A tiger butterfly flitted by as if on strings.

"Little fox," called Ingrid.

"I don't answer to that," he called back.

"I thought you lost your way," Ingrid answered, leaning against the Saturn, eyes on him as he approached.

"I was appreciating the scenery."

Chamomile yelled again back at the lake, followed by Micah's stern rebuke and a series of splashes.

Ingrid reached to the roof of the Saturn and carefully picked up a small skull in her long fingers. "I found this last night in the forest," she said, soft, reverent. She brushed off a lingering piece of soil. The mango-sized head was yellowed with age and spiderweb cracks ran from the large eye sockets up over the dome of its forehead. It had a mouthful of fangs intact except for one of the front incisors.

Andrew gasped.

"It's a bobcat. We found it while foraging, and I felt inclined to bring it back with me. Now I see why." Placing the skull in her spot in the backseat, she straightened and stared at it for a moment with her hands on her hips. Then she took a deep breath and shook her head, rounding the back of the Saturn to the trunk. She pulled out a plain black dress that went midway down her thighs and shrugged into it, and then pushed a few stray curls behind her pointed ears.

In the trunk, fresh-looking animal hide was neatly folded near the back of the compartment. He shuddered, but he was slightly impressed by what Ingrid and Chamomile seemingly accomplished just overnight. It didn't seem likely that the wildlife were altogether expecting to be hunted by Fae.

He dug his own change of clothes and then checked both his wrists. "Damn," he muttered.

Ingrid raised a brow.

"I lost my hair tie last night. In, uh...some activity."

Unruffled, she nodded, and then reached into the backseat. She emerged with a short strand of glittering black string that she tied off and handed to him.

"I feel like this is enchanted," he said.

"Maybe."

"Is it a good enchantment?"

"Yes."

Then she turned as Micah dashed back into the clearing, Chamomile in hot pursuit, with their peals of laughter ringing in the pure mountain air. They were cherubic in their nudity and joy.

Chamomile shrugged into a lemon-yellow cropped camisole and a flowing white skirt. Her eyes were alight and she pinched a handful of Micah's rear. Andrew shooed her away and she danced off to greet the cats where they lounged in the sun on the sleeping bags. She sprawled beside them with a contented sigh. Ingrid snuck up on her and then gave the sleeping bag a fierce push so it rolled up around Chamomile like a burrito. The smaller faerie squawked and the cats fled. Andrew laughed in surprise.

As he and Micah dressed in clean jeans and shirts, Micah gave him a sidelong look and said quietly, "What were you two talking about, hm?"

Andrew thought for a moment, watching the females roll up the sleeping bags and shepherd the cats back to the Saturn. "Everything," he finally said.

As the sun spilled golden light over the mountains and shafted through the trees, the Saturn rumbled back onto the interstate with Micah behind the wheel.

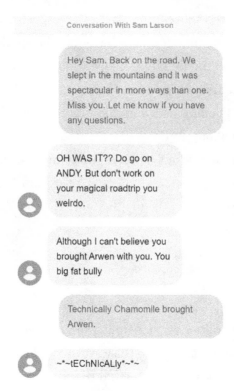

Conversation With Sam Larson

Hey Sam. Back on the road. We slept in the mountains and it was spectacular in more ways than one. Miss you. Let me know if you have any questions.

OH WAS IT?? Do go on ANDY. But don't work on your magical roadtrip you weirdo.

Although I can't believe you brought Arwen with you. You big fat bully

Technically Chamomile brought Arwen.

~*~tEChNIcALly*~*~

Grinning, Andrew rolled his eyes and set his phone on the dash.

"Micah," said Chamomile, "get me fast food."

"No."

Chamomile kicked the back of his seat for emphasis as she repeated, "Fast! Food!"

With a glance over his shoulder at Chamomile, Andrew patted Micah's knee and said gently, "Breakfast is probably a good idea. However—" He glanced back at the goblin. "—Now seems as good a time as any to note how disappointed I am by how decidedly *un*-soothing you are compared to your namesake."

Chamomile cackled. When Micah took them into a drive-thru, Chamomile dropped a slab of bark onto Micah's shoulder, winking at Andrew when he cast her a curious look. The unsuspecting cashier didn't even question it, accepting the bark as tender for their abundance of greasy foods and cheap caffeine.

With a mouthful of a muffin and sausage sandwich, Chamomile held out a hash brown in paper to Ingrid and said, "Try."

"Absolutely not." Ingrid curled a lip.

Sipping from an iced coffee, Micah said, "Aw, c'mon, Red. Live a little."

Andrew shook his head. "Pressuring people to eat junk food. Who even are you?"

Micah grinned at him around his straw.

Ingrid wrinkled her nose, took the hash brown between her thumb and forefinger, and took the tiniest bite. Then she stuck out her tongue and let it fall back off. "Ugh. No thank you." She wiped her fingers on the back of Andrew's seat, fortunately when he wasn't looking. Then she leaned over and resumed ignoring them all, intent on what she was working on.

Andrew twisted in his seat and watched her in silence for several minutes. She either didn't notice him, or didn't care.

Micah glanced at Andrew, and then back at Ingrid. "A

new project. What is it? I love watching you work." He looked over at Andrew. "She makes all her own jewelry. I think she uses art to avoid the violence." He grinned when he caught her scowl at him.

"This is for you," she said.

"Ooh!" Micah exclaimed, his eyes lighting up. "Really?"

"You're putting the bobcat skull in that?" Andrew asked. "That's amazing."

On Ingrid's lap she held the bobcat skull and a pair of small antlers she was stringing together with small bones to make a circlet. She had a pouch bursting with flower blossoms beside her, which overpowered the smell of fast-food and made the car smell like a garden. She was pinching a golden crystal between her fingers and sliding it into the eye socket of the skull.

"You found a bobcat skull? What the hell? Did you know a bobcat found me this morning?"

Nodding, Andrew said, "I told her. It seems like some kind of synchronous spiritual experience for you two."

"Yes," agreed Ingrid. "It's a message. Nature has chosen your side." She used her long pinky finger and fished around to move the crystal in the eye socket, to macabre effect. She had a little pouch with what looked like more tools including the thread she'd used for his hair tie, and tiny bones and glinting crystals. "The Redwood Queen doesn't get to decide anymore whether or not you can wear a crown. You're not the same as the boy you were twenty years ago."

Micah looked over his shoulder at his sister for a long moment. Softly, he told her, "You're not the same either."

When Arwen climbed from the backseat and onto Andrew's chest, he propped his knees against the glove compartment, draped his flannel over himself and his cat, and fell deeply asleep. The soft flow of the air conditioner kept Andrew's loose red hair floating like he was underwater, and occasionally he'd reach up and slap his cheek as if the tickling got into his dreams. Soft orange stubble grew on his sharp jaw. It was white around the corners of his lips, but everywhere else across his cheeks was still fiery orange.

"He's very Fae-like," said Chamomile, leaning over the seat and inspecting Andrew. Ingrid gave Chamomile a sharp look.

"Oh, I've noticed," said Micah with a grin. "You guys will help me get out of a speeding ticket if we get pulled over, right?"

"Obviously," sniffed Chamomile.

"Yes," said Ingrid. "Would you like me to kill them?"

"No thanks, but it's sweet of you to offer." Micah met Ingrid's gaze in the rearview mirror, a sparkle in his eye.

The terrain changed from rocky and green to gray skies

and emerald hills. It started to drizzle on them, and the sound put both Chamomile and Ingrid to sleep in the back-seat.

Micah fixed the image of Julian's face in his mind. If he were to guess what was happening in the Redwoods, he assumed Julian was intoxicated on Fae-spelled foods. He didn't know what was happening or what happened in the kitchen before he disappeared—he was just somewhere else, lost in a lie. But if Micah were to entertain his deepest fears, it was that his mother was tormenting his father. Torturing him, humiliating him. And...

And...

He'd kill his mother if he had to.

Micah shook his head slightly. The thought was almost involuntary, startling. Foreign to his pacifist approach to relationships. Hardly human.

He sighed, glancing in the rearview mirror at Ingrid and Chamomile. He refused to tell them—they'd just say they told him so.

Chapter Thirteen
The Redwoods

Micah pulled into the campsite next to Lake Sylvia at twilight. With the windows rolled down, the air outside was heavy with rain and heat. The cedars around the little clearing were tall and red but slender, and some of them were dead. He had missed their smell, he realized, as they didn't grow in Minnesota and were found more often built into clothes closets. There was a little picnic table and a fire pit with a cooking grate, and behind that were the shores of a narrow lake. A styrofoam cup bobbed against the shore next to a dead fish with a cloudy eye pointing to the heavens. There was a rope of buoys past the shallows, barely visibly in the failing light. He wished the park wouldn't allow swimmers. In the twenty years Micah lived in the Redwoods, he knew of at least five swimmers who drowned in Lake Sylvia—and he knew the Folk who were responsible.

He looked at Ingrid in the rearview mirror; she had both white hands clenched into fists. With no other reason to delay, Micah leaned over to the passenger seat and touched Andrew's cheek with his palm. "Hey." He stroked the pad of his thumb against his high cheekbone. "We're here."

Andrew took a deep breath and blinked his eyes open. His hand went automatically to Arwen, stroking her back until she purred. "Oright," he mumbled, tongue thick with sleep. "Let's go." He fumbled with his door and nearly fell out of the car. Chamomile happened to be there, squawking as she caught him around the waist.

"Hm, questionable start," said Chamomile. Andrew yawned and stood upright, patting Chamomile appreciatively on the head. She swatted his hand and left him alone as he rubbed his face. Arwen trailed after her as Chamomile rapped her knuckles on the trunk, Micah searching for the button on the dash that popped it open. She shouldered her gear after checking each of the arrows inside her quiver and testing the tension of the string on her bow. Then she slipped a leather guard onto her left forearm. All of the silly wild girl was gone from her face. Her biceps rippled as she adjusted her bow as she became a warrior instead of a childlike friend.

Andrew shook off sleep and stretched his shoulders, then touched his toes. He tightened and knotted his flannel around his waist, redid his ponytail, and adjusted the vial of Micah's blood around his neck. On the opposite side of the Saturn, Ingrid surveyed the campsite with narrowed eyes.

But Micah was still in the car. Frowning, Andrew bent to

peer back inside. Micah clutched the steering wheel with both hands, his expression blank, eyes wide and staring at the dashboard. Andrew knew that expression. He crossed to the driver's side and opened the door. Crouching, he pressed his hand against Micah's sternum, where Micah's heart pounded like it was trying to crack through his ribs and climb out.

"Slow down," Andrew murmured. "Take a deep breath. You're in control."

Andrew's words were almost lost over the rushing of his blood in his ears.

"In through your nose. Out through your mouth."

Micah obeyed, squeezing Andrew's fingers. He finally said, "I just don't know if I can do this."

Chamomile appeared at Andrew's elbow. "Sure you can." She clonked Micah with the shaft of an arrow, making him jump and stick his tongue out at her.

Ingrid leaned over Andrew. Her elbow dug into his shoulder, although he didn't dare say anything. She told Micah, "You lived in there for twenty years. And you're even stronger now."

Andrew nodded in agreement and said, "You're not alone, okay? I swear on that."

With a tremulous smile, Micah cupped Andrew's cheek in thanks.

"Go prepare your weapons," Ingrid ordered Andrew. He was prepared to argue as he glared up at her, but her gaze was fixed on Micah. Begrudgingly, Andrew yielded and shrugged her off so he could stand. Chamomile pranced along beside him, whether to keep him company or to shoo him away.

Taking Micah by the elbow, Ingrid murmured, "Come on then." She drew him out of the car and onto his feet. She had a smear of blood behind her ear from her hunt, her hair barely restrained in a loose bun and scattered with wildflowers from Montana. She searched his impassive, wide-eyed face with her irises brightened to a rosy pink.

"I wish I could be more like you, Nightshade Boy," Ingrid said in a whisper drenched in wistfulness. "Your softness is your armor and you mustn't forget that when you're facing the Queen. You aren't like her. You aren't like us." She reached around the driver's seat and picked up the circlet she made.

Micah beheld the finished ornament with wide and eager eyes, sucking in a breath as he trailed his fingers over it. Fixed as the centerpiece was the bobcat skull, fangs sharpened to points, chunks of topaz glinting in the dark eye sockets. Antlers and flower stems formed the circlet, lashed together with Ingrid's glittering black thread. Pieces of amethyst and tourmaline sparked among the antler points. Framing the bobcat skull were a pair of star-shaped nightshade blossoms, spelled to stay in bloom. She settled the circlet against his head—it was a snug, strange, but perfect fit—using her fingers to smooth down his turquoise bangs underneath. The bobcat skull settled over Micah's brow, its topaz stare complementing his violet irises.

Clasping her hands in his own, Micah told her, "Thank you. But you know you're not like her, right?"

She stared down at him, a tiny crease appearing between her eyebrows. "I—"

He grinned. "Silly Red. Look where you are. Tell me if the Queen would even dream of being in your position."

Casting her eyes toward their feet, Ingrid opened and closed her mouth in silence for a moment. She glanced back up, her eyes finding Andrew over Micah's shoulder preparing for a fight on Micah's behalf, despite...her. "You give me too much credit," she said to Micah, shaking her head.

"Just because I *can* lie," Micah said, "doesn't mean I do."

Ingrid let out a little sigh. "Why are you so stubborn?" Abruptly, she threw her arms around his shoulders and squeezed him tightly against her chest, dimpling her cheek against the sharp points of his circlet. He gasped, but then wrapped his arms around her and buried his face in her sweet-smelling shoulder. As if needing to stymie her overwhelming emotions, she moved away so quickly that she stumbled over a jutting stone. In front of the trunk, sniffing slightly with eyes downcast, Ingrid pulled out a rapier and drew it from its scabbard, revealing a blade black as night. Andrew hummed in admiration, leaning closer to inspect the blade as Ingrid hooded her gaze and smiled slyly at him.

She strung a black braided holster around her hips. Then she fixed two small daggers to her wrists.

Andrew reached past her and strapped his sword between his shoulder blades. Then he picked up his crossbow. It was small and sharp and black, made from steel. The bolts were the length of two fingers, lined up and ready to be shot off with savage speed.

Chamomile appeared at his elbow. "You should let me use that."

"No! You have your own bow." Andrew lifted it out of her reach.

"Well, are you any good with it?"

"One time I almost shot off my big toe."

"Mm, so, no." To Ingrid, Chamomile said, "Don't trust this man with a weapon."

Andrew cast her a dubious look and said, "I don't know...I got a sword to your throat pretty quickly, didn't I?"

Chamomile scowled, swatting Ingrid when she stifled a snicker. "I believe all you have going for you is the element of surprise—from your diminutive physique," Chamomile said in a growl.

Andrew gazed down at her. She was barely tall enough to reach his navel. "You're one to talk," he told her dryly.

Chamomile huffed at him and stamped her foot, making him laugh as he resumed checking his weapon. She looked up when Micah slunk around the side of the Saturn, hands in his pockets. Groaning, she said, "Micah, for real?"

Andrew turned to him. "What?"

"He doesn't have any weapons," sighed Ingrid, arms crossed where she leaned against the Saturn. "Of course."

Micah shrugged, looking sheepish. "They're just not really my thing. But, uh, you three look pretty cute, gushing over all your ouchie makers."

Chamomile scoffed. Then her eyes went round. She raised her bow and shot off an arrow over their heads. But she swore and spat, "Missed. Move—"

With a shower of leaves, a body dropped from the canopy and thudded behind Micah. He gasped and flinched away, but too late; a charcoal-colored arm pinned his hands behind his back and a bronze dagger appeared at his throat. Micah yelped and froze, eyes bulging as he felt the blade against his skin.

He was held against the body of a towering male faerie wearing red slacks and no shirt, adorned with oiled bronze cuffs and a choker. The male had a head of seafoam green curls he tossed back over leaf-green eyes, which danced with cruel delight as he clicked his tongue and said, "Ah, ah, ah."

Swords drawn and aimed at the male stranger, Andrew and Ingrid froze mid-lunge.

Micah's expression darkened. He knew that rumbling voice, the scent of this male, and the dark gray skin scalding hot to the touch and taut over bulging muscles. "Sivarthis," he spat.

Sivarthis smiled, showing sharp white teeth behind full lips. He bent down to Micah and said with his mouth against his neck, "How sweet. You still recognize my scent."

Micah squirmed and elbowed the male, but he barely flinched. Instead, the male slid a hand around Micah's stomach and up under his shirt. "You must have missed me," the male purred.

"Unhand the son of the Redwood Queen," Ingrid exclaimed.

Sivarthis lifted his angular head enough to blink slowly at Ingrid. "Beg pardon, Your Ladyship, but I cannot."

Struggling again, Micah dug a heel into Sivarthis's bare foot, but the blade pricked the soft skin under his jaw as a consequence. Blood oozed from a thin cut, and Micah bit back a whimper.

Andrew lunged again, but Ingrid grabbed him by the bicep and yanked him back beside her, sharply shaking her head.

"You, my little halfling," purred Sivarthis, lifting emerald eyes and gazing indifferently at Andrew, "smell like *him*." Sivarthis jutted his chin at Andrew. He held Micah as if in an embrace, dagger still poised against his tawny neck.

Andrew bared his teeth and spat at the ground. "Let him go or I'll slice you open from belly to chin," he growled.

Serrated white teeth appeared again. "That would amuse me to see you try," Sivarthis said thoughtfully.

"Sivarthis," said Micah, "you big stupid oaf, I want to see the Redwood Queen!" Knocking his jaw into the faerie's cheek, Micah growled, "Obviously she wants to talk to me too, since your dumb ass showed up. You can let me walk."

Sivarthis shook his head, but he straightened and at last moved away from Micah's face. "I cannot, little halfling."

Chamomile trained her bow on him over Micah's shoulder. "If you would please note, you're outnumbered."

Sivarthis looked down at her and said with a sneer, "Is that what you think, goblin?"

Following the sound of splashing, Ingrid turned her blood-red glare toward the lake. From the depths rose six Folk moving out of the shallows onto shore. Dripping, they raised sabers and rapiers and bows as they approached the Saturn and closed into a ring around them. They were all dressed in wisps of wet clothing which clung to toned chests and muscled thighs. Their eyes glowed eerie and cold in the oncoming night.

Sivarthis turned his head, gazed at the drenched Fae, and then whistled through his teeth. In answer, a lavender faerie twice Chamomile's height fought her easily into submission. Ingrid flinched when the faerie backhanded Chamomile across the face. Someone approached Ingrid and reached for her arms, but she fixed them with such a dangerous stare they remained motionless, long-fingered hands hovering over her in a stand-off.

Sivarthis drawled, "Now that you understand the circumstances..."

Then he pulled back the dagger and cracked the butt of
the weapon into the back of Micah's head. Yelping, Micah's
violet eyes rolled back. He crumpled. Sivarthis caught him
with his forearm across his belly, slinging him easily over
his shoulder.

Sivarthis smiled, cruel, bemused. "Shall we be on our
way?"

"Micah!" cried Andrew. He lunged at Sivarthis and evad-
ed the grasping hand of another faerie. He swung his
blade in a glorious arc toward Micah's captor, but then
Ingrid checked Andrew in the chest with her shoulder. She
was strong and solid, gripping his biceps. She jolted him
enough to snap his teeth together, his sword flailing as he
tried to stop it from touching her skin. As soon as he froze,
so did she.

She said softly in his ear, "Be still. For his safety."

Someone grabbed Andrew by the elbows and hauled
him off Ingrid. Still held by the lavender-skinned female,
Chamomile bled from a scrape over her brow, and her face
was hard and bright with fury.

The sight of Micah dangling over that male's shoulder
made Andrew sick and hot and ready to murder everyone.
The only relief was that by some magical force, the bobcat
crown stayed fast to Micah's head.

With a prominent swagger, Sivarthis fell into the front
of the pack of Folk. As if he felt Andrew's burning glare,

Sivarthis looked over his shoulder and flashed his sharp teeth at him, his tongue darting out over his lips. Andrew growled at him till the male faerie hanging onto his elbows gave him a vicious shake, kneeing Andrew in the small of his back and urging him forward. The darkness became thick and inky. Blindly, Andrew fought and spat curses till his lungs burned. He knew better than to believe he could escape, nor did he have any intention of leaving Micah dangling unconscious over someone's shoulder. But he'd be damned if he was going to stop fighting. Nobody had taken his weapons, cementing the impression they did not consider him a viable threat. That may be the case, he thought, but he was going to be a viable pain in the ass then. The yellow-eyed faerie who held him kept grunting, pinching his arm, jerking him around—so he knew it was working. Sivarthis turned and spat an insult at him, understood by tone and expression, but with words incomprehensible to Andrew. His faerie captor growled and wrenched Andrew's elbows at a terrible angle. Andrew bit back a groan of pain and finally gave himself a rest. Motionless in the manner of a poisonous snake, Chamomile watched Andrew with a smirk of amusement while her lavender captor held her by the nape of her neck.

The trees seemed to spread as they got deeper into the woods, the branches dripping with moss. All traces of humanity were gone. They'd left behind the campsites and the walking paths, stepping over the trunks of fallen trees and avoiding rabbits and confused deer that intercepted their path. Lizards skittered past, ferns climbed up to their knees, and leaves brushed them with beads of rainwater as they passed.

Ahead, in the slats of darkness between the trees, something gleamed bright and sinister, making his stomach turn. He blinked and for once stopped struggling, his eyes trying to convince him nothing was there. When he glanced to the side, to Ingrid, the red sheen in the air brightened on the periphery of his vision. Ingrid cast her glowing ruby eyes toward him and sighed through her nose.

So he wasn't imagining it.

As the misty red barrier grew nearer, it clarified into a great arching tree draped in moss and decay. It was almost a full circle. Andrew frowned as Sivarthis lifted a long elegant hand and traced the arc of the tree into a tighter and tighter spiral. Fiery sparks chased his finger. Beyond, the Redwood Queen's domain emerged. Andrew couldn't cut off a gasp of awe. It made Ingrid sigh louder.

He beheld splendor of a thousand faerie lights floating, plentiful as raindrops, soft white and faint red like stars. Their trembling light cast manic shadows on the faces of several dozen Folk standing at attention, lined up shoulder to shoulder to make a clear processional aisle that stretched forward a hundred yards. The ground changed from packed dirt to bronze cobblestones.

Great mushrooms colored cream, red, brown, and green climbed out of the dense red soil off the cobbled path. All around them Redwoods soared toward the heavens with trunks so wide they were like pillars in a giant's manor. It would take fifty people at least with fingers stretching to link together. A soft, warm drizzle started, raindrops catching in Andrew's lashes and forcing him to blink rapidly to keep his limited vision clear.

From every direction, the Redwood Folk watched them with myriad eyes, some bright and gleaming like when headlights catch a dog's stare, others small and black and beady. Many showed rows of pointed ivory teeth as they gawked at the prisoners and gestured with sharp clawed fingers. Some looked in surprise at Ingrid, walking erect, staring straight ahead with her brows low over her scarlet eyes.

Overhead, in the boughs of the massive Redwoods, domed houses decorated with windows and gleaming lanterns and dripping strings of yellow light perched. Sloping bridges closed in with shoots of thick vegetation strung between the Redwoods.

The largest of all the Redwoods was a true obelisk, easily the square footage of a manmade skyscraper. Set back in a circular cobbled plaza, stairs of mossy redwood ascended to the doors of a massive domed manor with arched windows all lit from within by blinding light. Ivy climbed over bright fire-colored logs. Explosive blossoms of all hues grew in the crevices, and tiny fireflies blinked in and out as they landed to rest on the petals.

At the foot of the stairs beneath the manor was a dais of redwood and gold. And at either end there was a tree trunk turned into a torch bearing floating orbs of blood-red and nightshade purple. Both cast eerie colorful shadows onto a dozen steps leading to a large throne carved to depict hounds and branches all gilded with gold. On the step beneath it was a smaller redwood throne, and finally beneath that was a backless seat carved from a stump into a flurry of leaves. Both of the smaller two thrones were mossy with disuse. Andrew assumed these belonged to Ingrid and to Micah, and seeing a throne for the people he'd spent the last thirty hours traveling with was surreal.

Two enormous golden doors groaned open as they approached. A tall silhouette appeared against the brilliant light from within and strode down the steps toward them. The Folk behind Andrew crossed fists over their chests. Slightly to the right of the dais, the Folk who had captured them pushed Andrew and Chamomile roughly to their knees. Andrew exchanged a look with her as she pressed her rosy lips into a thin line and then lifted her gaze to the trees.

Sivarthis dumped Micah onto the cobblestones at the foot of the staircase. Micah landed with a sickening thud on his stomach, groaning. Sivarthis bent and pulled Micah to his knees using a fistful of his hair. He gave him a savage shake; Micah cried out as he regained consciousness. He clawed at Sivarthis's fist, writhing in pain. Andrew twitched with the urge to run to him, but the yellow-eyed faerie grabbed him by the collar to keep him in place.

"My son," said a female voice, deep, contemptuous, angry, and startlingly pained, as if her feelings had been hurt. The Redwood Queen stepped down the stairs and into the plaza. The Queen's eyes reflected both of her children. Her right eye was blood-red, like Ingrid's, the pupil so small it was barely visible. Her left was deep plum, like Micah's when he was angry. The impression of her stare struck Andrew like a blow. She had really borne Ingrid and Micah. She was really their wicked, feral mother.

With easily over six feet of languid height, the Redwood Queen had the long and slender face like a deer, lips painted black, curled and sneering. She wore a dress like scarlet spiderwebs and just as insubstantial, revealing peeks of small breasts and rounded white hips. The crown atop her head of floor-length wine-red hair was an echo of the Redwoods with golden branches and leaves burned into oxidized copper. It was an immaculate piece of jewelry, layered and tangled and almost like a living thing. She was flanked by two red hounds on bony legs with eerie long faces and blinking golden eyes. The Redwood Queen waved Sivarthis off and he dropped Micah back to his hands and knees.

Sitting back and straightening his spine, Micah jutted

out his chin and glared up at her. "Your *Majesty*." He clenched his fingers into fists. He could have gone a hundred years away from this wretched female and it still wouldn't have been long enough. Not to mention the stinging throb of his scalp was a distraction he didn't need right now.

The Redwood Queen looked toward Ingrid, mismatched eyes reproachful. Her gaze lingered with a quirked eyebrow on the flowers in Ingrid's hair. She lifted her fingers, long and tipped in green with sharp pointed nails. Plucking a purple aster from Ingrid's curls, the Redwood Queen crumpled the blossom in her fist and let it rain to the ground. "What is this costume you're wearing? For shame, daughter."

Ingrid stiffened visibly, but she kept her mouth clamped shut. Micah narrowed his eyes.

"Go and get her dressed appropriately," the Queen said to a tall green nymph standing at her elbow. Floating on creamy green moth wings, the nymph grabbed Ingrid by the shoulders and steered her past the Queen and up the stairs to the manor.

Ingrid roughly shoved the nymph off. She planted her feet and whipped out a dagger from her wrist when the faerie reached for her. "Touch me again and I'll take your hands. I know the way." Leaving the nymph behind, she swept up the stairs to the manor and disappeared inside.

The Redwood Queen watched her leave with a faint

smirk. Then she turned back to Micah. Reaching down and grasping his chin so hard that he bit his tongue, she lifted him to his feet like he weighed nothing. She made him look small, like a preteen boy rather than a grown man. Staggering, Micah shoved her hand off his face and stepped away. Sivarthis snatched Micah's bicep with a dark hand.

Micah spun to face him. "Back the fuck off, Sivarthis." He jabbed a finger into the male's chest. "I don't care if you got a promotion. You're not allowed to touch me anymore."

Sivarthis scowled. The Queen shooed him away. Reluctant, muscles in his chiseled jaw jumping, Sivarthis bowed and stood back at the foot of the stairs, his venomous green eyes burning.

Micah turned back to the Queen and demanded, "Where's Julian? Give him back and let us leave."

The Redwood Queen showed pointed teeth and laughed. The sound was cold and hollow. "I think not," she said. "But you're welcome to see him. He has been quite happy since his return." She twitched a hand.

A small rose-skinned pixie stepped out the doors of the manor and tugged on a long golden leash, which looped around Julian's neck like a collar. His wrists were bound with glinting thread—thread Micah recognized immediately as something Ingrid had woven herself.

"How *dare* you," Micah said in a voice drenched with horror, sharp with rage.

Gold smeared Julian's lips and his amber eyes were

glassy, unfocused over his drooping smile. His button-down was rumpled and smeared with dirt. He stumbled barefooted down the stairs, the faerie using his leash
to keep him from falling—but barely. Micah dashed over
to catch him, to reach out and hold him, even if Julian
didn't know what was happening. But the Queen raised
her arm and struck Micah with the back of her hand. His
head snapped to the side and his body twisted away so he
staggered and landed on his knee. Stunned, seeing stars,
Micah lifted his head and wiped away a trickle of blood from
his lip.

Erupting with protective fury, Andrew bent his knees
and ducked. He twisted his arms and clasped the wrists of
the yellow-eyed faerie, who yelled in surprise as Andrew
pitched the faerie over his head and onto the ground at
his feet. With a vicious kick of his boot to the faerie's
chin, he lifted his crossbow and shot off an iron bolt with a
resounding *thwang*.

The Redwood Queen flinched out of the way at the last
second. The arrow pierced a fluttering hem of her spiderweb dress and shredded it. It clattered against the foot of
the dais.

The Queen's eyes widened. She picked up the torn edge
of her dress over her ribcage and inspected it in silence. If
she hadn't dodged, Andrew would have gotten her in the
lungs.

Gasping, Micah grabbed Andrew's waist and used him

as leverage to clamber to his feet. His head spun and a wave of nausea hit him. Grabbing Andrew's arm, he hissed, "Andrew, that was great and all, but she's gonna want you dead for that."

Still pumped full of adrenaline, Andrew said with a lopsided smirk, "Why else did we bring so many weapons?" He reached out and nudged Micah's antler crown straight, and then gently wiped his lip clean with the pad of his thumb.

Sivarthis nodded to the ring of faeries who'd accompanied them from the campsite. They readied their weapons, staring down the fox-faced, auburn-haired assailant and waiting for orders. Andrew raised his blade in his off hand, crouching in a defensive pose, with a taunting raise of a single eyebrow.

The Redwood Queen smiled and wagged her head, slow, deliberate, unruffled. Her guard relaxed almost imperceptibly, glaring at Andrew like they were disappointed he was still alive. She strode closer to them, her hooded gaze inspecting Andrew with obvious curiosity. Her lids were coated with an oily black paint extending past her lashes in wingtips, with bronze studs flashing along her eyebrows. "Now, you are a surprise, human."

"So I've been told," said Andrew with a smile.

Chamomile's blue eyes glinted where she stood aside from the fray.

"Let him be," Micah said, holding onto Andrew's waist, pushing at the crossbow as if hoping Andrew would lower it. He didn't.

She circled them with an elegant finger on the point of
her chin. Then the Queen reached out and touched a bolt
in the crossbow with one finger and hissed. She rubbed her
finger against her thumb, and her smile widened.

On his leash, Julian's eyes tracked her hungrily. He made
no indication he registered Micah's presence at all.

A murmur from the gentry watching alerted Micah that
Ingrid had reappeared. He looked up at his sister in the
doorway of the manor with the faintest feeling of relief.

When she descended the staircase, practically floating,
Ingrid looked almost unrecognizable in her royal splendor. Her eyes were smeared with black paint and lined
with sharp magenta tips. They'd painted her lips deep
mahogany. Iridescent rosy pink glimmered on her cheeks.
They'd pulled all the flowers from her hair, oiled her curls,
and arranged them in a loose veil over her shoulders. On
her head they'd placed a jagged bronze circlet, studded
with rubies, with the thornlike branches of the bronze
burned to black. They'd dressed her in two lengths of
ruby chiffon, tied over her chest like a bandeau and around
her waist in a long flowing skirt. It connected over her
bare midriff with silvery threads. A different nymph with
quivering ivory wings held Ingrid's skirts off the ground,
expression cold.

Ingrid's gaze slid to Julian. Her expression darkened,
and when she looked at the thread around his wrists, a

muscle rippled in her jaw. She looked at the Queen as one might behold an infected wound, her eyes narrowing. "Mother," she said flatly.

The Redwood Queen's attention finally left Andrew. He felt as if a dagger had pulled itself free from his side in a sweet and sharp relief.

"My daughter." The Queen stroked Ingrid's cheeks with her long fingers. "My heir. How much better you look now, dressed as you should be, like royalty. Welcome home."

Ingrid flinched away from her, expression hardening. She said nothing.

"I'm fascinated," said the Queen, turning slowly back to Micah as he stood pressed to Andrew with an arm protectively around his waist. "You return after twenty years with my daughter and this...hostile human, and only because your sire *wanted* to come back here, *wanted* to forget his life with you."

"It's not true," growled Micah. "He doesn't want this."

With a silent snort, the Queen took the leash from the rose faerie and pulled it toward herself. Giggling, Julian stumbled into her side, the Queen draping an arm around him. She squeezed his cheeks between her hands and asked, "Do you want to go home, my pet?"

"Stop," Micah pleaded.

His father released a shuddering sigh of pleasure, eyes fluttering shut as she held him aloft in her grip. "I am home," he breathed. "My Queen."

The Queen eyed Micah sidelong, thoughtful. Still staring at him, she said to Julian, "Kiss my feet."

"*Stop* it!" Micah lunged.

She was ready; she nodded to Sivarthis, who clapped his arm around Micah's chest. Micah snarled and kicked, his face blotchy with fury.

Andrew raised his bow, but an arrow whistled through the air, snicked his wrist with a splatter of blood, and struck the shaft of the crossbow so it flipped out of his grip and clattered away. He growled in pain and dropped to a knee to reach it, but another arrow shot and whipped his hand with the fletching. Andrew looked up sharply, teeth bared.

Chamomile had another arrow trained on him, crouched low to the ground, fixing him with cool blue eyes as she said evenly, "Leave it."

His shoulders sagged. "You're kidding me."

Horrified, Micah said in a voice that broke, "Chamomile, what—"

"I can see it serves me to honor the Redwood Queen," interrupted Chamomile. She touched her forehead and cast her frozen gaze to the Queen.

Standing behind the Redwood Queen, Ingrid stiffened, mouth dropping open.

The Queen beckoned Chamomile, who rose to her feet and padded up to her. Andrew caught her eyes lingering on Julian, who swayed on his feet as the rose-colored faerie fed him a bite of moist purple cake. Then her expression resolved and she looked away, shouldering her bow, tilting up her chin. Ingrid's lips curled in a silent snarl as she glared at Chamomile.

Sagging against Sivarthis's forearm, face crumpling, Micah moaned, "We yield. Tell me what you want. Anything. Just send my father away from here. Send him back to Saint Paul."

Still with her gritted teeth showing, Ingrid's eyes grew round and fearful, which shot a cold bolt of terror through Andrew.

The Redwood Queen stroked the head of one of her hounds, looking pleased. "Have a meal with me, my halfling."

"Let him go," Micah repeated, not looking at her. Despondent.

"You must miss our feasts," said the Queen. "Human cuisine cannot compare."

Micah shook his head, silent.

"You can sup with your father. It's late," said the Queen. "You must be weary."

"I hate you," he whispered.

Andrew nursed his bleeding hands, still down on one knee. The look on Micah's face—the resignation—made Andrew nauseous. This couldn't be over so quickly.

Then Chamomile spun a copper dagger in her hand and stabbed it into the neck of Julian's captor. Blood spurted in a crimson fountain. The rose-colored faerie crumpled, releasing the golden thread holding Julian. Chamomile caught it. The Redwood Queen began to turn toward her at the sound of the body thumping to the ground.

Sivarthis yelled and lunged toward Chamomile, but Micah kicked his leg back and wound it between Sivarthis's calves, tripping him and capturing him in a headlock. Micah's feet left the ground as Sivarthis struggled, but he couldn't get the smaller man's arms off his neck.

Chamomile wrapped the golden rope around her forearm and then heaved Julian onto her back, hooking her hands under his knees, his arms flailing around her neck. Then she stuck her tongue out at the Queen. Quick as her arrows, she sprinted into the cover of trees, Julian bouncing against her shoulders as they vanished.

Sivarthis broke free from Micah's hold and turned on his heel, but the Queen stopped him with a guttural noise. Fist raised to strike Micah, Sivarthis froze. She held the captain of the guard in her gaze for a moment, and he slowly stood up and clasped his hands, chest heaving.

Fixing his circlet himself, Micah looked up at Andrew. A smile spread on his lips. The heat of his gaze shot through Andrew's quailing spirit like liquid sunshine.

The Redwood Queen snapped her fingers. Her two hounds bayed hungrily, arching long silky backs, licking long ivory fangs. Then like twin flames they careened into the woods after Chamomile.

Andrew leapt back to his feet. He drew his iron sword

and thrust it toward the Queen. "I challenge you," he said. She froze.

Sivarthis barked a laugh.

"Fight me," said Andrew.

"No, no, no." Micah clapped a hand over his own mouth, and then Andrew's mouth, grabbing his shoulder. He hissed, "Shut up! Shut up! What're you doing?"

Gaze unwavering, Andrew lifted Micah's hand off his mouth, lacing their fingers together and saying to the Queen, "I win, you let me, Ingrid, Chamomile, Julian and Micah leave unscathed."

"And when I win?" the Queen said with a sneer.

Ingrid straightened, her expression resolving. "I stay," she said firmly. "That should satiate your greed, Your Grace." She clenched her fists, the misty rain sticking her coiling curls to her cheeks. She glanced back at Andrew and told him expressionlessly, "You're an idiot."

He grinned at her. Then he cast his eyes to the taller, sharper, colder version of Ingrid. "Do you accept?" demanded Andrew of the Queen.

The Queen looked thoughtful.

Still shaking his head, Micah whispered harshly, "This goes beyond reckless, man!"

"Definitely," said Ingrid.

"I mean, yeah," agreed Andrew.

"I accept," said the Queen, folding her hands in front of her, face splitting into the smile of a shark about to feast.

Kicking the cobblestones with his heel, Micah spat a string of profanity, covering his face with his hands.

Andrew gently lowered Micah's hands, hooked his finger under Micah's chin, and tilted back his head till their eyes met. "I don't care if it's a mistake," Andrew told him as he pushed back Micah's damp turquoise bangs. "I'm a fool for you. And besides, I took three years of fencing back in Liverpool. I'm practically an expert."

"I should not have brought you," said Micah, unamused.

"You could not have stopped me," said Andrew, not for the first time. "This means something to me. *You* mean something to me."

"Just..." Micah pressed his lips together. "Do *not* die."

"If you insist." Andrew's bravado only quavered when Micah drew their faces close with fingers on his chin. They kissed briefly, fearfully, with an unspoken promise that it wouldn't be their last.

Behind them, the Redwood Queen's eyes narrowed.

Ingrid gently pulled them apart and tugged Micah by the waist towards the dais. He held onto Andrew's hands as long as he could, breathing growing shallow again. Tension coiled in Andrew the further away Micah got. The circular plaza emptied out. Only he and the Redwood Queen remained.

The children of the Redwood Queen moved onto the dais, slippery with moss and mist; Micah slumped onto the smallest and lowest seat. He hugged his arms across his stomach. Ingrid laid both her hands across his shoulders, choosing to stand behind him rather than taking her own seat above him.

Glancing back at her, Micah said breathlessly, voice barely audible, "Ingrid, he's not going to survive a duel with her. I—I shouldn't have let him come here. He can't really understand what he's getting into."

"The challenge has been made and accepted," Ingrid told him. Her deep voice quavered, just slightly, on the last syllable. "You can't stop this now."

"Tell me I'm wrong. Tell me this'll turn out okay."

Ingrid said nothing, eyes downcast.

His throat tightened painfully at her silence. Micah said, "And she just let Chamomile and dad go. She could have stopped Chamomile in her tracks if she wanted to."

"She's not interested in them," said Ingrid. "She wants us."

Andrew took three measured steps away from the Queen. He still had his brown flannel around his waist, his hair back and secured by Ingrid's black thread. Raindrops beaded on his auburn locks. His heavy Docs were caked with mud, and his hands, clasped behind his back at the elbows, were both already red with his blood. Despairing, Micah dropped his face into his hands.

Sivarthis approached the Queen with a black velvet bundle. He unwrapped it, looking serious, and bent a knee with two rapiers extended toward her. She chose the one with the black and red leather hilt. As she weighed the blade in her hand, two child-sized Fae vibrated gossamer wings to float up and loop her braids through golden rings dangling from her crown, making her look like a weeping willow.

Sivarthis held the other rapier out to Andrew. His eyes were alight with anticipation as Andrew took the plum-purple hilt in his fist. It was a beautiful blade, shining white in the faerie lights, razor-thin by the tip. Andrew whistled and ran the pad of his index finger up its length.

"Tell me why you face down your death so shamelessly for my whelp of a son," crooned the Redwood Queen, tracing a patterned knot in the air with her blade. She sidestepped in an arcing circle around Andrew, who mirrored her, until they were away from the doors of the manor and in the center of the cobbled plaza adjacent to the dais. Jagged, hollow fir tree trunks filled with mushrooms ringed them in, along with large orb lights casting uneven shadows. Many duels must have taken place in this circle, blood spilled and lives lost for entertainment.

As he whipped the light blade experimentally through the rain, Andrew told her with a shrug of one shoulder, "This is what I do. I protect people who can't protect themselves. Especially when their parents are abusive assholes. Oh." He jabbed the blade in the air. "And I'm crazy for Micah."

The Redwood Queen scowled.

The crowd of Folk settled in to watch, bearing drinks

and reclining on moss-covered branches or golden swings, murmuring and pointing at them. Andrew glanced up and confirmed the railings were filled with faces above. He imagined that to the spectators, the only satisfying outcome of this duel would be him bleeding out on the cobblestones. His heart climbed into his throat. He looked toward the throne and Micah stared back at him, unblinking, fingers steepled and covering his mouth. He tucked his legs up on his seat, making himself as small as possible.

Ingrid perched on the edge of her seat, hands folded over her knee, looking even more like marble than usual. The red torchlight reflected in her eyes like they were windows into a forge. When she met his eyes, she resolutely squared her shoulders. Her dark brows lowered. She nodded once, slightly, and clenched her fingers tighter.

Andrew extended his right foot and bent his left knee and bowed deeply, a mocking smile on his face. "Your Majesty."

The Queen looked annoyed again. She bent slightly at the waist. "To the death," she said.

Faintly, Andrew nodded. He swallowed and agreed, "I will happily die for your son."

Chapter Fourteen
The Duel

"I'm gonna throw up," Micah said, bending over his knees, massaging his sore scalp.

"Drink," said Ingrid, and forced his chin back up.

Micah made a face as he leaned past the goblet under his lips to where his mother and his lover circled one another, quickly becoming damp with rain.

"*Drink,*" she ordered, lifting the goblet to his lips.

Left with no choice, he tipped it back and took a long swallow. The rush of warmth down his throat steeled him somewhat, calming his frantic heartbeat to more of a steady, angry drumming. He smeared the back of his hand across his lips and muttered a thank you to her, and she patted his back silently.

Intent on not striking first, Andrew proceeded to step around the Queen, slowly, crunching on soft woodchips. He bent his left arm behind his back, sword crossed over his chest.

The Redwood Queen moved first with a piercing cry,

both hands wrapped around the hilt of her sword. Andrew arched out of the trajectory of her weapon and drove his elbow into her shoulder blade.

She staggered. She was rusty.

Ingrid said as she rubbed her chin, "That's interesting."

Their mother straightened with a flash of fury. She went in again quickly and their blades clashed with a spill of sparks. Andrew's lips pressed together. The Redwood Queen pulled back, and then dove again; Andrew parried her with a single-handed swipe. It felt like a video game tutorial before the real fighting began.

Standing at attention at the foot of the dais with hands clasped behind his back, Sivarthis flicked his bright green gaze up toward Micah. He said through one corner of his mouth, curled in a smirk, "I imagine you're enjoying this, being back in the Redwoods where pain mingles with pleasure."

Micah's cheeks exploded with heat. Sivarthis had...used him for a time, taken advantage of Micah's easy affections to win favor with the Queen, which had eventually led to being promoted to captain of the guard. He stammered, "I never—no, that's not at all—"

"Shut up, Sivarthis," said Ingrid in a commanding snarl. "Speak out of turn again and I'll cut out your tongue."

Unruffled, Sivarthis raised his thick black brows and inclined his head to her, sizing up Micah with a lingering gaze that made him squirm before returning his attention to the duel.

The Redwood Queen jumped in again for two quick slaps of the flat of her blade, one on the side of Andrew's neck and one on the back of his right knee, too fast for him to stop her.

She was toying with him.

"Damn it," Micah said. "We've got to get out of here."

"If you make him abandon a duel," warned Ingrid, "she will chase him down to the ends of the earth. He will never rest. You will never rest."

Micah groaned and curled up in his seat.

Out in the rain and glowing with faerie lights, Andrew was not taking the bait. He remained slow and methodical, pacing, blocking where necessary to save his skin, prodding at her but not following the stabs with his body. He still had his left arm behind his back. In the crowd, as if sensing his reserve, Folk jeered.

Micah kept drinking from Ingrid's goblet until he could breathe again.

The Redwood Queen spun around Andrew, forcing him to follow her and duck beneath the swipe of her blade, spraying raindrops like glinting diamond insect wings. Before he straightened, Andrew swept his blade between her calves and tripped her with his wrist. He managed to draw a thin line of blood on the back of her leg. As she collected herself, the Queen's eyes flared with blood-red light and the air darkened, the faerie lights blinking out around her.

Glancing up at the dramatic effect, Andrew snickered. He stayed down, running the pad of his finger along his blade and collecting her blood. He smeared it across his cheek with a quick smile.

The Redwood Queen lunged at him with a snarl, three quick strikes bouncing off his blade but knocking him off his feet. He rolled twice and pushed up off his elbows, clambering back to his feet and making it back around to face the Queen just as she struck again. He twisted, but her blade sliced his collarbone, cutting open his shirt and leaving a thick slash of blood in its wake. A spasm of fear crossed his features.

"Feel the terror," said the Redwood Queen in a growl, not a hair out of place in her crown. She jabbed and swung with such speed Andrew was forced to back-step, and back-step, and back-step to avoid her blade until he finally dodged and stabbed toward her. She arced out of the way, but her dress tore from hip to waist. Her arc turned into an elegant spin and she struck him in the small of his back with the hilt of her sword, sending him sprawling into the ground. His rapier spiraled out of his grip. Andrew shook his head clear and dove for it, but the Redwood Queen staked the back of his shirt and pinned him in place. She picked up his blade.

"No, no, no," Micah rose and stepped down toward the duel but stopped when Ingrid pulled back on his bicep. "Andrew, you got this! Get up! Keep your cool!"

Andrew lay on his hip with his brow set in a scowl, chest heaving, tendrils of escaped hair sticking to his neck and jaw. He tried to toss Micah a carefree smile, but it looked more like a grimace.

"I admit," said the Queen, "I thought you would be dead by now."

Andrew swept his hair back from his face and said, "Yes, that's my specialty." Then he rolled onto his shoulder, bending the blade pinning him down; it snapped out of the Redwood Queen's hand and he snatched it on its recoil. He scrambled back to his feet holding her rapier now in his dominant left hand, eyes narrowed with pain and his jaw set with determination. The Queen came at him again, hardly giving him a chance to get the ground under him, but using her red-hilted rapier he blocked, and blocked, and parried, and back-stepped out of her way to recover.

Ingrid said in awe, "He is much better than he has any right to be."

Micah took her hand and squeezed tightly. Ingrid didn't stop him.

Andrew leaned and stabbed, missed, and pulled back, and did it again. The Queen was moving faster now, discarding the pretense that Andrew could keep up with her unsettling speed. Still, he leaned and stabbed, paused to gather himself then parried and blocked with his forearm. The blood on his clavicle had congealed. She cut into his forearm in another strike. Then again, she sliced above his waist, and he stifled a cry. She was closing in on his vital organs with care and precision. She was making a ritual of his butchering.

Micah couldn't even stay in his seat anymore; he was

crouching, trembling, his mind's eye torn between images of Andrew bleeding to death and of Andrew cradled safely in Micah's arms outside of the Redwoods. He was ready at any moment to spring from the dais; Ingrid knew, holding onto his shoulders even though her palms were damp with sweat.

As stains bloomed dark on his shirt, Andrew's complexion paled. He started to back-step after every encounter with her blade, panting briefly before inhaling deeply and wiping his wrist across his forehead.

"I can end you now," the Redwood Queen offered.

In answer, Andrew crooked his arm behind his back again and turned a quick prod of his blade into a wide arc. It forced her to sidestep and when she was transferring her weight between feet, he managed to strike her leg. She hissed as blood rose to her alabaster skin and mingled with the rain slick on her thigh.

"Same goes for you," Andrew said brightly, but his voice was hoarse.

Strike. Strike. Strike. Strike. She threw him off balance in a flurry of silver. She followed him as he stumbled. Micah stood up, heart hammering in his ears. He shook Ingrid off.

The Redwood Queen got Andrew to the ground again.

His elbows sank into the mud. He scrambled away from her. Andrew raised his rapier to guard himself, but she hooked the tip of her blade through the pommel, ripping it savagely from his grasp and sending it spinning through the air. She raised her rapier over her head as she laughed. The sound was wild, gleeful.

Victorious.

Blood throbbing from his wounds and coating his arm and his shirt, Andrew's clarity slipped away from him. He only regretted he was going to die and hoped, with a glance in their direction, that Micah and Ingrid would find their way back out of the Redwoods. They'd done it once, after all. All their trip back here had done was turn back the clock twenty years. For immortals, maybe that wouldn't be so bad. Hopefully Micah would heal soon and forget him. After all, he'd barely known him for two months. Never mind that every day with him was brighter, bolder, happier, than all other moments of the rest of Andrew's life combined. Micah would be fine. He'd be *fine*. He met Micah's gaze and smiled. Then he looked away and closed his eyes.

Almost as soon as he saw the orange inside of his eyelids, he heard, "Abso-*fucking*-lutely not!"

The ground under his legs erupted. Tossed backward, Andrew rolled through a somersault that shook stars into his eyes. He was back on his hands and knees in an instant, blinking, trying to comprehend what the hell had just happened.

The faerie lights shook violently in the air. Right where he'd been waiting for the Queen's final blow, an enormous root bucked up through the cobblestones, crawling with beetles and fat yellow slugs. Feet spread apart, rapier hanging limply from her hand, the Redwood Queen stared at the wild wooded barrier before her, her expression one of bewildered delight.

At the foot of the throne, Micah stood between slack-jawed Sivarthis, and Ingrid, who cursed wildly. His eyes were molten amethysts burning in the dark. Tears streaking his cheeks, he screamed, "Fuck you, Redwood Queen."

His fingers crooked into claws. From the mud under his shoes erupted thick squirming roots cracking like whips. "Fuck your hate."

He strode across wildflowers sprouting from the thick underbrush and growled, "Fuck your sadism." The twining roots rippled, whistling like arrows, racing toward the Redwood Queen. "And fuck...your...power over me!" Evergreen ringed his jeweled irises in a flash bright and brief as a firework.

The Redwood Queen sprang back, but her speed didn't matter. Her feet left the ground but did not return. The roots twisted and tangled and webbed around the Redwood Queen's body, tightening enough so that her white flesh dimpled underneath.

The Redwood Queen gasped as she fell to her knees, bound and immobilized.

Sivarthis roared and drew his weapon. But Ingrid leapt

at him and tackled him. They tumbled down the stairs from the throne and when they stopped, she landed with her knees braced on his chest. A bright copper dagger appeared in her fist, and she slit Sivarthis' throat so fast her pale hand was a blur. A gasp of surprise burst from Andrew as he heard blood rattle in Sivarthis' throat before the male faerie stilled, eyes open and staring heavenward.

Micah ripped the purple-hilted rapier from the Queen's bound hand at a savage angle. She gave a cry of pain; her fingers bent like brambles.

Sweet as sap, the Redwood Queen said to him, "My darling, your lover agreed to duel to the death."

He pressed the rapier to her long ivory throat and said through clenched teeth, "Do you think I give a flying fuck about your archaic terms, *Mother*? The only thing I want now is to slice your head off your shoulders."

Hands stained with Sivarthis's blood, Ingrid climbed back to her feet and dashed from the throne. She reached Micah as he loomed over the Redwood Queen on her knees, tangled in roots that answered not to her but to her youngest child, her halfling, the Nightshade Boy.

Through half-lidded eyes with a lascivious smile on her lips, she crooned, "Look at my precious children, so savage and bloodstained."

Leaning on the root, Andrew struggled to his feet, huffing, and grimacing. Adrenaline had abandoned him and everything throbbed. But he ignored it. Ignored it for the sake of his lover, whose hair was leaf-green, stirring with a wind that touched only him. His lover, who had transformed from a gentle, attentive man trying to be human into a fearsome otherworldly faerie, glowing, powerful, and bent on saving Andrew Vidasche's life.

Micah's gaze flicked briefly toward Andrew as he stood up against the root, taking in his colorless, awestruck face. They exchanged a quick and private smile before Micah looked back at the Queen.

He still had the rapier against her throat, and the roots hadn't loosened from holding her secure on her knees.

He'd never looked down on her in forty years. She was always above, staring, laughing, lusting for violence. He asked suddenly, "Why did you want me?"

The Redwood Queen blinked.

"You had Ingrid. She's..." He glanced sidelong at his taller sister, who stared down at the Redwood Queen with impassive ruby eyes. "Deadly, and serious, and loyal, and...just spectacular."

Ingrid twitched her head toward him and quirked her lip in a sidelong smile. Then she socked his arm.

Micah grinned at her and shrugged, looking back towards his mother. His expression sobered. "Why me?" Raindrops beaded on his luminous green bangs and dropped into his lashes.

After a moment the Redwood Queen tilted up her chin. She said with affection, "To see how strong my weakest can be." In her mismatched eyes, true pride flashed. "How glad I am that my death will be at his hands."

Micah froze. His heart sank to the soles of his shoes.

Leaning on the root protruding from the plaza, Andrew tried to catch his breath but saw through his pain Micah's uncertainty as the Queen spoke. His humanity collided with his Fae instincts, tenderness at odds with the wild. He slowly looked away from the Queen and to Andrew.

In response, Andrew limped around the root, stumbling on the loose cobblestones and clods of mud. He stepped on a slug which squelched under his boot and made him cringe. Then he came to stand beside him, clasping Micah's shoulder, pressing his lips to his temple under the circlet. Though he wished he could, he couldn't speak; he was too weary.

But Micah realized Andrew didn't need to say anything. Stymied, he slid his glare back to the Redwood Queen wrapped in his vines.

Micah curled his lip. "I refuse to give you the satisfaction." He kicked off his soggy chucks so his feet were bare. Then he dug his toes into the earth.

"Uh—" began Ingrid, but he held up his free hand.

Eyes closed, Micah sent his thoughts down to the velvety moss under the tender skin of his feet. Down beneath the moss to the earthworms and the ants and the beetles tirelessly fertilizing the soil. Down to the rich soil mingling with the roots pumping water and nutrients to the trees stretching for miles around them. He took a deep breath, in through his nose, out through his lips.

"I ask for an ending," he whispered. Then he dropped the rapier at his feet.

The roots confining the Redwood Queen began to stir. They called to greater parts and drew from the earth more, and more, and more of themselves. Around the Queen they coiled and swirled and multiplied, ropes turning to rods, rods turning to flesh. They shot up toward the heavens, spring-colored spores making an aura around them as they grew buds and then sprouts and then branches. Flesh bound together and grew bright red bark, small scales at first and then fingers and then as long as arms.

The Queen screamed, "What—what are you—stop! Micah, my child..."

Her legs and waist vanished into the trunk. Her arms followed.

Ingrid took Micah's hand and brought him and Andrew with her as she stepped back, careful not to stumble on the chunks of loose cobblestones. The soil under the Redwood Queen was still splitting, still coiling out in a cyclone of rich brown earth. Fissures in the ground ate up the rapier.

Micah saw behind the growing tree that the Queen's subjects had fallen into a half-crescent formation, all shapes and sizes of faces turned heavenward toward the disappearing heights of the Redwood Queen's trunk.

All that protruded from the newborn Redwood was the

Queen's white face. Even her crown was consumed by the tree. She took labored gasps. Her hair clung to her cheeks, at long last unkempt. "You will just let me die in here?"

Micah shook his head. "Only your violence dies today." He lifted his eyes to the towering Redwoods. "You'll live on, with your trees. They're all you've ever really loved."

Looking toward the Folk of the Redwoods, he shrugged and then declared, "I don't care what happens here. I'm sure before long there will be a new Redwood Queen. Maybe you'll be better than her and maybe you'll be worse. But you will do well to remember not to mess with me, or my sister, or anyone in Lilydale, until the end of time. You will remember that the Redwood Queen's son did not kill today. I allowed nature to do its work."

When the last sound left his lips, the Redwood bark closed over the Queen's face. Her eyes, one violet and one ruby, went still and glassy, and a single tear fell from her lashes.

He looked to Ingrid, and then to Andrew. "Let's go home."

CHAPTER FIFTEEN
THE VICTOR

ANDREW'S KNEES BUCKLED AS soon as he heard the word *home*, but Ingrid and Micah didn't let him fall. He slung his arms around their shoulders and limped along with them as the Redwood Folk watched them leave. They bore a range of expressions from reverence to disgust to disbelief. All remained still and silent as they passed. Flickering spring-green light sparked under Micah's bare feet. As they crossed the barrier back into the Hoh rainforest, Ingrid and Micah looked at each other over his head, hands outstretched.

Ingrid closed her fist on the shadows, Micah her mirror with but the slightest lag.

Folding the shadows was like running through thick and heavy curtains. Micah caught glimpses of the forest beyond; they startled a herd of elk, and sent birds flapping skyward, and almost collided with a cedar. Then past a curtain ahead of them in the dark was a little secluded campsite, and in the campsite sat Andrew's undisturbed beige Saturn, waiting for them.

Andrew let the rolling darkness carry him, stomach turning, and when it dropped him back out, his body wanted to keep going. He doubled over, patting Micah's arm in warning just before he vomited next to his feet. The quick gesture made pain shoot up and down his body. His head throbbed. He groaned, but Micah held him tight with both arms around his chest. He helped him straighten and rubbed his shoulder blades as he did.

"Look," said Ingrid.

A ring of enormous mushrooms colored white, violet, and scarlet had sprouted around the Saturn. Beyond its boundary lay the two red hounds, arrows lodged into their skulls, blood pooled under their maws.

On the roof of the Saturn, Chamomile knelt with an arrow nocked in her bow, the sharp point trained on the three of them as if in disbelief. "Are you free? Are you alone?"

"Yes," Ingrid answered, a jubilant note making her voice rise like a song.

Chamomile threw down her bow and arrow and dropped to the ground. "You're free!"

The cats scooted out from under the car, twining between her legs, their tails sticking up like flags that quivered at the tips. Ingrid stepped over the mushrooms and stooped to speak in hushed tones to Chamomile, whose eyes brightened and brightened until they almost glowed.

Through the window of the passenger side of the car, Julian was slumped forward in slumber, a sleeping bag draped over him and tucked behind his shoulders.

"Is—is he okay?" Micah asked.

Chamomile nodded. "He'll think this was all a dream, unless you tell him otherwise."

Micah carried Andrew past the ring of mushrooms. Within it, the air was quieter, a bit warmer, and the rain was repelled as if by an invisible umbrella. "You gave me a fucking heart attack, Chami," said Micah.

"Andrew gave me the—" She cut herself off, peering up at Andrew, grimacing. "Damn. That's a lot of blood."

Andrew groaned with his eyes slitted open, "That's a lot of sass." He grunted and flinched against Micah, his head drooping. "Sorry. I'm okay. Sorry."

"Now who apologizes too much?" Micah murmured with a smile, cupping Andrew's cheek in his hand.

"You, Your Grace," mumbled Andrew with a drunken grin, before his eyes rolled back as he collapsed.

Micah yelled and caught him under his armpits. Ingrid pulled open the door to the backseat of the car. Chamomile helped maneuver him by the hips as they laid him over the bench and set his head down on the seat. He grumbled, head lolling, clutching his bleeding waist. Ingrid crossed to the other side of the car and slid onto the seat, lifting his head and resting it on her thigh. Then she picked up her basket of herbs and began digging through them.

"Micah," said Chamomile firmly. "Move. We need to treat his wounds."

Yielding, Micah backed away and went to sit in the driver's seat. He reached over to Julian and touched his hand, and Julian sighed and murmured something incoherent. Micah inspected his face and chest and hands, but Julian seemed unharmed. So he really had been brought back to the Redwoods just to be intoxicated, just as bait to bring Micah and Ingrid back. Micah sighed, shaking his head, patting his dad's hand. Then he turned his attention back to Andrew, wet, bleeding, muddy, and barely conscious in the back of his Saturn.

Slipping through the open door, Chamomile climbed on top of Andrew's legs and straddled him.

"Oh," Micah intoned.

Andrew yelped and slurred, "What're you doing?" He lifted his head, shakily, and tapped her knees where they rested over his hips.

"Hush." Chamomile shoved Andrew's shirt up and wriggled it over his head.

Micah remarked dryly, "This is weird for me."

Taking the proffered bundles from Ingrid's hand, Chamomile bit off a mouthful, chewed for a long moment, and then spat them back into her hand.

"I don't think I'm hurt that bad," said Andrew hurriedly, holding up his hands. "Please don't spit on me."

She squished it between her fingers and then picked up

his wrist, using the slurry to coat his wrist and hand where she'd cut him with her own arrows.

Andrew gagged and grumbled, "S'that pesto?"

She smeared it over his collarbone. He hissed through his teeth. When she touched the wound in his side, he let out a ragged cry that ended in a whimper. He covered his eyes as Micah reached back and held onto his shoulder.

"Yeah. The Queen meant to do damage here." Chamomile's fingers spent longer working the herbs into his side while Andrew saw white stars behind his eyelids and felt himself teetering toward unconsciousness.

Chamomile massaged each injury and her lips moved silently, eyes bright with concentration, brow furrowed. The sharp pain of the wounds dulled like they'd been numbed with a shot. Then the pain was nothing but a memory. Andrew's tight muscles relaxed; his head lolled back, and he realized with a start that he was draped over Ingrid's thigh. She blinked down at him, expressionless, but when their eyes met as his vision cleared, the severe curve of her lips relaxed.

Andrew let out a ragged breath and carefully lifted his neck, but it didn't force an ooze of blood out of his collarbone. He gazed woozily at Chamomile. "This is more contact than I've ever had with women."

Micah snorted, leaned over the console, and kissed Andrew's damp cheek.

"Now," said Chamomile sternly, "this doesn't mean

you're not injured. It simply helps your body know how to heal. Don't do anything stupid for a week. Goblin's orders."

"That was amazing," Andrew told her.

"Yeah," Micah agreed, chin in his palm, "she's good."

Chamomile made a face at them both and then climbed out of the backseat. She lifted Andrew's knees onto the cushion and then slammed the door. "Get out of the driver's seat, Micah. I'm about to do some drag racing." She held up the keys to the Saturn.

Andrew blinked. "Those were in my pocket."

Chamomile shrugged. "I was in the area."

Micah made a choking sound. Despite himself, Andrew blushed.

"You're insatiable," sighed Ingrid. "I don't know if you should drive."

"It's *fine*," groaned Chamomile. "One time I drove some-one's Maserati. *That* I did crash. It was awesome."

Andrew began to struggle upright. Ingrid pushed against his shoulder blades and helped him settle in the middle seat, as Micah climbed over the center console and gingerly settled with his hip against Andrew's, arm against arm. Ingrid and Micah effectively kept Andrew upright, as he grimaced and adjusted his feet to fit the cramped space better.

Fadil and Arwen were crouched behind his head next to the windshield. Arwen leaned over the headrest and sniffed Andrew's stringy hair, the Queen's blood across his cheek, and then his ear, where she planted a sandpaper kiss. Andrew reached back to stroke her cheeks, but she stretched past him to sniff at the salve on his wrist.

"Chami," began Ingrid as she leaned into the car window and hugged her arms over her chest, "how did you protect the car for that long when the Queen sent the hounds after you?"

As she turned over the engine, Chamomile grinned wickedly. "She didn't think I had the cats, who ambushed her hounds halfway back to the Saturn. From how it sounded, the cats very much did a number on them, cursed canines. They bought me the distance to make it back and set up a ward before the hounds reached me. The rest was obvious." She fumbled around the side of the car seat until she successfully scooted it as far forward as she could. Then she stuck her left leg under her so she could see over the dash.

Andrew said, "This's a promising start."

"Don't make me kill you," said Chamomile. The car lurched to a start, and everyone in the backseat jumped.

"The cats were the secret weapon," said Micah in awe. "And you brought them with us out of sheer stubbornness." Fadil padded over Ingrid and Andrew and curled up on Micah's lap. Arwen followed close behind and melted into the slim space between Andrew and Micah.

Chamomile shrugged a small gold-green shoulder. "Stubbornness, or foresight? We'll never know."

"The will of cats and wild girls," mumbled Andrew, and then he dropped off to sleep.

Andrew could never sleep through nausea. He blinked his eyes open and swallowed the extra saliva that had pooled on his tongue, groaning softly. He gingerly straightened in the center seat, legs splayed awkwardly between Micah and Ingrid – who was also as leggy and cramped as him. The herbal paste dried against Andrew's skin thick and stiff, which in addition to his cramped muscles made him basically immobile.

Micah had fallen asleep with his cheek against the window, legs tucked up against the seat in front of him, arms crossed over his muddy green shirt. His circlet was askew on his brow, so the bobcat hung over his eyes like a toothy hood.

Beyond them, in the dim predawn light, flat fields sloped away from the car until they faded into the gray-blue of the sky. Short puffs of trees dotted the horizon. Occasionally, they zoomed past a farmstead, with barbed wire fences around grazing cattle.

He looked through the front windshield, puzzled, but the view remained the same. The prairie had never looked so...startling. "Where are we?"

Andrew tried to estimate when they'd left the Redwoods and the time it would take to drive clear through Montana and Idaho and back to North Dakota. The effort made his forehead pound.

"No idea," said Chamomile.

"This...is...slightly concerning. I mean—" He looked in the front seat where Julian still snored softly. "How long is Mr. Stillwater going to be asleep? What happens when he wakes up, and we're lost?"

Chamomile scoffed, "Stop being a paranoid baby. We'll be home within two hours."

"How? You can't tell me Micah and I were sleeping for...twelve hours or something."

Chamomile ignored him.

"She folded some shadows a bit," supplied Ingrid, curled up against the window next to Andrew. She was wearing Micah's purple shirt over the provocative dress they'd put her in at the Redwoods. When he noticed, she smoothed the hem down with a dismissive eyebrow raise. With her other hand, she was fidgeting with the vial of blood Micah had turned into a pendant. She must have taken it off his neck when he'd been unconscious.

Andrew felt a brief thrill of fear, but yet some certainty that the ground had shifted between him and his haunt.

She twirled it between her slender fingers and held it up so the light glinted on the fluid inside, turning it crimson. "I think this might have acted like a boon. Not to say you don't have *any* fighting skills, but my mother could have slain you in two minutes."

"Mm." He leaned back and slitted his eyes at her.

"She's a thousand-year-old faerie queen fighting on her own turf." She raised her slender brows and made a face back at him. "You're a thirty-year-old mortal."

Andrew huffed out a breath through his nostrils. He wanted to tell her he was actually thirty-two, but he was afraid that would prove her point. Ingrid held out the vial, and Andrew took it back and looped it onto the cord around his neck.

"I think Micah's blood protected you." She peered past him and her expression softened as she looked where Micah slumbered by the window. "Even more so because of his affection for you."

Micah woke with an inelegant snort. "What'd I do?"

Nodding faintly, Andrew touched the wound under his collarbone. The scab was still soft. "Yeah. That sounds about right."

As Micah stretched and yawned, Andrew strung his arms around his waist and nuzzled into the nape of his neck.

When they arrived back in Saint Paul under a cloudless afternoon sky, Chamomile managed to park them mostly on the curb outside Micah's brownstone on Saint Claire. She got a bit close to the trunk of one of the linden trees with the front bumper, a wheel riding the curb, but otherwise everyone was intact. She was the first around the front of the car to help Julian to his feet, who blinked blearily and slurred his words, leaning heavily on the small goblin and patting her head. Tossing his house keys at Chamomile, Micah gingerly helped Andrew out of the car.

Ingrid leapt out of the backseat with obvious delight. She stretched out like a long white sunbeam, smiling heavenward. She slid out of Micah's purple shirt and set it on the boot of the car. Without it, in the setting of a busy modern street with the smell of restaurants and garbage once again in the air, she looked like a celebrity preparing for a red-carpet event.

She smoothed the dress, fixed her hair, and then nodded to Andrew and clapped her hands on Micah's shoulders. "Perilous circumstances aside," she began, "I greatly appreciated this journey with you." She looked over and met Andrew's eyes. "And you as well. Truly."

Andrew held out his hand toward her. She frowned at it for a moment, and then set her fingers in his. He swept her hand up and kissed her knuckles. "Lady of the Bluffs."

Ingrid grinned in a meek, almost girlish way. Her cheeks even turned a bit rosy. It was so far from the expression she'd used to haunt him that it was hard to believe she was the same. She tugged on her curls and said cautiously to

Micah, "I have a hope that...things will be different now. That maybe you might come to enjoy being in Lilydale with me."

Micah's breath hitched. He looked past the corner of his brownstone where the trees opposite the river marked the beginning of the bluffs. Slowly, he started to smile, and he nodded. "How about I come up and visit tomorrow night?"

"Yes. I'll prepare you a feast. Of ordinary food. Nothing Fae-spelled. Do you still like those chicken wings with the sauce?"

Brow furrowing, Micah looked confused. Self-consciously, he pushed the circlet up on his forehead. "Uh, a feast? Why?"

Ingrid shook her head fondly and tapped the bobcat skull on his brow. "You vanquished the Redwood Queen, Nightshade Boy."

"Oh." Micah looked vaguely away.

Ingrid went on, "We will sing songs of it and weave tapestries. Of you and your brave knight."

Micah released a noisy breath and blinked a few times. "Right."

Andrew slung his arms around Micah's shoulders and kissed his cheekbone. "I'm honored to serve you as your awkward, not super talented knight."

"Stop," Micah flapped his hands at Andrew until he laughed and withdrew. "I—I think you're greatly exagger—"

"No," interrupted Ingrid. "I'm not exaggerating." She stared down at her young half-brother, her face still fine with faerie cosmetics, her hair turned frizzy as it dried. "Do not sell yourself short of this, Micah."

"O—okay," he murmured.

"I am eager to get back to the bluffs," said Ingrid. She nodded to Andrew, and then smiled tenderly at Micah and nudged his chin with her knuckle. "See you soon."

In flannel pants and bare-chested, Micah sat on the edge of Julian's bed as his dad finished a microwave dinner. Cinnamon, Arwen, and Fadil all sat and stared at him as he took a bite with shaking fingers. Julian's face was haggard, the lines deeper than before, with purple bags under his downcast eyes.

"Just remember to take it easy," Micah told him. "I'm ordering you on bedrest for a week, okay? The cats will tattle on you."

Julian gave a grumbling sigh. After he swallowed, he asked, "Was I in the hospital?" He rubbed his temple. "It's all so fuzzy."

Micah hesitated, his blood pounding in his ears. Then he said after a moment, "It was a bad spell, Dad." He reached out and squeezed his forearm. "But I think things are going to be better now." Then he took the empty meal tray and his fork and started to get up.

Julian looked up and scrutinized Micah with his sharp amber eyes. His gaze always made Micah squirm, like Julian could see through his attempts to protect him. Then Julian smiled faintly and nodded. "I believe you."

Shutting off the bedroom lights, Micah left and padded down the stairs. It was dusk, and everything in the living room was tinged purple. Andrew stood by the coffee table, freshly showered with his hair unbound and still damp. He unloaded white Chinese takeout boxes from noisy plastic bags. He'd changed into a plain black tee and a pair of maroon sweats with the golden logo for the U of M near the thigh.

When Micah came down the final stairs, Andrew looked up. His foxlike face lit up with sunshine as if Micah parted the clouds in his eyes. "Come, feast with me." Andrew's eyes sparkled in the faint light as he tugged Micah onto the cushion next to him. He held out disposable chopsticks in a red paper sleeve.

As he took them, Micah switched on a table lamp next to them that looked like an old Edison bulb. The light glinted off Andrew's hair like flecks of gold. Micah swallowed and asked cautiously, "Will you come with me tomorrow? To Lilydale."

Andrew paused, his chopsticks floating in front of his mouth with a tangle of noodles on the end. He lowered it and glanced over. "Yeah. Of course. If you want."

"As my date," Micah told him hurriedly, touching his arm. "To a banquet. Not as a knight."

"Yeah." Andrew shot him a tremulous smile. "It'll be weird."

"You're telling me." Micah helped himself to some beef and broccoli, using one of the ceramic bowls Andrew had grabbed from the kitchen. When he had a bowlful and had taken a few bites, he noticed Andrew had gauze around his hand and a big square bandage taped over his collarbone. "Who wrapped you up? Sam?"

"Ah, yes." Andrew rubbed his wrist as he took a swig of soda. "He insisted. I think it was helping him cope."

With a sigh, Micah said, "I wish I could have brought you home without a scratch."

"He'll be all right. I told him he can move into my extra bedroom. Keep a better eye on me. I think he forgave me then."

"Oh. Neat. He can hang out over here too whenever he wants. My dad would love the company."

Andrew's lips twitched faintly. He picked at grains of fried rice with his chopsticks, blinking a few times.

"What's wrong?"

Twirling his chopsticks between his fingertips, Andrew said quietly, "Nothing. That would make me really happy."

Suddenly confused, suddenly paranoid, Micah blurted, "But maybe I'm getting ahead of myself."

Andrew's head snapped up. A crease appeared between his brows.

Micah stammered, "I...I just—I don't want to assume. We've skipped like...a lot of relationship steps. Not that I know anything about typical relationships. You're my first human partner. So I'm in the—I'm—I'm rambling. Anyway, yeah, we've had an unusual go of things with all the, um...Folksy stuff."

"What?" Andrew blinked and gave him a sideways smile. "I mean, yeah. For sure. And that makes you...*less* sure about things?"

"No, no!" Micah waved his hands and then slapped his forehead. "Oh, god, that's not it at all. Words. I struggle. Andrew, I—" He grasped his knee. "I would do literally anything to make you happy. Like, I turned my mom into a tree. Cuz I was like, oh. That bitch is gonna kill my boyfriend and that won't do."

Andrew's smile broadened into a grin. "So you...you really killed your mum for me."

"My *mom*, yes."

Andrew rolled his eyes toward the ceiling.

"I mean...yes, and she—just took and took and took. My dad, and me, and Ingrid, and she was ready to take Chami. She corrupted everything like a moldy fucking piece of bread."

"Ah. Gross."

"But the craziest part is that now that we're home, and

we're alive, and you're sitting in my living room and you bought us Chinese food and..." Micah set aside his bowl, turned to him on the couch, and continued emphatically, "I want to do *all* of it with you. I want to buy you increasingly expensive gifts the longer we're together."

"I've always wanted a big crock pot," remarked Andrew.

The two of them burst into giggles that stole their breath for some time.

Then finally Micah wiped his eyes and he continued more seriously, "I want us to go to dinner and see movies we don't want to see. I want to wake up with you in my bed until we get sick of each other, and then miss you as soon as you're gone, and, and..." Micah trailed off, staring at the rug under the coffee table. "You've let me live the future I was always too scared to imagine. Like if I daydreamed about this, it would snuff out the tiny little flame of hope I had that it could ever really happen." He looked up, tentative. "And that's why I'm afraid I'm getting ahead of myself."

Andrew sat back in the corner of the couch, a silly smile on his face and tears dotting the corners of his eyes. He sniffed and started to laugh again.

Micah stiffened. "Hey, there's no need—"

Cutting him off, Andrew used his spindly limbs to capture Micah and pull him against his chest, arms wrapped tightly around his neck. Flooded with relief and joy, Micah let himself be effectively strangled for a moment before he got his knees under him so he could pivot to kiss him.

Andrew didn't feel the pull of his wounds as they kissed. He just felt the way the vibration of this half-human matched the frequency of his own. The flames of their hope, and their fear, and their faith in one another, burned perfectly in time. Everything else but their kindling affections disappeared, as they clung to each other on their way out of a nightmare and into a dream.

Chapter Sixteen

The Question

"Hey, Ingrid?"

Ingrid pulled her gaze from out over the lake and the river and the stars. They weren't as awe-inspiring as the raw wilderness in the mountains in Montana, but they were...familiar. Hers. Below her, Andrew was allowing Chamomile to give him a half-braid with a Celtic flavor. He wore a black sweatshirt and the vial of Micah's blood dangled above his collar. Andrew tried to tilt his head back to look at Ingrid, but Chamomile slapped his temple. She sat with her knees on either side of his shoulders on the edge of a slab of limestone, and ignored him when he protested when she pulled the braid tight. She was dressed in a cropped white tank top and a loose flowing skirt Ingrid had given her that matched the cornflower blue of her eyes. Her hair was in two twin braids and she wore a crown of bright orange tiger lilies.

Watching the braiding with a trace of amusement crinkling her eyes, Ingrid said, "What is it, Andrew?"

Andrew said, "What if I have someone in mind I want to check on, in your glass? I haven't seen her in almost twenty years, but—"

Laying across Andrew's lap, Micah opened his eyes and looked up curiously.

"It's my mother," said Andrew after a moment. "She...honestly is kind of like Julian. Only..." Andrew paused. Chamomile's fingers briefly stilled at his scalp. "I guess I didn't stick around for her like Micah did."

"That's not the same thing," Micah said quickly. He sat up. Under the collar of his half-buttoned flannel, the tip of an antler was visible. Last month he'd gotten a large black tattoo on his chest depicting a bobcat skull and antlers decorated with nightshade and lilies. The skull had bright yellow points in the eye sockets.

Resting her chin on her palm, Ingrid looked sidelong at Andrew. "Of course. If you're sure you want to know."

Andrew looked away over the bluffs. Behind them the creek ran north to south and just past it most of their little village of Folk had gone to sleep in their treehouses. Syabira was softly playing a ukulele and humming, legs tucked up under her, sitting under an oak tree and beside a glowing jar of faerie lights. Andrew thought of Julian, who still didn't know what had happened in Washington was more than a recurring nightmare of the Redwood Queen, and who still didn't know that the taste of faerie food on his tongue was more than just a whisper of a craving he'd never forget. Julian was at peace, most days. He was teaching Andrew how to cook better and enjoyed watching the same familiar movies over and over, mostly British romantic comedies or eighties science fiction flicks. Maybe his mum could have turned out like Julian. Not unblemished or without nightmares, but...normal. Satisfied.

He thought of Sam, whose life had gone on marching since discovering that the Folk existed. Sam had moved into the second bedroom in the flat over Magic's Repair as soon as it became apparent that Andrew was spending more and more of his time down the street at Micah's brownstone.

Andrew looked away from the quiet interstate, which was dark and void of streetlights where it crossed over the wild marshland and the river. Micah's luminous violet gaze was already on Andrew, as it so often was. The attention warmed the pit of his stomach, as it so often did. He leaned forward and kissed the half-faerie prince, waiting as long as he could to let his eyes close, trying to get a glimpse of Micah's soft brown features for as long as he could.

When he pulled back, Micah stroked his cheek with the pad of his thumb.

Finally Andrew looked back at Ingrid. Chamomile resumed pulling his hair into a braid. She softly hummed a harmony with Syabira. With a faint shake of his head, Andrew Vidasche said, "Yeah. I guess I'm not sure yet."

TO BE CONTINUED

RETURN TO LILYDALE WITH Micah and Andrew in *Relinquish Me, The Wayward Knight*, the sequel to *Deny Me, The Nightshade Boy.*

ACKNOWLEDGEMENTS

THIS JOURNEY INTO SELF-PUBLISHING began on Twitter. When I finally dedicated my time to building a social media platform, I was led to the Writerly Wyverns discord server, where I essentially met the entire team of people who drove me to self-publish and helped me get there. Vic, I don't know how I'd have gotten here without you as my hype man, my confidante, and my writing soulmate, if I may. It's been a while since my soul has been on the same vibration as someone else, and it feels like we've known each other forever. Olive, thank you for teaching me as much as you did in between all the awesome stuff you've got going on in your life. Dinah, thanks for being the first person to give me an art critique in 12 years, for being so generous and encouraging in doing so. Quinton Li, my editor, began as someone who was brought into my discord to act as a sounding board for people who wanted to go the indie publishing route, which at the time was just me. Because of this special opportunity, the night I met Quinton was the night I decided to publish The Heartwood Trilogy myself.

Another inspiration for this decision was RK Ashwick, whose kindness and wisdom on nothing other than Tumblr cemented my choice. Thank you also to every other beta who helped refine *Deny Me* from its earliest stages. The indie writing crew has been truly amazing, rich, and inspiring support and I wish I'd found you all sooner.

I also want to say a special thank you to Zsasa, my typographer, who has been so patient and diligent in working on *Deny Me* with me. She revised, made me extra touches for the inside of the book SO fast, and answered stupid questions and was patient with my confusion. She really brought my cover to life and I cannot wait to work on the next two books with her.

Beyond my online crew, I have a band of truly unrelenting supporters in my real life too, the most important of which being my husband Ryan. I wouldn't have the emotional bandwidth to write a damn thing if not for his support and encouragement even if he has absolutely no interest in my genre. He's been patient with me in my late nights, my year-long hyperfixation on this project, my inability to do ANY unrelated art, the money I've had to put into giving this project the treatment it deserves, and...yeah, all of it. And yes, I am willing to admit that he's right about my slow frog-in-boiling-water efforts to turn him into Micah, hehe.

My parents and my closest friends (online and in person) have always got my back, no matter how much my plans have changed. They support my stubborn creativity and have never made me feel dumb. My therapy office has been so great from my clients to my boss to my colleagues, and I have never felt more accepted for my authentic self anywhere else.

Obviously, none of this would have been possible without my OCs, who have been bouncing around in my brain since I was 11, helping me understand myself and the world and remaining my one true constant as I have ventured into life.

ABOUT THE AUTHOR

MARY VANALSTINE (THEY/SHE) IS a writer, artist, and therapist. Writing and art have been a hobby for some twenty years now since they were a goofy little middle schooler, which is actually when both of *Deny Me*'s protagonists were created. Mary fell in love with fantasy as soon as they were listening to their dad read C.S. Lewis before bed, and grew up devouring tales of dragons and sassy princesses, city magic and the Folk. Mary is fierce advocate for social justice.

Mary lives in the city in Minnesota with their nerdy husband, a dramatic preschooler, a very dumb puggle named Bilbo Waggins, and two perfectly angelic cats.

Stay Up to Date

To make sure you don't miss any updates on the release of more from The Heartwood Trilogy, find me on social media.

goodreads.com/author/show/41617849.Mary_VanAlstine

twitter.com/artcoffeecats

Also head to http://www.heartwoodtrilogy.com/ for extra character art and to subscribe to my newsletter for updates.

Printed in the USA
CPSIA information can be obtained
at www.ICGtesting.com
LVHW090451091223
766094LV00015B/29